"DO YOU KNOW A DIANE FLYNN IN CHICAGO?"

The nightmare David had worried about since the day of Kurt's funeral was here. "Should I know her?" he replied carefully.

"I just thought you might. Of course, Chicago's a big city."

Janice paused, awaiting his response, but he couldn't come up with a thing to say.

"I just don't know what to think, David," she finally continued. She briefly told him about finding Kurt's separate checkbook, and a rent receipt for a Chicago apartment.

He tried to sound casual. "Maybe the best thing you could do is to forget it. What can be accomplished after the fact, after the man's dead?"

"I'm surprised you don't understand," Janice replied, and his heart sank. "Betrayal can be very difficult to live with. Once you lose trust in a man, you may never be able to trust another."

Special thanks and acknowledgment to Pat Warren for her contribution to the Tyler series.

Special thanks and acknowledgment to Joanna Kosloff for her contribution to the concept for the Tyler series.

Published August 1992

ISBN 0-373-82506-4

SUNSHINE

SUNSHINE

PAT WARREN

Harlequin Books

TORONTO • NEW YORK • LONDON
AMSTERDAM • PARIS • SYDNEY • HAMBURG
STOCKHOLM • ATHENS • TOKYO • MILAN
MADRID • WARSAW • BUDAPEST • AUCKLAND

TYLER

TYLER

American women have always used the art
quilt as a means of expressing their views on
life and as a commentary on events in the
world around them. And in Tyler, quilting has
always been a popular communal activity. So
what could be a more appropriate theme for
our book covers and titles?

SUNSHINE

This local variation of the ever-popular Amish
Sunshine and Shadow quilt is distinguished
by contrasting diagonal rows of squares
reflecting light and dark colors. Female
settlers learned to make the most of the dark
times and relish those bathed in light.

Dear Reader,

Welcome to Harlequin's Tyler, a small Wisconsin town whose citizens we hope you'll come to know and love. Like many of the innovative publishing concepts Harlequin has launched over the years, the idea for the Tyler series originated in response to our readers' preferences. Your enthusiasm for sequels and continuing characters within many of the Harlequin lines has prompted us to create a twelve-book series of individual romances whose characters' lives inevitably intertwine.

Tyler faces many challenges typical of small towns, but the fabric of this fictional community created by Harlequin will be torn by the revelation of a long-ago murder, the details of which will evolve right through the series. This intriguing crime will culminate in an emotional trial that profoundly affects the lives of the Ingallses, the Barons, the Forresters and the Wochecks.

There's new glamour at the old Timberlake resort lodge, which has recently been purchased by a prominent Chicago hotelier, a man with a personal interest in showing Tyler folks his financial clout, and a private objective in reclaiming the love of a town resident he romanced long ago.

Folks at the newspaper office are flattered that Chicago financial adviser David Markus has decided to subscribe to the *Tyler Citizen*. That's how he learned that it's winter-carnival time in Tyler. Marge will be serving up her famous Irish stew at the diner. The Kelseys never miss it. And you can bet Britt Hansen's kids will be first in line for the bobsled run. So join us in Tyler, once a month for the next seven months, for a slice of small-town life that's not as innocent or as quiet as you might expect, and for a sense of community that will capture your mind and your heart.

Marsha Zinberg
Editorial Coordinator, Tyler Series

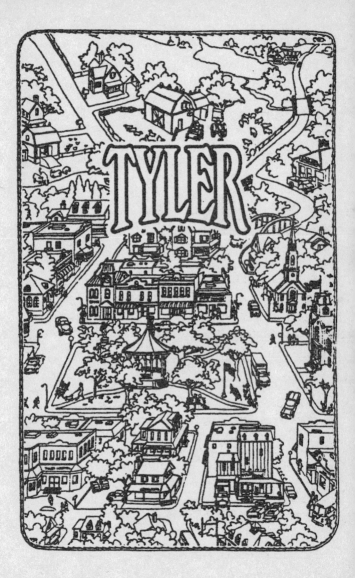

CHAPTER ONE

EMPTY. She felt empty inside, lost and bewildered. And alone, despite all the people she'd left sleeping back at her house. The big, two-story house she and Kurt had lived in together for all but two years of their twenty-three-year marriage. The house that she would now occupy alone.

Janice Ingalls Eber gathered the collar of her winter coat closer about her throat and stared out at the icy center of Lake Waukoni. She'd awakened early and driven out here to one of the peaceful places she and Kurt had visited often. Only half an hour's drive from Tyler, the small lake wasn't nearly as popular as Wisconsin's Lake Winnebago, which was one reason they'd liked coming here to fish, to picnic, to lie on the thick grass in the summertime.

In her mind's eye, Janice could picture Kurt rowing away from shore, his strong, tan arms moving rhythmically, his dark eyes laughing at her because she'd insisted they wear life jackets. She'd always been the cautious, careful one, while Kurt had loved the excitement of challenges, physical and otherwise. As a young man, he'd raced cars, learned to fly single-engine planes and skied every chance he had. He'd had a restless energy that seemed to drive him to swim regularly, even late into the season, to jog daily and to compete fiercely in tennis matches with friends.

At forty-six, slim and wiry with not an ounce of spare flesh, Kurt Eber took care of himself and was the picture of health. Or so Janice had thought until five days ago when she'd received the call. Kurt had died of a massive coronary while playing handball.

The rising sun shimmered on the surface of the lake and would probably melt much of the accumulated snow on this unseasonably warm January day. The day she would be burying her husband. Despite the mild morning, Janice shivered and thrust her hands deep into her coat pockets.

Fragmented thoughts drifted through her dazed mind. The frantic phone call from Kurt's office manager and handball opponent, Tom Sikes, urging her to rush to the hospital. Her best friend, Anna Kelsey, offering to drive, her solid presence keeping Janice from falling to pieces. Dr. George Phelps, an old friend and their family physician, holding her hands as he gravely told her that Kurt had been dead almost before he'd hit the floor. She should cling to that, George had said— that Kurt hadn't suffered more than a moment's swift pain.

Janice had wanted to lash out at him, to shriek a denial that surely he had to be wrong. Kurt couldn't be gone so quickly, so unfairly. He wouldn't leave her like that. He'd always been there for her. Always, since they'd met at the University of Wisconsin so long ago.

Just after she'd finished her sophomore year, Kurt, newly graduated, had persuaded her to quit college and elope with him, to leave her father's house and become his bride. Surely this had to be some cruel joke.

But it hadn't been.

Hunching her slender shoulders against a sudden gust of wind that swirled powdery snow at her, Janice turned and walked slowly back to her station wagon. She'd best return, for her children would be wondering about her absence. She'd left a brief note on the kitchen counter explaining that she'd gone for a short drive, but they'd worry anyhow.

Kurt, Jr.—K.J. as he'd been affectionately labeled as a youngster—a junior at his father's alma mater, undoubtedly would be pacing the kitchen and drinking black coffee as Kurt so often had. His sister, Stefanie, only two years older and believing herself to be much more mature, would be calmly making breakfast for everyone. In her disoriented state, Janice had insisted that her father as well as her sister and brother-in-law, Irene and Everett, stay at the house, and now she regretted the impulsive invitation. She dreaded being alone, yet she craved it, an odd dichotomy of emotions. Perhaps they would sense her mood and leave right after today's funeral service.

Janice got behind the wheel and turned the key. After a few rumbles, the engine caught. She and Kurt had talked about going shopping next month for a new car for her. With a trembling sigh, she wondered if she would be able to make such a large purchase on her own. She'd never picked out furniture or anything major without him. Swallowing back a fresh rush of tears, Janice headed for home.

SHE WAS SHAKY, but holding up well, Anna Kelsey thought as she stood studying Janice Eber across the funeral bier. Her long auburn hair was coiled under a black felt hat and her wide gray eyes were hidden behind huge sunglasses. Anna's heart went out to the slim, fragile woman who'd been her close friend for more than twenty years. It was difficult enough burying the very elderly; to bury a husband in the prime of life was a travesty, Anna believed.

Needing a moment's reassurance, Anna slipped her hand into her husband's, and felt his strong fingers tighten in response. The death of a friend was a stark reminder of everyone's mortality, she thought. Of course, Johnny and Kurt had not really been friends, not the way she and Janice were.

With his thriving insurance business and his near-obsession with competitive sports, Kurt was quite different from Anna's husband. Johnny was a foreman at Ingalls Farm and Machinery and preferred quieter activities such as fishing, camping and a game of touch football with their grown children and expanding family. With Anna's help, Johnny also operated Kelsey Boardinghouse, while Kurt had owned a large Victorian-style home, driven a Mercedes and worn five-hundred-dollar suits. Quite a difference.

A chill wind blew across the snow-covered hillside cemetery where the large gathering of mourners stood by the grave. Anna had known the townspeople would come in droves, for Tyler was a friendly place to live, a supportive community. Though Janice Eber had never worked outside her home, through the years she'd volunteered at her kids' school, the library and the hospital, and she was well liked.

She was a sweet woman, Anna thought, a good wife, caring mother and wonderful homemaker. Anna had never heard Janice raise her voice nor give a dissenting opinion. She simply didn't like to make waves, which often annoyed Anna, who felt Janice ought to speak out more, be a little more assertive.

Anna watched the solemn-faced minister move to the head of the casket and begin reading the Twenty-third Psalm. Shifting her gaze, she felt Janice's face turn even paler as her son gripped her hand on one side and her daughter gripped the other. Kurt had been from Boston, an only child whose parents had died some years back, so there were no Ebers to mourn his passing. But the Ingalls clan was well represented, flanking Janice on both sides under the dark green canopy.

The Ingalls family had been involved in the early settling of Tyler. Inventive and industrious, they were still the wealthiest folks in town. Janice's father, Herbert, ran the company lab in Milwaukee and seemed friendly and down-to-earth to Anna. His wife had died years ago and Herbert had raised both Janice and Irene. No two people could be less alike than Janice and her sister, Anna thought as she watched Irene clutch her full-length mink coat more tightly around her ample bosom.

Then there was Janice's uncle, Judson Ingalls, Tyler's patriarchal figure at nearly eighty. Tall and dignified, he stood next to his widowed daughter, Alyssa Baron, and her three children. In truth, they were no longer children. The oldest, Dr. Jeffrey Baron, was thirty and already being mentioned as the next chief of staff at Tyler General Hospital.

Next was Amanda, a couple of years younger, sweet and unaffected and a practicing lawyer in Tyler. And the youngest, Liza, a fun-loving, spirited young woman, a decorator who'd recently married a somewhat reclusive fellow named Cliff Forrester. A striking family, attractive and intelligent and, with the possible exception of Liza, dignified in their bearing.

Had the Ingalls family, with their wealth and style, made Kurt into the man he'd become—a restless superachiever and self-made businessman who'd never quite felt accepted despite his best efforts? Anna asked herself that question as she heard the minister winding down. Kurt had married Janice when she was very young, obviously wanted to exceed her family's achievements, to make her proud of him. Anna wondered if Kurt ever knew that Janice would have loved him just as much if he'd been a used-car salesman.

Stepping back with Johnny, Anna stood among her own children, watching the many citizens of Tyler file past to say goodbye to Kurt and offer a word of comfort to Janice. She saw her two married daughters, Laura and Glenna, walk over with their husbands to talk with their cousins.

Looking up at her husband, Anna squeezed Johnny's hand. "I think you should phone the office for an appointment," she said quietly. "You haven't had a checkup in a long time." As Dr. Phelps's receptionist, she knew the health history of nearly everyone in town, yet she had trouble persuading this stubborn man to take care of himself.

"I will," Johnny answered in the vague way he had when he didn't want to argue the point. Obviously he had no intention of complying. "Are you going to Janice's when this is over?"

"Yes, of course. You remember last night, all that baking I did? I had Patrick run it over to Janice's earlier."

Johnny frowned. "What about the rest of the town? You have enough to do without—"

Anna stopped him, raising a hand to caress his cheek. "Lots of people are bringing food. It's already done, so don't fret. We *wanted* to do it this way. Alyssa dropped off several platters already and Marge Peterson sent two boxes of covered dishes from the diner. You should stop and have something to eat."

"I can't. We've got a lot of people out at the plant with this damn flu bug." Johnny glanced up at the early-afternoon sun. "Freezing one day, then almost sixty the next. Half the town's sick with it."

"It's still the middle of winter," Anna commented as she frowned at her only son. "Patrick, why aren't you wearing a topcoat?"

Patrick Kelsey smiled at his mother. "I'm married now, Mom," he answered as he slipped his arm around his wife's slim waist. "You can't boss me around anymore."

"As if I ever could," Anna muttered. "Pam, you need to take a firmer hand with your husband."

Pam Casals Kelsey looked up into her husband's vivid blue eyes. "I try," Pam answered. "I insisted Patrick bring his coat and he insisted we leave it in the car."

"That's because my son thinks he's a macho man," Anna responded with a smile. But then her gaze shifted back to Janice.

There was a weary slump to her friend's shoulders and her hands fluttered nervously as she accepted the condolences of a well-dressed man Anna had never seen before. Obviously Janice was still struggling with the shock of Kurt's sudden death. Maybe if they got her home now, she'd have time for a short rest before having to put up a brave front during the luncheon.

Quickly, Anna said goodbye to her own family and moved unobtrusively until she was next to Janice. Taking one of her cold hands, she smiled gently. "Why don't we move along to the house now? You can talk with the rest of the people there."

"Yes, yes, fine." Janice sounded tired. Slowly she turned for a last look at the coffin that held her husband's remains.

She hated to leave, yet she wasn't certain how much longer her legs would hold her. She was so cold, cold clear through. Her feet, her hands... It should have rained today, Janice thought irrelevantly. You shouldn't bury someone on a sunny, crisp day but rather on a gloomy, rain-filled one. Much more appropriate.

Her thoughts were rambling, disjointed and a little frightening. She needed to get out of here, to be home, to be safe and warm again. She would not cry here in this grim, desolate place. Moving woodenly, as if she were sleepwalking, Janice placed the rose she'd been holding on top of the casket, then closed her eyes a long moment, fighting the quick flash of pain. When she felt her son's hand on her arm, she straightened and let herself be led to the waiting limousine.

SHE LOOKED TIRED, David Markus thought as he stood at the far end of the living room watching Janice and the seemingly endless stream of neighbors and friends who kept coming up to her. Women with reddish-brown hair usually looked good in black, but today, Janice's pale skin was too stark a contrast. Yellow was her color, a preference he'd shared with her years ago.

Sipping his coffee, he studied her from his unobtrusive corner. The dress was somewhat shapeless and not terribly flattering to her willowy figure. She'd wound

her thick hair into a haphazard upsweep that was
nonetheless appealing. Her face was oval, with high
cheekbones, a small nose and a generous mouth. By far
her best features were her wide-set gray eyes. Without
the sunglasses, they appeared huge and terribly vulnerable, fleetingly reflecting a myriad of emotions as
they settled on first one person, then flitted to another. He doubted if she'd remember much of what
was said today.

She'd changed, David decided as he settled himself
on the arm of a nearby chair. But who hadn't in the
past twenty-plus years? Changed, and yet she was in
many ways the same. A little hesitant, her voice still low
and husky. He'd been enamored of that voice back
when he and Kurt and Janice had all three been attending the University of Wisconsin at Madison.

David had just started his junior year when Janice
had arrived as a bright-eyed yet shy freshman. In a
bevy of sophisticates, she'd stood out as a guileless innocent. He'd gravitated to her and they'd started dating. It wouldn't have taken much for him to have gone
off the deep end over Janice, and he'd recognized that
quickly. But he'd been nearly penniless then, financ-
ing his education with scholarships, and on what his
mother managed to scrimp together. He'd had nothing to offer a girl from a moneyed background.

She'd come from a sheltered home and a watchful
father. Finding herself suddenly on her own, she'd
gradually moved out of her shell, and David knew
she'd dated others besides him. After a while, he'd

stopped asking her out, telling her he had too many obligations to allow much time for dating. She'd accepted his news calmly, though he'd thought she looked disappointed. Or had that been wishful thinking? The next thing he knew, she'd been all wrapped up in his roommate, Kurt Eber.

Kurt's parents had died, leaving him with a decent nest egg that he hoped to parlay into even more money. The Ingalls family didn't seem to intimidate Kurt, though he'd mentioned to David that they appeared to disapprove of his brash confidence. David had wondered if Janice would succumb to Kurt's heated pursuit of her, and indeed, she'd been overwhelmed by his charm. Over her family's objections, she'd run off and married him. David had chosen not to go along to stand up as Kurt's best man.

So much water under the bridge since then. Finishing his coffee, David stood and set the cup aside as Herbert Ingalls walked over to him, squinting through his bifocals.

"I know you from somewhere, don't I?" Herbert asked, extending his hand.

"Yes, sir," David said, shaking hands. "We met some time ago. David Markus."

"Ah, yes. You were involved in a government program that my lab was working on about five or six years ago." Herbert ran long fingers through his unkempt white hair.

He was a big man, tall and thick through the chest, even though he had to be in his mid- to late-seventies.

Compared to his well-groomed older brother, Judson Ingalls, Herbert in his baggy tweed suit looked a little like an unmade bed, David thought.

"You still with the Feds?" Herbert asked.

David shook his head. "Twenty years was long enough. I've got my own firm now. Financial adviser."

"Out of Milwaukee?"

"No, sir. Chicago." He nodded toward Janice. "I went to college with your daughter. And Kurt, of course." Janice had taken him to her family home once, but David was certain her father didn't remember meeting him then.

"Football, right? You played college ball. Pretty good, as I recall."

So he did remember. A sharp old man. "That was a long time ago."

Herbert wrinkled his brow as he glanced over at his daughter. "Damn shame about Kurt. A quick heart attack like that—easy on the victim, hell of a thing for the family to handle."

"Janice looks pretty shaken up."

"She is, for now," Herbert went on. "She's stronger than she looks, though. I've been telling her for years to get out of that man's shadow. Not healthy. Janice has this stubborn streak. But now she's got no choice."

David's gaze took in the crowds of people filling the downstairs. "It looks as if she's got a lot of supportive friends and relatives."

Herbert's shrewd eyes moved to study David. "Always room for one more, son." He clapped David on the shoulder. "Good to see you again."

"You, too, Mr. Ingalls." David watched Janice's father wander over to a small cluster of people by the door. Was he reading too much into their brief conversation or did Herbert seem less than grief-stricken over his son-in-law's death? Perhaps the family's early disapproval of Kurt had lingered through the years. How, he wondered, had Janice coped with all that?

Reaching for his cup, David strolled to the dining room for more coffee. As he poured, someone spoke from behind him.

"Excuse me, sir. Are you David Markus?"

David turned and looked into the dark brown eyes of the young man he recognized as Kurt's son. He was taller than Kurt had been, his shoulders broad in a dark sport jacket. "Yes, I am. You're K.J., right? Your father mentioned you to me often. He was very proud of your excellent grades."

The young man flushed with pride. "Thank you. I've wanted to meet you. You're kind of a legend around school. They've never had a running back as big or as fast as you."

It had been the only sport, the only diversion from work and his studies, that he'd allowed himself. The young man before him seemed as intense as he'd been in those days. "I used to love the game."

K.J. jammed his hands into his pants pockets. "I sure wish I could have made the team. Dad wanted me to in the worst way. I'm big enough, but I don't have the feel for it, I guess."

"Not every guy's meant to play football." David sipped his coffee. "What do you like to do?"

His expression became animated. "I'm interested in art. I like to draw. Cartoons, mostly. Political satire, that sort of thing. I've had a couple published in the university press. Dad said drawing was okay as a hobby, but that I'd never make a lot of money at it."

David leaned back against the buffet. "Is that what you want to do—make a lot of money?"

"Well, yeah, that's important, isn't it? But I just wish I could make a good living doing what I like to do best."

"Maybe you can. Are you majoring in art now?"

"No, business administration. Dad thought that would be best. But I take as many extra art courses as I can squeeze in."

"Well, K.J., I'm not sure I'm the right one to advise you, but it's been my experience that the most successful men are those who work at doing what they like best. Your dad was a success because he honestly loved business—making deals, beating the competition. However, that may not be for you."

"I think he wanted me to follow in his footsteps. You know, take over when he was ready to retire and all that."

David nodded. "My dad owned a butcher shop and loved what he did, cutting the meat, joking with customers. I worked there after school for a lot of years and hated every minute. We're all different. Maybe you should talk this over with your mother. She might be in favor of a change.''

K.J. cast a hesitant glance through the archway at his mother. "I don't know. She always went along with my dad."

David laid a hand on the boy's arm. "She's going to have to make several important decisions without him from now on."

Swallowing, K.J. nodded. "Yeah, I guess so. Anyhow, it was good meeting you finally. Dad talked about you a lot, told me he saw you often in Chicago on his business trips. How come you never came to Tyler before?"

David shrugged. "I have a client in Whitewater, and whenever I'm in this vicinity, I usually end up there rather than Tyler."

"You know my mom, too, don't you?"

"I did, years ago." David hoped he didn't sound as nostalgic as he suddenly felt. Gazing into the eyes of Kurt's son, he also felt a pang of regret for opportunities lost and things that could never be. "Good luck, whatever you choose to do."

K.J. smiled at him. "Thanks."

As the boy walked away, David searched the room, his eyes drawn to Janice, deep in conversation with the buxom woman who'd been introduced as her sister. He vaguely remembered Irene from their college days, though her hair color was different now and she was carrying an extra thirty pounds. Wishing he could take

Janice aside for a talk, even a short talk, he carried his coffee over to the window seat and sat down.

TRAILING A CLOUD of expensive perfume, Irene Ingalls Bryant came up to Janice and hugged her. "I really hate to leave you, but it's a long drive home and Everett has to stop in at his office."

Stepping back to rub at a spot above her left eye, Janice nodded. "I understand."

Not satisfied with the natural reddish highlights in her hair, Irene had gone on to cosmetically enhance them, winding up with a brassy look. She patted the lacquered curls and frowned. "You really should get some rest. You've had a terrible shock."

Janice wanted everyone to leave, *everyone*. But that would be rude of her and ungrateful. She put on a small smile. "I'll be fine. Thank you for coming."

"What is family for?" Irene asked rhetorically. "Hayley wanted to make the trip with us, but I wouldn't hear of it. Her baby's due any day. She sends her best." Irene and Everett's only daughter was expecting her first child.

Janice nodded again. She'd been nodding all day, it seemed.

"Maybe, after you rest awhile, you should come to Milwaukee for a nice long visit. We can catch up."

It occurred to Janice that people said a whole lot of things at awkward times like this. She and Irene had never been close and had rarely exchanged long visits, but she supposed her sister's invitation was heartfelt.

Fortunately, she was saved from answering as Everett joined them, already wearing his topcoat and carrying Irene's mink. Everett was a successful stockbroker in Milwaukee, a big man who liked sailboats, silk ties and smelly cigars.

"You ready to go, Mama?" he asked in the clipped tones of a man with a cigar clamped between his teeth.

Janice could recall few instances when she'd seen Everett without one of his imported cigars. She'd once remarked to Kurt that she wondered if Everett showered with his cigar, slept with it, made love with it in his mouth. They'd laughed over the foolish thought. She swallowed past a lump.

"You're looking pale, Lady Janice," Everett went on as he helped his wife into her coat. "Got to take care of yourself better. Those two fine kids, they need you now more than ever."

Janice ground her teeth and hoped he wouldn't notice. Everett's habit of giving everyone a pet name annoyed her suddenly. Had she lost her sense of humor and her level of tolerance, as well as her life partner? Everett was nice enough and she was being unfair. With his florid face and his excess fifty pounds, he seemed a more likely candidate for a heart attack than Kurt. Was she reacting so badly because Kurt was gone and Everett was very much alive?

In a rush of remorse for her thoughts, she placed an apologetic hand on Everett's arm. "I'm sorry we didn't have more time to talk today." Her glance took in Irene. "Perhaps I will drive to Milwaukee soon."

Irene gave her a smile and another hug. "Take care of yourself and call me if you need anything. *Anything.*"

"I will." Janice watched them leave, then paused a moment to catch her breath. The crowd was thinning out at long last. Her father had left some time ago, walking out with his brother, Judson, the two of them deep in conversation. Now if only the others would leave.

She turned to find her cousin Alyssa's concerned eyes studying her.

"How are you holding up?" Alyssa asked softly, slipping her arm around Janice's waist.

"All right." Janice drew in a deep, steadying breath. "It's odd but I never once pictured this scenario." Alyssa's husband had died about ten years ago, and though she'd not given it much thought before, Janice now found herself wondering about many things. "How on earth did you cope after Ronald's death?"

Alyssa shrugged her slim shoulders, her expression unchanged, though there was a hint of sadness in her blue eyes. "You just do, somehow. One day at a time. You have your private moments, and the nights are very long, very lonely at first. It helps to stay busy." She smiled then, trying for a lighter note. "I have loads of committees I can use your help on. In time, my dear."

Charity work and volunteering. She'd done her fair share of all that, Janice thought. More of the same held little appeal. Yet what would she do when there was no one to cook a special meal for, or redecorate a room for, or plan an outing around? She would find *something,* but this wasn't the day for decision making.

Janice indicated the dining room table, still laden with food. "The luncheon was lovely. You and Anna did a wonderful job."

Alyssa shook her head. "You didn't eat a thing, did you?"

"I'm not hungry, truly." She squeezed Alyssa's hand. "I need to say a word to Tom Sikes. Excuse me a moment, please."

She found him in the dining room at the dessert bar. She'd known Tom, Kurt's office manager, for years and found him to be earnest and honest, if a shade pedantic. He also seemed to feel a measure of guilt, since he'd invited Kurt to play handball with him at his apartment complex on the outskirts of Tyler on that fateful day, though she'd tried to reassure him that Kurt's heart attack had been no one's fault.

Janice touched his arm. "Tom, I'm sorry we haven't had more time to talk."

From behind thick, horn-rimmed glasses, he blinked at her. "I want to say again, Janice, how very sorry I am. I'll really miss Kurt."

"I know. Thank you."

"And I want you to know that I'll be at the office every day, at your disposal, when you're ready. I know this isn't the time or place, but..."

Janice frowned. "I'm not sure what you mean. At my disposal for what?"

Tom stroked his thinning blond hair. "To go over the books. Some decisions will need to be made about the business, about who will run things. What about the satellite office Kurt had set up in Chicago, the plans he had for expansion? We have several large policies coming up for renewal soon. We need to work up bids since...well, since Kurt's gone, some of our clients may not automatically renew with us as they have in the past."

Rubbing her forehead, Janice felt light-headed. She hadn't given a thought the past few days to Kurt's work. "I...we didn't discuss the business much, Tom. I know very little about how the agency operates."

Tom nodded understandingly. "It's all right. I can update you when you're ready. In the meantime, I hope you'll trust me to keep things running smoothly."

Tom had been with the firm almost from the day Kurt had opened Eber Insurance Agency. He and Kurt had also become jogging buddies and had gone skiing together often since Tom's divorce. Looking at him now, Janice realized she hardly knew the man. But Kurt had trusted him and that was good enough for Janice. "Yes, I do trust you. And I'll be in as soon as I...well, soon."

"No hurry. Take your time."

She watched Tom walk away and turned to get herself a cup of coffee. But when she picked up the cup, her hands were shaking so hard that the cup rattled in its saucer.

"Here, let me help you with that." David Markus poured coffee for her, then led her to the window seat where he'd been sitting watching her.

Gratefully, Janice took a bracing sip, closing her eyes briefly. "Thank you," she whispered.

Up close, he saw a light sprinkling of freckles on her nose that he remembered from an earlier time. They gave her a youthful look that touched him. "Rough day. I know you'll be glad when we all leave."

She opened her eyes to look into his steady blue gaze. She saw empathy and concern and something else she couldn't identify. Having David Markus appear at the cemetery after so many years had surprised and unnerved her. He was so big, his shoulders in his pinstriped dark suit so broad, his hand as he took it from her elbow large and tan.

He'd changed from boyishly handsome in his college football days to a deeper, more mature attractiveness. She'd dated David as a freshman, but she'd quickly learned that he had goals, commitments and obligations, and he wasn't about to let a woman sidetrack him. Yet he was looking at her now with a warmth that she couldn't help responding to.

"It's been a very long time, David," she said.

"Yes, it has." He indicated the house, the people. "Good years for you, I see."

"They have been, until now."

"Your daughter is lovely. She reminds me a great deal of you when we were in college."

"Oh, she's far prettier. Stefanie lives in Boston now and just became engaged to a Harvard law graduate. I still miss having her around."

"I can imagine. I had a talk earlier with your son. Nice young man."

"I think so." She paused, trying to remember. "Your wife died some time ago, isn't that right?"

"Yes, twelve years ago."

Janice's expressive eyes reflected sympathy. "An accident, I believe Kurt said."

David nodded, angling his body on the window seat so he could look at her better. "She lost control of the car on an icy road." He decided to change the subject, to probe a little, hoping he wasn't getting too personal. "Will you be all right?" A man who spent his life in the insurance business probably had good coverage on himself. But as a financial adviser, David was well aware that many men had all the trappings of wealth, yet were mortgaged to the hilt. And, although Janice's family had money, he didn't know if she had an interest in their holdings.

Janice finished her coffee and set it aside, deciding that his politely worded inquiry was about her financial situation. "I'm embarrassed to tell you that I haven't any idea. Since you were his friend, you're probably aware that Kurt was the kind of man who liked to run the show, to take care of everything. And I let him." She glanced over at Tom Sikes with a worried expression. "Now, I wish I'd at least asked more questions about the business. But I never dreamed...I mean, he was only forty-six." Her voice ended on a ragged note.

David took her hand, threading his large fingers through her slim ones. "Life takes some funny turns, doesn't it, Sunshine?"

For the first time in days, she felt a smile tug at her lips. Sunshine. She remembered going on a hayride with David back when she was a starry-eyed freshman thrilled to be asked out by a football hero. They'd all been singing, and one old song, "You Are My Sunshine," had been given a particularly rousing rendition. After that, David had often called her Sunshine.

"That sure takes me back," she told him.

"You remember then?"

"Of course. We had some good times together."

"That we did."

He was so solid, Janice thought, his presence so calming. For a fleeting moment, she wished she could lay her head on David's broad chest, to let him comfort her and ease her fears.

Instead, Janice shifted her gaze out the window. The wind had picked up in late afternoon and the sky was gray, the clouds heavy with snow. She felt a chill skitter down her spine, reminding her of the reason they were all gathered together today. "It's so very hard to accept that he'll never come home again." She spoke softly, almost to herself. "Kurt traveled a great deal, but I was seldom lonely because I knew he was coming back. Being alone and knowing there'll be no one returning ever again is very different."

David had lived alone most of his adult life, yet there were times he felt the same. "Fortunately, you have your children, family, friends."

Yes, there were people, plenty of people. But would they be enough? Surprised to find her hand still in his, Janice pulled her fingers free and stood, suddenly uneasy. "I have to talk with a couple of others. David, it's good seeing you again."

He did something then that he'd been wanting to do since he'd stood watching her at the cemetery. Rising, he placed a hand at her back and drew her close to his body for the space of a long heartbeat, then pressed his lips to her forehead, finding it cool to the touch.

Her hands rose to his chest in surprise, then lingered a moment. She inhaled the clean scent of soap and smoke mingled with the outdoor smell of a wintry day, a decidedly male combination. Stepping back, she realized she was trembling.

David took a card from his pocket and pressed it into her hand. "If you ever want to discuss a business matter, or if you just need to talk, my office and home numbers are on here. Call me."

Janice nodded. "Thank you."

Brushing a strand of hair back from her forehead, she watched him make his way to the door and find his overcoat. In moments, he was strolling down the snowy sidewalk toward a long, gray Lincoln.

David Markus had been widowed for years and seemed to be coping fine. She would, too, Janice thought as she slipped the card into the pocket of her black dress. Somehow.

With a weary sigh, she turned back to mingle with her remaining guests, wondering if this very long day would ever end.

CHAPTER TWO

IT WAS ALL pretty overwhelming. Janice sat at her dead husband's desk in his paneled study, with piles of papers stacked everywhere, wondering where to begin.

The house was too quiet, even though Stefanie was curled up on the leather couch across the room reading a book. Janice had always enjoyed this house; yet now the rooms seemed oppressive, the emptiness mocking her.

K.J. had had to go back to school shortly after the funeral, but she'd been delighted that Stefanie had been able to stay longer. It was two weeks since they'd buried Kurt, the days filled with people coming and going and the pleasure of having her daughter home with her. And the nights filled with restless tossing and vivid memories.

Swallowing, she bent to her task. It felt strange going through Kurt's desk, which had been his particular domain. She'd located the will he'd made out, leaving everything to her. Just what "everything" was she hadn't determined yet. As she looked at the insurance policies, stock certificates and files on their personal household bills, Janice felt like crying.

"Something wrong, Mom?" Stefanie asked, getting up and coming over.

Janice blinked back the tears. She'd done far too much crying lately. Forcing a smile, she pointed to the stack of bills and mail that had accumulated since Kurt's death. "There's so much to go through."

"How about if I help you?" Stefanie gave her mother a quick hug, then pulled up a chair beside her.

Janice opened the electric bill and studied it. The amount didn't seem very high. She flipped open the checkbook. There was less than two hundred dollars in the account since she'd paid the funeral expenses.

Stefanie peered over her shoulder. "Is that about what your electricity usually runs?"

"I have no idea," Janice admitted. "Dad handled all the bills. He used to write checks every couple of weeks. He always told me not to worry, that he'd take care of them." Chagrined, she looked at her daughter. "I should have insisted he at least keep me informed, right?"

"Probably, but don't blame yourself. I know how Dad liked to run things." Stefanie picked up the next notice. "The mortgage coupon, due on the first of the month. Do you know what you still owe on the house?"

"Not really." Janice was studying a credit card bill and another from Gates Department Store. Had she run up nearly three hundred dollars' worth of purchases? Or had Kurt bought some things? She'd usually just given him the receipts and he'd taken it from there. Pretty stupid, she was beginning to realize.

The next envelope was from a different mortgage company, a reminder of a past-due amount. Janice frowned. "I wasn't aware we had two mortgages on the house." She remembered clearly Kurt ushering her into the bank for the closing when he'd purchased their home. Stefie had just been born and he'd been so proud to be able to provide such a lovely place. Three years later, Kurt had quit the branch office of a major insurance firm and opened his own agency, telling her that the only way to get ahead was by owning your own business. He'd worked hard and they'd prospered. But she'd paid little attention to his financial dealings.

Stefanie took the notice from her mother's hand. "There's nearly nine hundred dollars past-due. Surely Dad couldn't have just forgotten to pay."

Janice became aware that Stefanie was looking at her as if she could scarcely believe her mother had so little knowledge of the running of the house. "I can't imagine that he did." She sat up taller. "It's probably an error. I'll call and get it straightened out tomorrow. And I'll transfer some money from our savings to the checking account and pay the rest of these." She felt a little better having decided that.

She hadn't located a savings account passbook in Kurt's desk, but he'd probably kept it at the office, Janice decided. She had to order new checks to be printed and find out the up-to-date balances on the accounts. Surely there was enough money. They hadn't lived lavishly, though they were comfortable. Kurt had rarely refused a request she'd made for a purchase or an improvement on the house. But then, she hadn't asked often. So much to see to, to think about.

Stefanie had been sorting through the rest of the mail. "This is mostly trivial junk. A magazine subscription renewal notice, a request for the return of an overdue book from the library and a coupon offering a large pizza at a discount. Three more notes of condolence—these names don't look familiar."

Janice sighed. "Probably from Dad's clients. There's a whole stack on the dining room table."

"And here's a notice that the tires on Dad's car are due to be rotated next week." Stefanie brushed back her long hair. "Have you decided what you're going to do about the cars, Mom?"

Janice leaned back, her eyes filling. "How Dad loved that car." A very impractical Mercedes convertible that seated only two. Kurt had bought it in Chicago and driven it home, so pleased with his purchase. Janice smiled at the memory. "He'd have it washed weekly, and afterward he'd take a rag and polish it even more. I wonder if I should sell that or my station wagon."

Stefanie stacked the mail in a neat pile. "Why not get rid of both and get something you *really* want?"

"I don't know, Stefie. It seems kind of...frivolous." Janice sat back wearily. "I'll decide later." Why hadn't she paid more attention to things? Why hadn't Kurt taken the time and trouble to explain all this to her before he died? Why had he left her with this dreadful mess?

"All this has taught me a valuable lesson," her daughter said, rising to return to her book. "When Ross and I marry, I'm going to make sure we handle the household accounts together."

"That's a good plan." Hers had seemed like a good plan at the time, too. She'd done what her husband wanted her to do. If he'd lived, there wouldn't have been a problem. But he hadn't lived.

In a burst of unreasonable anger, she shoved back the chair and went to stand by the window. It was snowing again, a light sprinkling, and quite cold out. She'd hardly left the house since the day of the funeral. Yesterday the dry cleaners had phoned, asking when she'd be picking up Kurt's shirts. She'd had an urge to tell them to keep them, that he would no longer be needing them.

The windowpane was cool on her forehead as she leaned forward, trying to swallow her anger. It was stupid to be angry with someone for dying. Kurt, she was certain, hadn't wanted to die, had loved life immensely. Why? Why had this happened to them? It wasn't fair.

Stefanie came up behind her, slipping an arm around her slim waist. "Mom, are you all right?"

Janice nodded and cleared her throat. She had to get a grip on herself. Stefanie was a worrier and was going home tomorrow. The least she could do was put on a brave front for one more day. "I'll be fine." She glanced toward the fireplace. "Why don't we build a fire?" She was always cold lately, even wearing her gray sweatpants and a heavy sweater.

"We used up the last of the wood last night, remember? Want me to call around and see if I can get some delivered?"

Kurt had always ordered the wood and had it stacked. Janice didn't even know where he'd gotten it, or who to call. Annoyed, she shook her head. "Let's forget it. I think I'll make a cup of tea. Want some?"

"No, but I'll make it for you," Stefanie suggested.

"That's all right. I need something to do." In the kitchen, Janice turned on the small radio and put water on to boil. Opening the refrigerator, she looked inside, wondering what to make for dinner. Nothing appealed to her, but she'd have to produce something for Stefie's sake.

She shuffled covered dishes around, leftover food her friends and neighbors had brought over. Taking the lid from a familiar blue dish, she found tuna salad that had gone bad. Kurt had loved tuna and had undoubtedly made it some time ago, then promptly forgotten it was there.

Angrily, she scraped the moldy salad down the drain and turned on the disposal. Why hadn't he eaten the damn tuna? Why had he let it spoil when he knew food was expensive? And why had he left her here to cope with all this alone?

A rush of guilt flooded her and she felt the heat creep into her face. She had no right to be angry with Kurt.

He hadn't meant to leave her. Yet he had, and she would have to stop feeling sorry for herself and get on with her life. *Dear God, where was she going to find the strength to go on?*

The music from the radio grew suddenly louder, taunting her. Janice's head shot up as she heard Johnny Mathis singing, "It's wonderful, wonderful. Oh, so wonderful, my love." She and Kurt had danced to that back in college. Only Kurt was gone now and nothing was wonderful. Nothing.

Her back against the kitchen cupboards, Janice slid to the floor, hoping her daughter wouldn't wander out and see her like this. Resting her cheek on her bent knees, she closed her eyes and let the tears fall.

KELSEY BOARDINGHOUSE was a warm and wonderful place, a place Janice had always felt welcome. Losing her mother at an early age, she'd gravitated to Anna Kelsey when Anna had first arrived in Tyler. Though Anna was only about ten years older than Janice, she seemed to personify everything a mother should be. As Janice entered Anna's big kitchen the next evening, she hugged her friend a bit longer than usual, absorbing Anna's warmth like a favorite quilt wrapping around her.

"I'm so glad you stopped in," Anna said, stepping back to look her friend over. The pale skin beneath Janice's eyes was dark with fatigue. Not sleeping well yet, Anna guessed. And she was wearing those shapeless, unflattering sweats she dragged out every winter. "Take your coat off."

"I came to coax you out for a walk," Janice said. "Maybe we could stroll over to Marge's Diner and have a piece of her sinfully rich pie." She wasn't really hungry, but she thought Anna might not want to just go marching around on a snowy evening after working all day.

"Good idea," Anna said. "Johnny has a meeting tonight and I've just finished the dishes. Let me grab my jacket."

"I don't know how you do it," Janice said a few minutes later as they headed down the street, their booted feet crunching in the hard-packed snow. "A full-time job and running the boardinghouse with Johnny and always being there for your children. I wish I had your energy."

Anna linked her arm with her friend's. "I don't feel very energetic tonight. I really should do a thorough cleaning in my two vacant rooms upstairs, but I don't feel up to it."

"Did you lose a couple of boarders?"

"I didn't think of them as boarders really. You know my nephew, Brick Bauer, don't you?"

"Sure, I know Brick. Didn't he get married recently?" She'd been so self-involved lately that she hadn't kept up with what had been happening around town, Janice realized with dismay.

Anna chuckled. "He sure did. Karen's the police captain, which technically makes her his boss, since

Brick's a lieutenant. They each had a room with us. Their wedding was a disaster, but at least they're finally together." Anna looked up as they turned off Gunther Street and onto Main Street. Snow was gathered on the limbs of a bare maple tree under the street lamp, silhouetted against a dark sky. "Isn't that pretty?"

Janice inhaled deeply. "Yes, it is." She was so glad she'd come out tonight. She'd been cooped up entirely too long inside that house filled with memories. As they walked across the town square toward the diner, she gazed around at the familiar scene—the library and across the way, the post office. On the next corner was the Hair Affair where she should be making an appointment for a cut. "I wish I had a nickel for every time I've walked across this square—with the kids when they were young and with Kurt."

She was getting melancholy again, Anna decided, and rushed to divert her. "Did you get Stefanie off to Boston?"

"Yes, this morning. I'm surprised she stayed as long as she did. That girl is so in love. Every night she'd call her fiancé and they'd talk for a good hour. Then Ross would call her during the day." Janice sighed. "Do you remember being like that, Anna? So crazy in love that all you thought about was Johnny, all you talked about was Johnny?"

Anna shrugged. "We were both eighteen, Janice. A couple of kids, really. But yes, I remember when he was my every thought and I probably bored my friends to death talking about him. In that first rush of passion, I think we all feel as if we invented love. Didn't you?"

"I suppose I did, but it all seems so long ago. Kurt's been gone such a short time and already sometimes I have trouble remembering how he looked, how he sounded."

Anna squeezed her friend's arm. "Give it time, Janice." She stomped the snow from her boots and opened the door of Marge's Diner, smiling as a rush of warm air fogged her glasses. "I love the way it smells in here," she commented as she waved to Marge, who was behind the counter as usual.

The restaurant wasn't crowded on a frosty Tuesday evening. A couple of teenagers were sipping hot chocolate across the way, and one of Joe Santori's carpenters was finishing his dinner at the counter. Anna walked to a booth and slid onto the red vinyl seat as Janice seated herself opposite her. She shrugged out of her jacket and concentrated on polishing her glasses.

"Good to see you, Janice," Marge said as she handed them each a menu. "You, too, Anna."

"Don't you ever take time off, Marge?" Anna asked as she put her glasses back on. "Seems like you're here night and day."

"Married to my work," Marge commented wryly.

"I don't have to look at your menu, Marge," Janice said with a smile. "I want a piece of your wonderful apple pie and a cup of coffee." It must have been the walk, for she was suddenly hungry.

"Make mine the same," Anna said, handing back the menus.

"Coming right up."

Janice watched Marge walk away, then leaned toward Anna, keeping her voice low. "I've always felt a little sorry for Marge, deserted by her husband so many years ago, then her daughter leaving. Always alone and having to work. And now I find myself in basically the same boat."

Anna frowned. "Are you in trouble financially?" She'd always thought that Kurt made plenty of money and assumed that he'd have lots of insurance.

Janice shrugged. "I don't think so. I've got to go to Kurt's office and go over the books, check things out." She brushed back a lock of hair. "I hate to think of all that."

"Maybe you need some help. You could ask Judson or your father perhaps." Seeing her friend wrinkle her nose at those suggestions, Anna grew thoughtful. "How about David Markus? I talked with him for a while at your house and he said he's a financial adviser. He also said he's known you for years, yet I've never heard you mention his name."

"The three of us went to college together. It was a shock seeing him after all these years." A picture of David sitting with her on her window seat came to Janice, the way he'd taken her hand, then kissed her forehead. A lot of Kurt's friends had hugged her that day, but oddly, it was David's touch she remembered.

Feeling unaccountably guilty, she pushed the thought away.

"He's very attractive," Anna said as their dessert and coffee arrived. Nodding her thanks to Marge, she picked up her fork. "Is he married?"

Janice took a careful sip. "She died in a car accident twelve years ago."

"And he's never remarried? Hard to believe." Anna took a bite of warm pie.

"I don't know why we're talking about David Markus. I'll probably never see him again."

Anna had had enough. She touched Janice's hand and waited until her friend met her direct gaze. "Listen, Kurt died, you didn't. Now, I know you're grieving and I'm not suggesting you start dating this week. But you're only forty-three and far too young to talk as if your life is over. I was merely suggesting you call an old college friend for some financial advice, not that you run off with him."

But Janice wasn't listening. "I believe some women love only one man and if something happens to him, that's it."

Her grief was making her melodramatic, Anna thought with a sigh. "I'm not sure I agree."

"Tell me honestly, Anna. If something happened to Johnny, would you want to go on?"

"I would be devastated, as you are. But I would go on, because of the children and grandchildren. And for myself, because I'm not one to give up."

"Could you love anyone after Johnny? I doubt it. Why, look at Alyssa."

Anna took another bite of pie, wondering how she could steer this conversation to a lighter vein. "What about Alyssa?"

"We've talked about this before, of how Alyssa was wildly in love with Eddie Wocheck when she was young. You said you didn't think Alyssa's been truly happy since her father broke up that romance."

Anna shook her head. "I don't believe those were my exact words."

"Pretty much. I know that you and Johnny were close to Alyssa and Eddie. I remember you said that Johnny warned Eddie that Uncle Judson would put a stop to any wedding plans, but you advised Alyssa to elope with him."

"You're right, I did. But today I'd probably advise her differently. Eddie had nothing then and Alyssa was the only child of the richest family in town. It's hard for a young man to take on all that. Perhaps if they'd married, the strain on Eddie, having to prove himself, would have ruined the marriage. Didn't Kurt ever feel intimidated marrying into the Ingalls clan?"

Janice thought that over. "Maybe a little, at first. But he drove himself and did very well rather quickly. They were never close, but Dad respected Kurt."

"But the two of you eloped. Was that your idea or Kurt's?"

"Kurt's. He said he couldn't afford a big wedding and he didn't want to accept one paid for by my family." Janice set aside her plate. "You know, I've had a lot of time to think lately and I realize now that from the beginning, I let Kurt make all the decisions. His only concession to me was finally agreeing to move to Tyler."

"He wanted to stay in Madison?"

"He wanted us to live in Milwaukee, but I didn't want to be that close to my father." She let out a small laugh that had a bitter edge. "I went from one dominating man to another." She took a sip of coffee and tasted regret.

Anna finished eating and raised her eyes to study her friend. Janice was a bright woman, but had always had a head-in-the-sand approach to life. Perhaps Kurt's death was causing her to question and to face some harsh realities. Anna wasn't sure Janice was altogether prepared for that. "Maybe what you need next is a man with whom you can be yourself, someone to really share with."

"I think I have enough to cope with just recovering right now. To think of another man is not only premature, it's ridiculous." She stared down into her coffee cup. "Besides, what on earth would a worldly man like David Markus want with a small-town creature like me?"

Ridiculous, was it, Anna thought. Yet it was Janice who'd brought David's name up again. "Eddie Wocheck's been all over and yet I believe he's very interested in seeing Alyssa, who's lived her whole life in a small town. It isn't where we're from that matters as much as who we are."

Janice waved a dismissive hand. "That's different. They knew each other way back when and..."

"Didn't you just tell me you went to college with David?"

"Yes, but we only dated a few times. He had this sense of obligation to his widowed mother and this burning need to succeed."

Anna gave her a mock scowl. "Terrible traits in a man."

But Janice was determined to make her point. "I'd be willing to bet that Eddie and Alyssa will get back together. She's always loved him, always will. A one-man woman. Like you. Like me."

Amused, Anna smiled. "You should be writing books, with your imagination. I don't think it's all that simple. Thirty years have passed. Alyssa's not the same woman she was at nineteen and Eddie's changed. They've both had a less than perfect marriage. I don't think either one is impulsive enough to jump into anything." Again, she met her friend's eyes. "And I'm not convinced you're a one-man woman, either."

"Why do you say that? I had a good life married to a wonderful man who loved me."

Anna had never cared very much for Kurt, but this was no time to mention that to his widow. She'd never been able to say why. There'd just been something about Kurt that had kept her from warming up to him.

"Yes, you did have a good life. I only mean to point out that it is far from over."

Janice finished her coffee thoughtfully. "I suppose you're right, to some extent. It's just that I feel so unfocused. I need to meet with Tom Sikes, to see what's happening at the office. Maybe I should go back to school."

"You really should," Anna said encouragingly. "You're so good with colors and fabrics that if you got your degree, you could open your own interior design studio. Liza thinks you're a natural and she should know. She's worked everywhere."

"I'll have to wait to see what the money situation is. Maybe I'll *need* to get a job."

Confusion and ambivalence were not uncommon after losing someone close, Anna knew. "It's not too late to do either. Or both. Eber Insurance is a going concern. You could learn that business, if you feel so inclined. You know, there's nothing quite like earning your own money to give you a sense of accomplishment, a feeling of independence."

Janice ran a hand through her hair. "I've got to get a haircut, too," she commented absently. "I know you're right. I've been too dependent on Kurt, but he wanted it that way and I . . . well, I just drifted with it. It was easier. Now I regret not taking more of an interest."

Anna rose. "As I said, it isn't too late. Perhaps Kurt's manager can help you. Or David Markus."

There was that name again. Janice scooted out of the booth and went to the counter to pay Marge. Outside again in the chilly night air, she turned to Anna. "Thanks so much for coming with me and letting me bend your ear. You're a good friend, Anna."

Anna gave her a quick hug. "Anytime. Talking things out helps."

About to start walking home, Janice paused. "Anna, why did you go to work for Dr. Phelps? Did you get tired of always being in the house or was it financial? I don't mean to pry."

"I *wanted* to. I wanted to do something that was mine alone. Johnny had his work at the plant and we shared the boardinghouse and the children. But I needed something of my own, and that independence I mentioned earlier. I think he began to respect me more, and my self-respect increased as well when I proved I could make my own way if I had to."

"I would have thought Johnny would object to his wife working."

"He didn't and still doesn't, because he knows that my working fulfills a need in me. Johnny doesn't have this thing about needing to be in charge and in control the way Kurt did."

She'd said it kindly, and with the best of intentions, yet it bothered Janice to hear the words. Probably because she knew Anna was right. "Kurt was a good man, Anna," she said softly. It seemed important to remind her. And perhaps herself.

"Of course he was."

Janice nodded. "Good night." She set out at a brisk pace.

Anna stood watching Janice for a minute, then turned toward her own street. It would seem that Janice Eber had a long way to go before she accepted Kurt's death. And, Anna thought with a sad shake of her head, it likely would be a painful journey.

SQUINTING, Janice leaned closer to the ledger spread out on Kurt's desk. The numbers blurred. She pulled back and they came into focus. Brushing back her hair, she acknowledged that she'd have to make an appointment for that eye exam she'd been putting off for too long.

But even glasses wouldn't clarify the columns of figures she'd been trying to make sense of since arriving at Eber Insurance several hours ago. Kurt's secretary, the bookkeeper, Tom Sikes and the sales staff who'd come in and out had all treated her kindly. They'd gone to great pains to explain the operation to her. She envied them their acquired knowledge and despaired of ever catching up.

Finally, she'd shut herself in Kurt's private office so no one would witness her private humiliation as she tried to make sense of the papers she'd been given. It would seem that the firm wrote insurance for commercial properties, plus auto, homeowners, and some life and health. A broad base. According to Tom, they were decidedly in the black. Janice would have to take his word for that, since the ledgers were beyond her understanding.

Tom had also pointed out several large policies coming up for renewal soon that she'd have to pay special attention to. Their representatives wanted to meet the person who'd be in charge, to be assured that the main thrust of Eber Insurance would be as before. Janice sensed that Tom thought himself the likely candidate to take over. He'd stopped short of offering to buy in or buy her out, yet she felt he was considering doing so.

She hadn't the foggiest notion which way to go on that.

Janice rubbed her forehead. She'd never suffered from headaches much until recently. Now they seemed to be her daily companions. Maybe what she should do was handle the immediate problems and take the rest of these papers home to read over at her leisure. Finding a large manila envelope, she shoved the stacks of papers into it. She filled two, then sat back with a worried frown.

Whom was she kidding? She could read all of this, study it till the cows came home, and be no further ahead than she was right this minute. She simply had too little understanding of the business world to be able to make intelligent decisions. She needed help, but whom could she trust?

Her father was out of the question. He was too far away and too opinionated. She ruled out her Uncle Judson as well, for though she liked him, he had a tendency to make decisions for people and then expect them to follow without question. Kurt had been a little like that and she wasn't certain she wanted to start up with another man who'd overpower her. Perhaps it would be best if she went outside the family for assistance.

Janice didn't know the men who'd advised Kurt—his attorney and his accountant. They'd both been at the funeral, offering to help in any way they could. But she hadn't particularly liked their somewhat condescending attitude toward her. Maybe she was being overly sensitive, but she'd rather have someone fresh on the scene.

Finally she zeroed in on the name that had been hovering in the back of her mind since her walk with Anna. Grabbing her leather bag, she rummaged around inside until she found what she was searching for. Leaning back in Kurt's chair, she studied the card David Markus had given her.

Had he meant it when he'd said to call him if she needed anything, or had he just been trying to be polite? A financial adviser with years of business experience seemed the right person to ask. Still, she hesitated.

She'd never called on a man other than Kurt for help. Never. Of course, she shouldn't think of David as a man, but rather as a business consultant. Janice smiled at her own silliness. Definitely difficult not to think of David Markus as a man first and foremost. However, she was certain he looked upon her as a friend's wife and nothing more.

Although he had once, for a short time. One long-ago autumn when they'd dated. But that had been when they were both young and carefree. Now, Janice thought of David more as a trusted ally.

With that thought in mind, she dialed his office number. In moments, his secretary came on and told her that David wasn't in, that he was working from home this afternoon. Before she lost her courage, Janice dialed his home number.

He answered on the third ring.

"David, this is Janice Eber," she said, hoping she didn't sound as nervous as she felt. "I hope I'm not interrupting anything important."

Spooky, David thought. Downright spooky to have the woman he'd been thinking about call just then. "Janice, good to hear from you. How are you holding up?"

"I'm doing fine. Personally, that is. But with the business end of things, not so well."

"How can I help?"

"I'm not sure. I'm sitting at Kurt's desk in his office, and I have to admit I'm overwhelmed. I don't understand the books, a second mortgage on our home, some investments. Kurt's office manager, Tom Sikes, is more than willing to explain everything, but..."

He caught the pause, the hesitancy, and understood. "But you don't know him and you're not sure you can trust him."

He'd about summed it up, though she hadn't spoken those exact words aloud. "More or less."

"Would you like me to meet with Tom Sikes, go over the papers and then explain everything to you?"

She felt relief flood her. That was exactly what she wanted. "If you're sure you have the time. I know you're some distance from here and I hate to ask. You must be busy."

"It just so happens I'm visiting a client in Whitewater tomorrow morning. I could be in Tyler about one. Could you ask Tom to prepare for my visit, to have the latest audited reports and tax returns available, and give him permission to show me all the books?"

"Yes, certainly."

"Leave the mortgage information and Kurt's insurance policies on the desk also and I'll check into those."

She was feeling better by the minute. "Fine. Feel free to look through the entire desk and files. Anything else?"

Leaning back, David smiled. "Yes. Invite me to dinner tomorrow evening. I should have a pretty good idea of how you stand by then, unless I run into something out of the ordinary."

Dinner. Janice hadn't thought that far ahead. But it was the least she could do. "Consider yourself invited. But understand that I mean to pay you as would any other client."

"We can discuss that over a glass of wine."

Now they were drinking together. Janice felt her pulse quicken, something that hadn't happened in a very long time. As the thought held, she felt herself flush with guilt. She was a widow, a woman *newly* widowed. She would do well to keep that in mind and keep this meeting businesslike. With no small effort, she put a touch of formality into her voice. "Then I'll see you tomorrow evening."

"I'm looking forward to it."

Something had been bothering her since he'd answered. "David, what's that noise I hear in the background?"

"Oh, that." He laughed. "That's water gurgling. I'm sitting in my hot tub. It's a great way to unwind after a long day at a desk."

She was caught off guard. "A hot tub," she repeated.

"I'll have to show it to you sometime."

Her errant mind went wild. She pictured him sitting in the sunken tub, hot bubbling water swirling around his muscular chest. They'd gone sailing together one balmy afternoon, and Janice remembered that David's chest was generously sprinkled with dark, curly hair. Was it still like that? she wondered.

Flushing, Janice stood up so quickly she nearly toppled Kurt's chair. Whatever was the matter with her? Grateful that David couldn't see her red face, she struggled for a nonchalant tone. "Tomorrow then, David. I appreciate your help."

"It's my pleasure. See you then, Sunshine."

Sunshine. Talking with him had warmed her like a ray of sunshine. Hanging up, Janice shook her head to clear it. She would definitely need to get a grip on herself by tomorrow. Her emotions had been unstable since that fateful phone call about Kurt. That would explain why she was acting so peculiarly, thinking thoughts she'd long ago discarded.

Quickly, she put the things David had requested on top of Kurt's desk. Fumbling through several drawers, she scooped up a couple of folders, notes and address books she thought she might look through at home later. She grabbed her coat, purse and manila envelopes and went to find Tom Sikes to set up David's visit.

CHAPTER THREE

STANDING IN FRONT of her closet, Janice frowned as she stared at the clothes hanging there. Odd how it hadn't occurred to her until recently that her wardrobe badly needed updating. Probably she hadn't thought much about what she wore because she spent most of her time at home and she had plenty of around-the-house things. The past couple of weeks she'd been out and about more than in the previous six months. She'd lost weight since Kurt's death, having no appetite and very little interest in cooking for only one. Next week, she'd definitely make it a point to get to Gates Department Store and look for a few good items of apparel.

Ordinarily, she just grabbed something comfortable and put it on. But this wasn't exactly an ordinary day. Tonight, David Markus was coming for dinner.

Not that this was a date. It was a business meeting. But it was taking place in her home and she hadn't spent an evening alone with a man other than Kurt in ... well, not since her college days. She felt strange entertaining someone, even for a business meeting, without Kurt.

Her meals lately had consisted of a quick salad or bowl of soup eaten at the kitchen sink or while reading a book. But not tonight. She'd planned a complete dinner and even set the dining room table with china and stemware, using a pale green Irish linen tablecloth her mother had left her. Not because she wanted to impress David, but rather because she wanted him to know she wasn't just some backward hausfrau. She did know how to cook elegantly and serve beautifully, even if she didn't understand the paperwork Kurt had left behind.

Janice wasn't sure why it was important to her that David not think her lacking talent and imagination, but it was.

She'd also gone in to the Hair Affair this morning for that long overdue haircut. Glancing into the mirror of her dressing table, Janice had to admit that Tisha had done a good job. She'd opted for a shorter look and found that, with her hair's natural tendency to curl, the feather cut flattered her.

After that, she'd driven to nearby Belton, where she'd seen an ad for a place that made glasses in an hour. She'd had her eyes examined, then she'd tried on frames. The oversize frames she'd chosen made her oval face seem smaller, but at least she could read more easily now. That would be important tonight when David explained the company books and papers.

But back to her skimpy wardrobe. After much deliberation, she decided on a soft yellow sweater and her brown wool skirt. Not exactly a knock-'em-dead outfit, but then this was her home, not some chic restaurant. Chic had never been her style anyway, Janice thought as she zipped up the skirt and slipped her feet into low-heeled, tan pumps. Chic was for young women on the make.

Sitting down at her dressing table, she watched her face grow pink. Where had that thought come from? It wasn't even an expression she used. Janice was widely read enough to realize that she was somewhat old-fashioned in her thoughts about sex. Hard not to be, having been raised by as strict a father as she and Irene had been. Janice knew that Stefanie, already sharing an apartment with her fiancé, probably had experimented far more than she ever had.

Still, she missed the sexual side of loving and living with a man, Janice admitted to herself as she removed her glasses and leaned forward to apply a bit of eyeliner the way her daughter had taught her. Married love was comfortable if not wildly exciting. Exciting was for the young. She'd enjoyed sex with Kurt, but it hadn't been the be-all and end-all of their relationship. They'd mellowed and taken a mature approach to lovemaking that had put it in proper perspective.

Janice threw down the makeup pencil and closed her eyes with a sigh. Why was she thinking along these lines tonight? She had never been one to dwell on the physical aspects of her marriage.

It was the prospect of seeing David Markus in a very short time.

Gripping the edge of the dressing table, Janice stared at her reflection. She saw a middle-aged woman, a shade too slender, with nice hair and large gray eyes that looked haunted and hesitant. That about summed it up. A woman who'd recently buried a husband she'd loved very much. *Still* loved very much.

Be that as it may, David was a very attractive man. A man who set a woman to thinking, even if she didn't want to think along those lines. He wasn't forward or bold or flirtatious. But he was enormously appealing and unconsciously sensual.

He'd been alone for years and probably had scads of women after him—glamorous, cosmopolitan women. Fortunately, she wasn't in the market for a man and therefore needn't concern herself with the man-woman thing.

Picking up her favorite cologne, she lightly sprayed her neck and arms and behind her ears, then applied a little lipstick. Stefanie was always telling her she ought to wear more makeup, but Janice didn't feel comfortable with more.

Standing, she examined herself one last time. Not gorgeous, but it was the best she could do for now. Who expected gorgeous at a business meeting anyhow? Grabbing her glasses, she went to check on dinner.

DAVID TURNED into the Eber driveway at five to seven and switched off his Lincoln's engine. He sat for a moment looking at the large Victorian house painted a pale gray. The streetlights illuminated the patches of snow clinging to the front lawn. The dining room bay window with the wide seat faced the street on the drive side, and he caught a glimpse of the table through the sheer curtains.

The house was beautifully decorated with expensive things, obviously done with a loving hand and a generous bank account. Kurt had often bragged to David about his home, his chest puffing with pride. David had wondered how his friend had managed to parlay a modest inheritance into a profitable business complete with an elegant home and expensive life-style. After having spent hours poring over Kurt's books, he had a pretty good idea.

Kurt had worked like a man driven, and David thought he had been. Driven to succeed, to impress his wife's family, to prove he was worthy of the Ingallses' approval. The signs were all there. Kurt also had had something to prove—that he was as good as an Ingalls. And he'd enjoyed the trappings of the good life—the big house, the snazzy car, membership in the right clubs.

But success had come with a big price tag. He had spent years robbing Peter to pay Paul, mortgaging everything to the hilt, no sooner paying off one loan than getting in deeper with another. Apparently he'd kept most of the details from his wife, probably because to tell her would have made their future solvency look iffy, causing Janice to question him. However, the strain had undoubtedly added to the deterioration of his health, which he'd obviously been unaware of.

Fortunately, Kurt hadn't left Janice and his family in ruin, though he'd been headed in that direction. David knew Kurt had had plans—big plans—for one day being very wealthy. But he'd died too soon. And now, as David climbed out of his car, he wondered how much he should tell his widow without tarnishing the man's memory.

Taking an uneasy breath, he left his car, stepped onto the porch and rang the bell.

Janice opened the door and smiled at his look of surprise. Self-consciously—for he was staring—she brushed her fingers through her hair. "I had it cut."

David moved inside and closed the door, setting his leather briefcase down on the floor. "I like it. Brings out the red." From behind his back, he brought forth a single yellow rose wrapped in cellophane.

Her eyes softened as she took the flower and held it to her nose. The first time they'd gone out, he'd brought her one yellow rose, telling her he wished he could give her the entire dozen he couldn't afford at the time. He could now, she was certain, yet the gift of one stirred shared memories. "Thank you," she whispered.

"I didn't know you wore glasses."

She whipped them from her face. "I just got those, too. My arms weren't long enough, so I decided it was time to admit that the years had caught up with me." She took his topcoat and hung it in the hall closet.

Standing close, he inhaled her scent. Something lightly floral and expensive. "Personally, I think the years have been more than kind to you."

She turned, leaning against the closet door. He wore a gray suit with a vest, a pale blue shirt and striped tie. His face was ruddy from the cold and his eyes even bluer than she remembered. "And to you," she heard herself say, then flushed. To cover the moment, she turned toward the kitchen. "Make yourself comfortable. Would you like a glass of wine?"

"Sure."

But in the kitchen, her fingers fumbled and she couldn't get the cork out of the wine bottle. Nerves, she thought, and took a deep breath.

"May I help you with that?" David asked from the doorway.

She stepped aside as he took over. "If you like. I seem to be all thumbs tonight."

As he inched the cork free, he looked at her over his shoulder. "You look very in control to me."

Unused to flattery, especially on such a consistent basis, she turned aside before he could see her cheeks heating again. She wished he'd stop, or her face would be flaming all evening. Getting down the glasses, she set them in front of him and watched him pour.

Handing her one, he raised his own. "What shall we drink to?"

"I don't know."

He screwed up his face thoughtfully. "How about a quick end to winter and a happy springtime?"

Janice found a nervous smile. "Sounds good." They sipped.

"That wouldn't be coq au vin I smell, would it?" he asked.

"It is." She smiled more naturally now, pleased that he approved of her menu choice. "Why don't we go sit down while it finishes cooking?"

David let her lead the way into the spacious living room and stood until she seated herself in a corner of the couch facing the fireplace. Noticing that a fire had been laid, he raised a questioning eyebrow. "Shall I? It's a good night for a fire."

"Please do." She watched as he removed his jacket and bent to light the fire. She'd gone through Kurt's address book yesterday and found the name of the man who furnished their wood. A quick call and he'd brought in a fresh supply this morning. "Does your home have a fireplace?"

"Yes. I love to sit and stare into the flames."

She did, too. But Kurt had always been too restless to be idle for long, preferring more active pastimes. Janice watched as David leaned forward to distribute the flame along the crumpled newspaper and kindling. He was a big man, yet he moved effortlessly, almost gracefully. His build reminded her of her father's in his younger days, and of K.J., whose physique resembled his grandfather's. She sipped her wine.

David dusted off his hands and sat down at the opposite end of the couch. He picked up his glass before turning to her. Yellow was definitely her color, he thought as he let the tart wine roll over his tongue. Her eyes were avoiding his, and he wondered if she was nervous over what he might have found at Kurt's office or because they were alone together in the cozy intimacy of her living room.

His gaze took in the decor. "Did you do this? It looks great."

She warmed under his praise. "Thank you. I studied design for a while."

"Ah, yes, I remember." She'd once confided her dreams of decorating palatial mansions. Apparently she'd put her dreams aside so Kurt could pursue his.

Uncomfortable under his scrutiny, Janice switched subjects. "Did you have any trouble finding Kurt's office?"

"No, none at all. Tom Sikes is very knowledgeable about the company."

"He's been very helpful. Kurt often said that Tom wasn't much of a salesman, but he made a very good manager."

David nodded. "Usually the best salesmen don't do well in management. Too much ego. Kurt, on the other hand, was a hell of a salesman. Usually the owner doesn't keep on hustling the way Kurt did, but he was getting new accounts regularly. The agency has an impressive book of business, and most of it's due to Kurt's hard work."

"My father often said that Kurt could sell ice cubes to the Eskimos." Janice relaxed fractionally, whether from the pleasure his reassuring words gave her or from the wine, she wasn't certain. "So then you found the company to be solvent and problem free?"

David crossed his legs, searching for the right words. "No company is totally problem free, but Eber Insurance is decidedly solvent. I was pleased to see that your name is on the incorporation papers, so business can continue as usual without too many forms needing to be filed."

"That's a relief. Kurt used to remark that insurance regulations are very strict."

"They are. Have you any idea what you want to do with the business?"

Janice set her glass on the small table between their chairs. "I've been thinking about it, but I just don't know."

"I'll go over the books with you later, but for now, let me spell out your options. First off, I get the feeling Tom would like to take over."

"I got that impression, too."

"Whether he has the money to buy you out, I'm not sure. Or perhaps he's considering a partnership, with you the silent member. Those are two options. Or you could sell to an outsider. Finally, you could run it yourself."

"I know very little about the insurance field and business in general." But as she shifted her gaze to stare into the crackling flames, Janice thought of Anna's words. *There's nothing like earning your own money to give you a sense of accomplishment, a feeling of in-*

dependence. Could that be what was missing from her life?

"You don't have to decide right now," David went on.

"I suppose I could learn," Janice said softly, almost to herself. Her mind racing, she looked over at David. "What would I have to do to run it myself?"

She surprised him. He'd guessed she'd back away from even considering that. Perhaps she would still when she realized what she'd be taking on. "You'd have to take the required insurance courses. I believe that the University of Wisconsin has an extension program at Whitewater, and the campus is only an hour's drive away. Eber Insurance handles a variety of commercial and individual policies."

"Are separate courses required for each?"

"Pretty much. Then you have to pass a state exam in each category in order to be licensed."

Janice leaned her head back, fighting the feeling of being engulfed that came over her so often lately. "I should have known it wouldn't be simple."

David leaned forward, wanting to ease her mind. "You don't have to keep the business, Janice. You can offer the company for sale, take the money and invest it. I can steer things along with Tom until the transfer, if you like. That would be a lot easier on you."

She knew he was trying to be helpful, to walk her through this as painlessly as possible. But a nagging little voice at the back of her mind kept whispering in her ear. "Easier," she said aloud. "All my life, David,

I've taken the easy way. It was easier to elope with Kurt than buck my family's objections and push for them to accept him and our marriage. It was easier to quit college as Kurt wanted me to rather than carry on a long-distance romance for two more years until I graduated. It was easier to let him run the business, the household, practically my whole life, than to fight against his need to be in charge. I'm finding out that the easy route isn't necessarily the best path to follow."

"Have you been unhappy?"

"Unhappy?" Janice considered that a long moment. "Not unhappy, no. But occasionally unfulfilled, I think, or is that too dramatic a statement?"

He shrugged, toying with his wineglass, swirling the contents thoughtfully. "For some women, marriage is enough. For others, it isn't. It's an individual choice."

"Would simply being married be enough to keep you happy? Wouldn't you feel unfulfilled without your work, the sense of accomplishment?"

"No to the first question and yes to the second. And besides, someone has to earn the money, to make a living."

"Exactly. And I no longer have someone to rely on to do that for me. Maybe I shouldn't have relied so heavily on Kurt during our years together. Maybe then he wouldn't have pushed so hard. Maybe he'd still be with us."

David shook his head. "That's the guilt of the survivor talking. I've been through that and I know. You can drive yourself crazy with the what-ifs and the maybes. You didn't push Kurt, demand more and more so he had to work harder. That need was in his personality and you didn't put it there. Believe me, because I knew him fairly well."

She'd been curious about something and wondered if he'd give her a straight answer. "All those times the two of you met in Chicago, did Kurt talk about me?"

David picked up his wine for a long swallow, allowing himself an extra moment to answer. "We talked mostly about business. When he did mention you, it was always to say how much he cared for you."

His face looked sincere enough, yet she sensed an uneasiness behind his words. "I was just wondering." Picking up her glass, she rose. "I think dinner should be ready."

He, too, was ready for a change of subject. "Can I help?"

Walking to the kitchen, she spoke over her shoulder. "You can pour more wine."

David removed his tie, placed it alongside his jacket and unbuttoned the top button of his shirt. He wanted to strip away the formality that was between them. Perhaps if he looked more casual, Janice would relax a little.

JANICE HAD PLACED the yellow rose in a crystal bud vase in the center of the table. David waited until she set out the serving dishes. Then, because it was his habit, he held the chair for her as she sat down. Taking his own seat, he saw that the small gesture had both surprised and flustered her.

The chicken was wonderfully tender, the rich wine sauce complementing it perfectly, while the salad was crisp and the rolls warm and fragrant. He told her so and watched the pleasure shine from her eyes. As he buttered a roll, it occurred to David that Janice likely hadn't had many compliments in her life, since each one seemed to delight yet embarrass her. Perhaps Kurt's other interests had overshadowed the attention he might have lavished on his wife. For that reason alone, David meant to let Janice know that he still thought of her as special.

"Tyler's a pleasant little town," he said, thinking they'd had enough business conversation for a while. "I haven't spent much time here, but I like it."

"Mmm, I like it, too. When we first moved here, though it was my idea after living in Milwaukee and then Madison, I was a little frustrated at not having more stores available, more activities. But I've gotten used to the peace and quiet, a worthwhile trade-off."

"I hope it won't upset you if I bring it up, but I overheard a couple of people at the agency talking about a body that's been discovered—one that had been buried for forty years. They said the woman's name was Margaret Ingalls. A relative of yours?"

"Yes, my aunt. I was an infant when she disappeared, so I don't remember her at all."

"Disappeared?"

Janice paused to pass the plate of vegetables. "So the story goes. You might recall meeting my Uncle Judson here at the house after the funeral. Margaret was his wife, a pretty wild lady, from what I've heard. She was from Chicago and hated having to move to a small town when Judson's father had a heart attack and he had to take over the family business here in Tyler. They spent lots of time at Timberlake Lodge, and evidently Margaret used to throw some rather unruly parties while her husband was hard at work. When he found out, he lost his patience. They quarreled and it's rumored that Margaret ran off with some playboy. However, it would seem she didn't get far."

"I assume they suspect foul play. If Margaret had simply fallen while running off, someone would have noticed."

"I'm sure they would have, because Uncle Judson employed several servants. Plus Alyssa, his daughter, was about seven. Recently, Alyssa's youngest daughter, Liza, who's a decorator, took it upon herself to renovate the lodge. Margaret's remains were discovered when some water pipes were being checked down by the lake."

"A real-life mystery happening right here. And all this time, your uncle's never remarried?"

Remembering her hostess duties, Janice topped up his wine. "No. My dad always said that Judson was crazy about Margaret, but that she never appeared happy."

Finishing the wonderful meal, David sat back, giving his full attention to Janice. In the dim light of the chandelier, her skin took on a golden cast. "They sound like a mismatched couple. So many who marry are."

His eyes had darkened and his expression was sad. Janice had the feeling that they were no longer talking about Margaret and Judson. "Is that how it was with you and your wife?" she asked, the wine making her more forward than usual.

David held her gaze. "In many ways. I was thirty and Eleanor was nine years younger when we married. She'd been raised in a small town and had been very sheltered. I'd been all over the world. I should have taken better care of her."

"Now who's feeling guilty? Anyone can lose control of a car, David. You weren't at fault."

He looked unconvinced. "If I'd been home, she wouldn't have had to go out in such bad weather."

"She was young, but she was an adult."

"She was pregnant with our first child."

Instinctively, Janice reached out and took his hand, lacing her fingers through his tightly. "Oh, David. I'm so sorry."

David glanced out the window at the wintry sky for a long minute before turning to her. "Was your marriage a good one, Janice?"

"Though it ended abruptly, I feel fortunate to have had a good marriage, yes."

His eyes continued to stare into hers and, for a nervous moment, she sensed he wanted to say something. "What?" she asked, her voice not quite steady.

"Nothing, nothing at all." He shifted his gaze and sipped his wine.

Perhaps it would be best not to press, Janice thought as she got up to clear the table. "I'll get the coffee."

While she did that, David went to get his briefcase. Over coffee, he spread out the papers on the dining room table and explained her financial situation.

"This one insurance policy of Kurt's could pay off that second mortgage, which is at a fairly high interest rate, and provide adequately for K.J.'s remaining college needs. The original mortgage is manageable and a good tax shelter, so I suggest you keep paying on that one. This second policy, although it's been borrowed on, will give you a good cash base. You can put that lump sum into the money market, or certificates of deposit, which are doing fairly well right now. The third and final policy he'd cashed in several years ago." Wondering how much of this she'd known about, David looked over at her. "Any questions?"

She hesitated, unwilling to reveal so much about her personal affairs to David, who was, despite their long acquaintance, not really a close friend. However, since she'd requested his help, it would be foolish not to ask. "Is it possible for one party of a marriage to take out a second mortgage on a property they jointly own without the other person's knowledge?"

"No. The lending institution requires both signatures. I found the original note in Kurt's office safe.
You signed the second mortgage as well as the first."
He watched her struggle with accepting that. "Maybe
you don't recall. A lot of men bring home papers for
their wives' signatures and most women sign without
question, trusting the men they married." He wanted
to give her the out, so she wouldn't feel bad about not
having noticed.

Janice nodded. "Kurt often did that. I imagine he
probably explained the need for the second mortgage
at the time, but I don't remember just now."

"Collateral for a business loan, perhaps. Most
companies experience cash-flow problems periodi-
cally. Or perhaps he used it to open the satellite office
in Chicago."

"Yes, that was most likely it."

She was agreeing, but she was beginning to question. And to doubt. David had an unreasonable desire
to take a hard swing at a dead friend for putting that
look of uncertainty on Janice's face. "I've made a list
of bills to be paid at the office, verified each one and
left it with the bookkeeper. You'll need to go in and
sign the checks in the next day or so. The accounts re-
ceivable is healthy and there should be no surprises,
provided all the salesmen remain."

A new fear was born. "Do you think some plan to
leave?"

"It all depends on where they see the company
headed. You'll need to come to a decision as to what

you plan to do with Eber Insurance, then share it with the staff as soon as possible. I checked with Tom, and most everyone seems to be pulling his own weight. Whether you sell or keep the company, you wouldn't want to lose good, productive people. Kurt's death is a shock to them, too, and they need to know who will be at the helm, who they can go to with problems."

Janice ran shaky fingers through her short hair. "That seems only fair."

"I've also taken the liberty of listing the personal bills so that—"

"What personal bills? Those always came to the house. I've paid most, and the rest are on Kurt's desk in his den."

He'd suspected as much when he'd run across the two items. Though he'd prefer to spare her, there was no backing down. "There are two credit cards listing the company address, both charged to the maximum allowable amount." He held the bills out to her.

Janice put on her glasses and studied the charge-account billings. A series of purchases by date only, revealing an amount owed of more than a thousand dollars on one and several hundred on the other. She swallowed hard, trying to keep her composure, trying to come up with an explanation. "These must have been used by Kurt to charge things for the company, perhaps during his travels, even though they're billed to him personally. I've never seen either one before."

"Entirely possible. I use one credit card for business charges and others for personal expenses."

Her mind was racing. "I brought home several envelopes filled with things from his desk drawers. I haven't had time to go through it all yet. There must be a savings-account book in there somewhere. I know we had one, but it's not in the house."

David hated to tell her, but felt she needed to know. He handed her the bankbook he'd found among Kurt's papers. "It was closed out more than a year ago."

Silently, Janice leafed through the passbook. Looking pale again, she removed her glasses and rubbed her forehead.

He tried to ease her mind. "There's always the insurance money, which is considerable."

"Yes." Nervously, she straightened the pile of papers before her, lining up the edges just so, her thoughts in confusion. "I suppose you run into this a lot when you probe into people's finances. The husband sort of melds the personal assets with the business holdings."

"It's not uncommon." It was, however, a dangerous practice. Going on instinct, he placed his hand over hers, stopping her restless movements. "I hope you're not worried. You're not in bad financial shape."

From somewhere, Janice found a smile. "I'm not worried. I'm certain that Kurt would never leave me in a fix. Not knowingly, anyhow."

She needed to cling to her belief in Kurt, David realized, in order to get through this. He would let her have that as long as humanly possible. "Of course not." He squeezed her hand briefly, then snapped his briefcase closed and stood. "It's getting late. I'd better let you get some rest."

Forcing herself to concentrate on the moment, Janice walked with him to the living room, where he put on his jacket and folded his tie before placing it in his pocket. "Are you planning to drive back to Chicago tonight?"

"No, I'm a little beat. Tom suggested I take a room at Kelsey Boardinghouse for the night, so I stopped in there earlier. Seems like a comfortable place."

"It is. Anna Kelsey is one of my closest friends." She took his coat from the closet and handed it to him.

"She remembered me from the reception. Her nephew moved out recently and she's giving me his old room for the night." He hated to leave her, but couldn't think of a single acceptable reason to stay. Besides, he sensed she needed to be alone, to sort through all she'd learned tonight.

"Will you be setting out early tomorrow morning, then?"

"Not too early, but yes."

Janice came to a quick decision, something she was unused to doing. "Why don't you stop by for coffee before you start back to Chicago? I've got a lot of thinking to do tonight. Hopefully, I'll have arrived at a decision by then, at least about the business. I can't put that off too much longer."

He took a step closer. "Don't push yourself. A day or two won't matter."

"I think I'll feel better once I make up my mind."

"I'll be glad to help you in any way I can."

She smiled up at him. He was so tall, so solid looking. "Thank you, David. You've been an enormous help."

He suddenly realized it wasn't gratitude he wanted. Placing his hands on her arms, he touched the sleeves of her yellow sweater. "Let me hold you, just for a minute."

Apprehension leaped into her eyes. "David, I..."

"Friend to friend, Janice?" he asked gently. "For old times' sake."

She let out a deep breath, then let him ease her close, his arms sliding around her. Her hands fluttered nervously at his waist, then quieted as she closed her eyes. His touch was light, offering comfort with no pressure. She gave in to the pleasure of simple human contact, of being held and feeling safe, if only briefly.

David bent his head, his face grazing her hair. She smelled wonderfully female, and she felt soft and giving. He scarcely breathed, not wanting to frighten her. The years dropped away and he remembered the last time he'd held her, really held her, back when he'd been able to touch her more freely. But she was here now, willingly in his arms, and David felt his pulse pound in reaction to her nearness.

"You're a very special woman, Janice," he said softly into her hair. "And you're going to be fine."

He drew back first, letting her know she could trust him, that he wouldn't push. This was a fragile woman who'd been buffeted by some heavy storms lately. He would not add to her anxieties.

Stepping back, David smiled down at her. "Thank you for the best dinner I've had in I can't remember how long."

Janice folded her arms over her chest, recognizing it for the protective gesture it was. She felt unaccountably close to tears and suddenly vulnerable to this very appealing man, and the knowledge was frightening. "I can't imagine that. I'm sure you eat in the best of restaurants in your many travels."

His hand on the doorknob, he shook his head. "I hate to eat out alone. I often stop at some fast-food place, grab a bag of burgers and eat them in my hotel room while I watch the news on TV. Some glamorous life, this traveling around."

She was certain he was exaggerating to flatter her. "In another minute, you'll have me feeling sorry for you and rising at dawn to make homemade muffins for your breakfast."

"That was my plan. Good night, Janice."

Though it was cold, she stood watching him through the open storm door. After a brief warm-up time, he backed the car out of her drive. He paused on the street, flashed his lights on and off at her, then drove away.

He'd left her with some uncomfortable things to think her way through. And he'd left her with the solid impression of his body close up against hers. How could she have enjoyed that when . . . when she loved Kurt?

Feeling guilty, she closed the door just as the phone began to ring. Distractedly, she walked to the den to answer. But before she got there, the answering machine picked up the call.

"I'm sorry we can't come to the phone right now," Kurt's recorded voice began.

Janice stopped in midstride, frozen to the spot, her heart pounding.

"Your call is important to us," Kurt went on. "Please leave your name and number after the beep and we'll get back to you as soon as possible."

Oh, God. Oh, God. Pressing the knuckles of one hand to her mouth, Janice sank into the nearest chair. *Kurt, Kurt.*

Irene's voice came on, saying she was just calling to check on her, that she'd phone back tomorrow. Good, because Janice couldn't have talked with her now if her life depended on it.

Leaning her head back, Janice closed her eyes. She felt the tears building, building. When would this terrible helpless feeling go away? When would her heart stop being so heavy? When would she feel like smiling again, genuinely smiling?

CHAPTER FOUR

DAVID ZIPPED UP his leather travel bag and carried it down the stairs at Kelsey Boardinghouse, following his nose toward the enticing smell of perked coffee. He'd slept well under a handmade quilt and had awakened early to the unfamiliar sounds of a busy household stirring. Dressed casually in a black turtleneck sweater over gray slacks, he walked into the Kelsey kitchen and found Anna bent over, loading the dishwasher. "Good morning," he said, laying his coat over the back of a chair.

Anna smiled a greeting as she reached for a cup. "I'll bet you could use some coffee."

"Yes, ma'am." David took his cup to the butcher-block table and sat down. He'd arrived last evening and found Anna and her husband, Johnny, sitting by the fire exchanging replays of their day. At their invitation, he'd joined them and spent a comfortable hour chatting. He'd liked Johnny Kelsey, finding him down-to-earth and quick-witted, while Anna was soft-spoken and undoubtedly the heart of her family. "I thought I was early but it looks like everyone's up and gone."

"Weekends are like that." Anna finished and re-filled her coffee cup before joining him at her table.

"Johnny had something to check on at the plant, a couple of folks had Saturday errands, and I believe my daughter Kathleen is sleeping in. We're sort of casual around here."

David glanced out the window at the wide porch, the sloping back lawn. "Your home is lovely and very comfortable."

"Thank you. We like it." Anna took a swallow, then set down her cup. "So, are you able to give some assistance to Janice? I know she's feeling confused."

Through her glasses, he studied Anna's intelligent blue eyes and remembered Janice mentioning that they were close friends. Still, he decided it was up to Janice to speak of her finances if she felt the need. "We're in the process of going through the papers. I did outline her options regarding the insurance agency. I imagine she'll decide to sell it."

"Do you?"

David sent her a questioning look. "Don't you?"

"I don't know, David. Janice has always had someone to depend upon, going from her father's house to her husband's home. She's never really had a chance to be her own person, to find out what *she* wants, because she's always too busy pleasing others. Maybe this is a good time for her to try a new path."

David was thoughtful. "She has absolutely no business experience, and insurance is a tough game, highly regulated, with a great deal for a newcomer to learn. It would take her months to be even minimally qualified to run Eber Insurance."

Anna leaned back, toying with her spoon. "She has the time. It might do her good to fill her hours with studies. It would take her mind off Kurt being gone. I consider her bright enough, don't you?"

David shifted in his chair, wondering why Janice's good friend would want her to follow such a difficult road. "Yes, I find her very bright. I thought so years ago when I dated her back in college. Bright and energetic and sharp. I think she should do *something,* but I'm not sure the insurance business is the answer."

"You don't feel women belong in business?"

"I think some of them do, but which business is the question. I somehow don't see Janice being happy selling insurance. I could be wrong."

So that was how it was, Anna realized, keeping her expression bland. David was attracted to Janice, yet looked upon her as too unsophisticated to succeed in such a difficult field. Perhaps she was, but there was more to Janice than David, who'd been absent from her life for more than twenty years, was able to see. "Maybe she'll surprise us both."

"Maybe." David finished his coffee and stood. "I think when we lose a life partner through death or divorce, it's best to make other changes in our lives gradually."

Looking him in the eye, Anna also stood. "I agree. Janice needs time to reevaluate her future. She doesn't need someone pushing or prodding her in one direction or another."

A good friend to have in your corner, David thought. He gave her a small smile. "I'm not that kind of man, if that's what you're worried about."

"I'm glad to hear it. Janice is very vulnerable right now."

"I'm aware of that and I'd never take advantage."

After a long moment, Anna nodded. "No, I don't think you would." Stepping back, she handed him his coat. "I hope the next time you're in Tyler, you'll stop to see us again."

"Thank you, I will."

As he walked to his car, it occurred to David that Anna was an expert at reading between the lines.

But he didn't think either woman knew what Janice would be up against stepping out into the business world, he decided as he drove toward Janice's house. His mother hadn't, either, and the necessity had aged her before her time.

David had been seventeen and his sister only ten when their father had died of a quickly spreading cancer that had insidiously moved throughout his body, killing him shortly after his fortieth birthday. Shocked and grieving, David's mother had put the butcher shop up for sale. But times hadn't been good and there'd been a big mortgage on the house. So she'd had no choice but to go to work as a dentist's receptionist.

The hours had been long and she'd had to take two buses home to the small house on the south side. Though the living had been lean, she hadn't allowed David to quit school, had in fact scrimped and saved to put him through college. It had hurt him to watch that good, frail woman grow old and weary with the weight of their problems. And it had inspired him, too.

He'd worked hard, graduated near the top of his class and qualified for a government job with lots of potential. He'd gone into fieldwork, and though there'd been some dangerous assignments, David had thought the risks worth it. The need to take care of his mother, to make her life easier, had burned in him. As soon as he was able, he'd bought her a better house in a nice suburb and had made it possible for her to retire. Soon after, he'd enrolled his sister in a good college, proud to be able to take care of his own.

He'd knocked around a lot of places by the time he'd met Eleanor. She'd been young and very lovely, a secretary in the Chicago office where he'd been based. He'd been wildly attracted to her and suddenly felt the lack of a loving home life. After a whirlwind courtship, he'd married her.

Turning onto Janice's street, David hit the button to lower the window and took a deep breath of the cold, wintry air. His work had involved a great deal of travel, which had left his young wife home alone too much. Though Eleanor hadn't complained, he'd felt uneasy about not being there to advise and guide her, especially after she'd gotten pregnant. He should have been there for her, and if he had, perhaps she wouldn't have died.

David sighed. An old struggle with guilt, one he still wrestled with too often. If he ever married again, he'd play it differently. He'd take care of his wife, be there for her, support her every decision, protect her.

Parking in Janice's drive, he set aside his musings and stepped out. He was on the porch, his hand stretched toward the bell, when she opened the door. She wore a roomy blue sweater over stone-washed jeans and white sneakers, the casual outfit making her appear more youthful. Her makeup consisted of a touch of lipstick only, something few women her age could get by with and still look morning-fresh and appealing. The unpretentiousness charmed him, he realized as he stepped inside.

He smelled cinnamon and smiled. "You did bake."

Janice led the way to the kitchen. "I couldn't sleep. Too much on my mind, so I thought I might as well be doing something productive." Directing him to the glass-topped dinette table, she busied herself pouring fresh coffee.

She hadn't been kidding when she'd said she hadn't slept. She'd tossed and turned and fought the covers all night, wrestling with a multitude of problems, wanting desperately to make the right decision. It was years since she'd had to make one strictly on her own. She wondered if it would get any easier as time went on.

Sitting down opposite David, Janice allowed herself a moment to look at him. The smattering of gray at his temples only added to his appeal. His cheeks were red from the cold and his eyes were sky blue this morning. She could see a tiny nick on his chin where he'd cut himself shaving and could smell the rich male scent of him over the baked goods on the table. Her hands not quite steady, she offered him a roll.

David bit into the cinnamon crust, then licked the buttery sweetness from his fingers. "Mmm. Where'd you learn to bake like this?"

Janice looked up from the dark liquid in her coffee cup. "From a cookbook. I imagine, if you put your mind to it, you can learn most anything from books."

Wiping his hands on a napkin, David watched her. "I feel a speech coming on."

She made a dismissive gesture. "Not a speech, but I have come to a couple of decisions. I'm going to ask Tom if he'll stay on as manager and give me as much help as he can while I see if I can learn something about the insurance business. Then I'm going to check into where and how soon the required courses will be offered. Probably I should consider some accounting and computer classes as well."

David leaned back. "Sounds like you're going to be pretty busy."

"I need to be, David." She swung her eyes around the room, then brought them back to his. "The walls are closing in on me. Besides, I should at least be able to understand what's going on in the company. I probably won't run it alone. It was always Kurt's dream that his son would want to take over after college. But for now, I need to do this."

He wondered if she knew about her son's love of art. "I'm proud of you. It'll be tough, but you can do it."

Janice knew her surprise showed on her face. "You approve?" She'd hoped David would be in favor of her decision, but she hadn't really thought he would be. That he was flustered her. Kurt had rarely encouraged her in new endeavors and she was confused as to how to react.

He took his time with a swallow of hot coffee, choosing his words carefully. "You don't need my approval, Janice, or anyone else's. This is your decision. I support whatever will make you happy and I'll do anything I can to help you."

She smiled. "Thank you, David. I appreciate all you've done for me already and I want you to send me a bill for your time. I also could use some investment advice for the insurance money, and perhaps a little help with the firm from time to time. Tom's knowledgeable, but I trust you more."

"I value your trust," he said. She seemed nervous, whether because he was here or because of her new commitment, he couldn't tell. Finishing his coffee, he rose. "If you need anything, you have my number."

"Yes." She walked to the door with him. Arriving at her decision left her feeling drained on the one hand, exhilarated on the other. She'd rather hoped David could have stayed to talk with her, let her toss around her ideas and see how they'd sit with him. But she hadn't the right to ask and he was probably anxious to get going. Though he'd protested to the contrary, she knew he must have a busy life back in Chicago.

Shrugging into his coat, David again felt a reluctance to leave her as he opened the inside door. It was a cold but sunny day, and he wished he could ask her to grab a jacket and walk with him in the crunchy snow, to show him her town. Or they could go for a ride out around that lodge her uncle had once owned and she could tell him a little about the area residents. He badly wanted to rediscover the qualities he'd admired in her so long ago, to renew their friendship. But her husband had recently died and he was an outsider. She also had a small-town reputation to protect.

Yet no one was watching them now. David gently cupped her chin, forcing her wide gray eyes to meet his. "Take care of yourself, Sunshine." Before he could change his mind, he gave in to an urge and brushed his mouth across hers. Caught off guard, she parted her lips in surprise and he lingered for another instant, his touch lightly caressing. Then he opened the storm door and hurried down the porch steps.

Too unnerved to react before, Janice now felt a flush of guilt stain her cheeks. Quickly, she shut the door, listening to her erratic heartbeat. Surely no one had been driving by, no one had seen them. She should have pulled back, shouldn't have allowed the kiss, amicable though it had been.

Yet she found herself touching her lips with her tongue to recapture the remnants of his taste.

Standing there twisting her wide gold wedding band, Janice wished she had more experience with handling conflicting emotions.

IT WAS EARLY EVENING during the first week of March when Janice stopped her station wagon in front of the house on Elm Street. The stately Victorian was much larger than her own. She stared at the big porch where she'd spent many hours sitting and chatting on hot summer days. Her Uncle Judson and Alyssa lived here together, and she'd felt the need to talk with her cousin. She'd phoned earlier, and Alyssa's voice had been warm as always when she'd invited her over for tea and sympathy, as she'd put it.

But it wasn't sympathy Janice was seeking, she realized as she got out of the car and went up onto the porch, a stiff winter wind hurrying her steps. Support, maybe, and an encouraging voice. Someone to assure her she was doing the right thing, she thought as she rang the bell. Someone to tell her she wasn't being an utter fool with her ambitious undertaking and her various worries. Alyssa had seemed the perfect person to see, for she'd never worked in the business world either, nor was she half as assertive as their friend, Anna Kelsey. Perhaps she was merely searching for validation, Janice thought as the door swung open.

"Alyssa, that front door has been squeaking on its hinges since you and I were both children. Why don't you or Judson get it fixed?"

Alyssa laughed. "There ought to be some constants in life, I feel, and that's ours." She drew her cousin inside. "Janice, I know I've told you before, but I really love how you're wearing your hair." Leading the way to the kitchen, she patted her own shoulder-length blond hair. "Maybe I should get mine trimmed. There comes a time when long hair on a woman just doesn't seem appropriate, don't you think?"

Janice slipped off her coat and tossed it on a chair. "I don't think yours is too long at all."

Alyssa poured boiling water into her cherry-red teapot, glancing up at her guest as she finished. Janice was wearing a dress in a soft shade of blue with a wide leather belt, one Alyssa couldn't recall seeing before. "Is that a new outfit?" Placing the lid on the pot, she carried the tea tray to the small table by the window. "What is this, the new you?" She smiled to take the sting from her words. Lord, she'd almost said the unforgivable, she thought, almost asked Janice if she was turning into the merry widow. Kurt hadn't been dead two months yet, and Alyssa knew how devoted Janice had been to him.

Still, as she sat down and looked her cousin over, she did think that Janice somehow seemed younger and more perky.

"I hadn't realized how country bumpkin my wardrobe had gotten," Janice explained. "Now that I'm going into the office nearly every day and attending classes in Madison, I had to go out and buy some clothes. I used to live in sweats, but things have changed."

Alyssa leaned back. "How are the classes going?"

Janice brushed a lock of hair from her forehead and frowned. "I've never found anything so difficult and complicated in my life. Going back to learning after all these years—well, it's a lot tougher than I'd thought. Then there's the hour it takes to drive round trip to the University of Wisconsin at Whitewater for my insurance courses. And after class, I go to the agency and Tom tries to explain forms and procedures, throwing all these terms at me." She laughed helplessly. "He might as well be speaking Greek."

"But you're hanging in there?"

"I suppose I am." Janice watched Alyssa pour the Chinese orange-scented tea that was her specialty and inhaled the familiar pungent aroma. "Actually, I'm kind of enjoying myself. I mean, I'm struggling through the material, but getting to know the producers and what they do is invigorating." She accepted the cup from Alyssa and reached for a slice of lemon. "Of course, most of the time I despair about ever catching on to everything."

"You shouldn't doubt yourself. It takes time, naturally, but you're an intelligent woman. You'll be fine." Alyssa swung her gaze out the window at the darkening sky. "Sometimes I think I should have done something more productive after... after Ronald's death."

Janice studied her cousin's profile. The tilt of her head was almost regal and there was obvious strength in Alyssa. Yet there were those who thought of her as somewhat flighty, though not as much as her mother before her. Janice envied Alyssa's elegance. Even now, wearing wool slacks and a silk blouse with simple gold earrings, she looked like the society matron she was.

But there was a lingering sadness in her blue eyes that never seemed to fade.

Because they were related and Alyssa was only six years older than she was, Janice knew her well. Knew that though she'd been a child when her mother disappeared, Alyssa had been greatly affected by the seeming abandonment. And then her father had broken up her alliance with her first love, Eddie Wocheck. But perhaps her husband's death some years later had devastated Alyssa the most. Facing financial ruin, Ronald had committed suicide.

Noticing that Alyssa's thoughts had slipped into the past, Janice touched her hand. "Your situation was different. You had three children still at home. My two are nearly on their own."

Alyssa squeezed her fingers. "I suppose you're right."

Glancing at their intertwined hands, Janice realized that both of them still wore their wedding bands. Was Alyssa still grieving so many years later for her dead husband? Unlikely, since Anna seemed so certain Alyssa had married Ronald on the rebound after Eddie had left town. If not that, then why was her cousin more moody and introspective tonight? "Is anything wrong?"

"Not any one specific thing," Alyssa said. "Just an uneasy feeling I have. Since Liza's return and then her marriage..."

"Yes, and now you're going to be a grandmother, Anna tells me. That must be an exciting prospect."

"It is, but Liza's so restless, you know. She's intent on dredging up the past and I'm not sure that's wise."

Janice watched as Alyssa sipped her tea. She'd have to tread softly here, but maybe talking things out with a family member would help her cousin come to grips with a buried past. "I've heard you say many times that you can't remember what happened the night Margaret disappeared. Are you afraid that all this is going to force you to recall something upsetting?"

"Yes, that's part of it. I think I've got a repressive nature, you know. My upbringing, perhaps. I scarcely remember ever talking with my mother. Certainly my father and I rarely speak about anything emotional. When Ronald was having his problems, he never confided in me. For years I've felt that if only I'd known, perhaps I could have helped him and he wouldn't have... have died. But lately, I've begun to wonder if I did suspect and just ignored the signs. If it was easier to pretend there was nothing wrong."

Janice let out a troubled sigh. "I know how you feel. I keep wondering if there wasn't something I could have done so that Kurt wouldn't have felt this compelling need for more and more. I believe his drive to succeed weakened his heart and ultimately killed him."

Alyssa's eyes were genuinely sympathetic. "I don't think you could have changed Kurt, Janice. I think he needed to prove to himself that he was as good as an Ingalls."

"But why? I never compared him to members of our family."

"Who knows? It isn't easy for a man, marrying into this family. Today's men seem more able to handle a wife from a wealthy background, but back when we were young, that wasn't necessarily so. Ronald had weaknesses, quite a few, and I wasn't strong enough to cope with them. Or to admit he even had them. Perhaps if I had . . ." Vaguely, she let the thought drift.

Janice found her hands not quite steady as she poured more tea. Alyssa had inadvertently led into an avenue she herself had been wondering about. "What kind of weaknesses do you mean?"

"Well, of course, financially, he made some poor decisions. But I think there was more." Folding her hands, she stared down at them. "I think there were other women."

"You think Ronald was unfaithful?"

"I have no proof, only this persistent *feeling.*"

Janice had heard the rumors about Ronald, too, but hadn't believed them. Or had she, like Alyssa, *chosen* not to listen? Were they two of a kind—trusting women unable to face reality? "I know what you mean. Kurt traveled so much—Milwaukee, Chicago, Washington, D.C., sometimes even New York. He was often gone a full week at a time. When he was alive, I rarely gave it a thought. But now . . ."

Alyssa switched her attention to her cousin's troubled face. "Is there some reason why suddenly now you suspect Kurt might have . . . have been seeing someone else?"

"I ran across something in Kurt's office desk. A checkbook register. For five or six years, there've been checks made out to someone named Diane Flynn. All for considerable amounts, all notations in Kurt's handwriting. My name isn't on the account."

Frowning, Alyssa leaned forward. "Have you checked with the bank that has the account?"

Janice nodded. "There's a balance of about four hundred in the account, but other than that, they couldn't tell me anything."

"Did you find the cancelled checks?"

"No. I've searched the office thoroughly. The bank had the latest packet, along with the end-of-the-month statement. I showed them Kurt's death certificate and they finally released it to me. Two checks, both made out to Diane Flynn, both endorsed by her. No other information except that they were cashed by a Chicago bank."

Though her voice was unemotional, Alyssa could tell Janice was upset. She knew only too well how distressing it was to learn something about your husband after his death. If she could spare her cousin that, she would. "You are, of course, jumping to conclusions. Diane Flynn may be a business professional Kurt dealt with, a woman representing a company where he purchased something. Or some insurance payoff on a policy or..."

"I totaled one twelve-month period," Janice interrupted. "The amount was nearly fourteen thousand." Her eyes, suddenly bleak, rose to meet Alyssa's. "Why wouldn't he have written a business check, if that's what it was, on his business account? I asked Tom Sikes, Kurt's manager, to look up the name in their files. He couldn't find a record of Diane Flynn anywhere."

"There's a logical explanation somewhere, we're just not seeing it, Janice. Kurt loved you, of that I feel certain." Alyssa picked up her cup, annoyed to find her hand shaking. Damn Kurt, she thought nastily. Janice had been devoted to him. What possible reason would he have for straying?

Janice finished her tea and pushed aside the cup. Maybe tea and sympathy was what she'd been after. Lord, but she didn't want to turn into a pitiful soul. Squaring her shoulders, she sat up taller. "I probably shouldn't have told you."

Alyssa touched her arm. "Why not? I won't tell anyone, if that's what you mean."

"I know you won't." She gazed out the window at a sliver of moon hanging in an inky sky. "I had half a thought to ask David Markus to see if he could find this Diane Flynn. He lives in Chicago. But I hate for him to know that Kurt..." Her voice caught and she swallowed.

"Perhaps it's best to let sleeping dogs lie." A change of subject was in order, Alyssa decided. "Have you been seeing David?"

Janice frowned. "Not 'seeing him,' in the sense you mean. I asked him for some financial guidance. He seems supportive, though I get the feeling he doesn't think I'm suited for the business world."

"Just what you need, another assertive man in your life."

Janice turned to her with a frown. "Is that how you saw Kurt?"

"Yes. Didn't you?"

Odd how both Anna and Alyssa had viewed Kurt the same way. "I guess so, but not in a harmful way." She felt a need to change the subject. Knowing frank confidences shared between women often led the way to more, Janice didn't hesitate to ask. Besides, half the town had seen them together at the Christmas party. "How are things between you and Eddie?"

Alyssa took her time answering. "Does any woman ever *really* forget her first love?"

"Probably not."

"Kurt *was* your first love, wasn't he?" Alyssa hadn't seen her cousin all that often when Janice had been away at college. She'd been busy with her own growing family at that time.

Had Kurt been her first love? Janice asked herself. She thought of the last time she'd seen David, the way he'd touched his lips to hers. She'd been attracted to him at eighteen, but when David had told her that he had too many obligations to get serious with anyone, she'd shifted her attention to Kurt. Had things been different, would she and David have fallen in love? She would never know.

Still, she chose not to answer Alyssa's question. "I don't believe I will mention this Diane Flynn to David. They say you shouldn't ask a question you don't want to hear the answer to. I should probably drop the whole matter. After all, what can I do about her now, even if it's true?"

"I think you're right. Put it out of your mind."

But could she? "Could *you?*" Janice looked at her cousin and saw the answer in her eyes. Suddenly tired, she glanced at her watch and stood. "I've got to get home. I have a list of insurance definitions a mile long to memorize and we're having a test tomorrow."

Alyssa walked down the hall with her, but the door opened before they reached it. "Dad," she greeted Judson. "I'm glad you're home."

"Hello, ladies. Cold out there." Judson Ingalls stomped snow from his shoes, then slid an arm about his niece. "How you doing, honey?"

"Surviving, Uncle Judson," Janice told him.

"That's all most of us can do." Turning to the hall closet, he reached for a hanger for his coat.

Janice hugged Alyssa. "Thanks for listening."

Alyssa nodded. "Take care and call me, anytime."

"I will. Bye." Janice made her way to her car, a weary slump to her shoulders.

ALYSSA CLOSED the door after her and took a deep breath. Her conversation with Janice had been unsettling, and she was about to have another, one she'd put off too long. "Dad, I've got some tea made. Will you come and have a cup with me?"

Judson rubbed the back of his neck. "I'm a little tired tonight, Alyssa."

"Please. I need to talk with you." She watched her father's face, seeing the flash of reluctance. He'd been the patriarchal figure of the family so long that everyone was used to doing things his way. But he gave in and walked to the kitchen. Alyssa followed, searching for how to bring up what she wanted to discuss.

Finally, when she'd made fresh tea and poured them each a cup, she sat down opposite her father and plunged in. "I've been trying to talk with you for some time. Ever since Edward came to our Christmas party."

Judson kept his eyes averted. "Are we going to re-hash all that again, Alyssa? I know I interfered in your life with regard to Edward, but you were so young and I really thought I was doing what would be best for you."

She waved a dismissive hand. "No, Dad, that's not what I want to talk about. I know you've been as upset as I am over the discovery of Mother's remains after all these years. Liza has really stirred things up by insisting on renovating Timberlake. And then there's Brick and that police captain wife of his poking around, determined to get at the truth." Only recently, Anna had confided that the captain thought Judson had done away with Margaret. Alyssa shuddered at the thought. If only she could remember . . .

Judson shifted impatiently. "I don't know as anyone has the whole truth of what happened the night Margaret disappeared."

"I've been having these dreams." With trembling fingers, Alyssa rubbed her temples.

"What kind of dreams?"

"They're disjointed, but very real. When I saw that old suitcase they found, I knew what would be in it before it was opened. Mother's clothes. I have this... this nagging sense of memory. I believe I know something, but I don't know what it is. The truth eludes me."

Judson's sharp eyes flashed to his daughter. "What exactly *do* you remember?"

Alyssa frowned, trying to recall. "There was one dream recently that was so real. I was a little girl again, about the age I was when Mother disappeared. I remember waking up one morning in my bedroom and I called out for her. But she didn't come and I started to cry. Then you came in and held me and you were upset, too."

Alyssa didn't even hear her father's sharp gasp, so caught up in the past was she. "You told me Mother was gone, that she'd left us, that she didn't love you anymore. I asked why and you didn't answer, just hugged me harder and rocked me. You called me your little princess."

Judson's sigh was ragged with emotion. "I remember that. It wasn't a dream." Running a hand over his face, he shook his head sadly. "I shouldn't have talked so much to you about all that. You were just a child. All these years, I've felt terrible, drawing you into my pain."

Alyssa blinked rapidly, then looked at him, realizing he suddenly looked older, more frail. "Why not? She was my mother. She left both of us."

"Maybe so, but it was me she was running from, not you. In her own way, Alyssa, Margaret loved you. It's just that she wasn't very maternal. But that wasn't your fault. I tried to make up for the loss of your mother, tried to be a good father."

She touched his hand. "You have been a good father. I don't want you to think otherwise. I . . . I'm just wondering why suddenly, after all these years, I remember things that happened back then that I couldn't recall before. Just before Christmas, when I was visiting Worthington House, Edward brought his father over. I hadn't seen Phil in some time and he called me *malushka*. He used to call me that years ago. It's Polish for little girl. That night, I had another dream in which I was a child. I was awakened at night in my bed by what sounded like a gunshot. Maybe hearing Phil call me by that childhood name triggered a memory. And I'm wondering what other memories I've buried that might come out. Is there anything else I should know about that night, Dad?"

His expression unreadable, Judson shook his head. "I don't remember every detail clearly myself. We tend to push aside painful memories, and Margaret's leaving hurt me badly. She made me feel like a failure—that I couldn't hold on to her, that I wasn't enough for her."

Perhaps it runs in the family, Alyssa thought grimly.

"After she left, I couldn't bear to think of her, to see her clothes. I ordered the servants to haul all her things up to the attic, out of my sight. Then I locked the door myself and never went up there again."

"No one else did either, until Liza's curiosity sent her up to rummage through her grandmother's things." Looking up, Alyssa saw the defeated look on her father's face and wished she hadn't put it there. "I'm sorry if I've upset you."

"I guess I always knew one day all this would come out. We can bury our memories and even our feelings, but when people come back into our lives, like Liza and now Edward, everything gets stirred up again." He put his large hand on top of hers. "How do you feel about seeing Edward again?"

She could tell him the truth easily. "Confused. I still have feelings for him, but we're very different people than we were back when he left."

"Be careful, Alyssa. Some hurts we never get over." Somewhat shakily, Judson got to his feet, touched her shoulder very lightly, then left the room.

Alyssa raised her cup and drank more tea she didn't want. It had been quite an evening.

She who had always avoided confrontations whenever possible had actually sought one tonight. She hadn't learned too much from talking with her father, but then, he wasn't a man to open up easily. At least she'd started them communicating, and perhaps, in the future, they would talk again.

Clearing the table, she moved to the sink to rinse the tea things. Funny how nearly everyone in town envied the Ingalls family with all their connections and wealth. Yet Alyssa couldn't name a single Ingalls who seemed trouble-free and happy, except the younger generation. The old saying about money not buying happiness was never truer than in Tyler.

When, she wondered as she dried her hands, would the curse be broken and happily-ever-after begin?

CHAPTER FIVE

DAVID DIDN'T ADMIT the real reason he'd suddenly decided to subscribe to the small Tyler weekly newspaper, the *Tyler Citizen*. He told himself it was because he'd met some of the townspeople and wanted to keep up with their activities. He told himself he had several clients in the area and it was the friendly thing to do. He told himself a variety of lies, until one day he admitted the truth to himself.

He thought he could keep track of what Janice Eber was doing that way.

But it wasn't working. Though there was a chatty column describing the activities of various locals, her name never appeared. There were a few social functions where attendees were listed, and her name was never among them. There were charity luncheons, and although her cousin, Alyssa Ingalls Baron, was frequently mentioned, Janice was not.

David was getting frustrated.

Until he read an early March issue. It seemed that Tyler hosted a winter carnival each year complete with bobsledding events, snowmobiling, ice skating and horse-drawn carriage rides throughout the picturesque area. This year, it was to take place a few weeks later than usual, on the St. Patrick's Day weekend. Just the ticket, he thought as he dialed her number that evening.

Janice answered, sounding distracted and tired.

"Janice, this is David Markus. How are you?"

"David, how nice to hear from you. I'm fine, and how have you been?" Her voice had warmed, sounding more like herself.

"Busy as usual. I just returned from a swing through southern Illinois visiting clients. Nice country down that way."

He felt foolish, talking about the countryside, which certainly wasn't why he'd called. Yet he knew he had to be cautious with Janice.

"I had no idea your client list was so spread out." Janice set aside the book she'd been studying and pulled her feet up under her on the couch. It felt good to sit back and talk to a friend.

"Several used to live in the Chicago area, but moved for one reason or another, yet retained my services."

"Well, that says a lot about your abilities." For a moment, she wished he were here seated on the other end of the couch, a warm presence in the house, someone to talk with. Ah, but what would she do with him when she ran out of things to say?

"How are your studies coming?" he injected into the silence. "Still at it?"

"Oh, yes. I have an insurance exam coming up Friday morning. I was just sitting here studying."

"I admire your tenacity. But all work and no play can make Janice a dull girl. Are you planning on going to Tyler's winter carnival this weekend?"

Janice ran her fingers through her hair, a habit she'd developed since it'd been cut. "I hadn't given it much thought."

"I'm ready for a break and I was hoping you would be, too. How would it be if I drive down Saturday morning and we go together?"

A date? Good Lord, he wasn't asking for a date, was he? Feeling a bit flustered, Janice didn't know what to say.

David spoke into the lingering silence. "I thought we could stroll around and watch the events. I've been to other winter carnivals in small towns and there's usually a restaurant or two at the end of the day featuring a special dinner, and along the way, booths offering hot drinks. Is that the sort of thing Tyler has?"

Despite her misgivings, she was being drawn in. "Yes. Marge's Diner is the local gathering spot, and she's open both days with a carnival menu. Probably corned beef and cabbage or Irish stew this year, since it's so late. We've never had it on St. Patrick's day before. And there are tents with hot coffee and fresh doughnuts throughout."

She was warming to the idea. David put a persuasive note in his voice. "Sounds great. What do you say? Will you take pity on this poor city boy and let him take you?"

Put that way, she couldn't see the harm. They'd be out in the open air with lots of other strollers. If anyone asked, she could explain that David was Kurt's friend, in town to give her business advice. Yes, she could use a break, especially after Friday's exam. "You talked me into it," she said with more enthusiasm than she'd suspected herself capable of at this point.

"Terrific. Around noon on Saturday?"

"Yes, that would be fine."

"See you then. Good night, Janice."

She hung up the phone, the sound of his deep voice ringing in her ears. Stretching out her legs, she propped her stocking feet on the coffee table in front of the couch. It was a little chilly in the house and she hugged herself, scrunching up her shoulders.

She hadn't had the energy to light a fire. It seemed such a waste for one person. A fire was meant to be shared by at least two people. And, Janice had to keep reminding herself, she was only one. It took some getting used to, no longer thinking of herself as half of a pair.

Leaning her head back, she conjured up a picture of David Markus the last time he'd been here at her home. He'd kissed her before leaving. A brief, almost friendly kiss, but a kiss nonetheless. She was sure he'd meant it as a comforting gesture and nothing more. After all, David was a man of the world, sophisticated and well traveled, a former government agent who'd undoubtedly brushed shoulders with many important people.

A quiet homebody like her would hardly appeal to him. He was just being kind to the widow of a friend.

Which was as she wished it to be. She wasn't interested in a relationship and doubted if she ever would be again. She'd been so *comfortable* with Kurt, so *accustomed* to him. To his ways, the nuances of his conversation, the expressions on his face.

New places and new people intimidated her. Last week, a middle-aged man wearing horn-rimmed glasses and a nice smile, someone who sat across from her at the insurance sessions, asked her out for coffee after a class. Startled, she'd quickly refused him. Beginning again with someone else—well, the very thought had her shuddering.

Janice released a sigh into the silent room. Two months since that fateful call about Kurt. Odd how still a house was when no one shared it with you. She remembered evenings when Kurt had fallen asleep reading the newspaper on the very couch she now sat on, and she'd been across the room curled up in a chair with a book. Silence was different when it was shared.

To be honest, she had to admit to a certain amount of loneliness. Not devastating loneliness, because she was busier these days than she'd been in years. Perhaps ever. The classes, the hours spent in the office with Tom and the sales staff, and her evenings studying kept her occupied, and usually tired enough to sleep. But there was an emptiness to her days, a desolate feeling to her nights, a melancholia that clung to her as the lingering aroma of Kurt's shaving lotion clung to the bathroom shower curtain.

Friends called occasionally, wanting to come visit, to go to lunch, asking her to dinner. Yet she seldom took up their offers, using the excuse of her busy schedule. The truth was, she didn't feel very sociable. She didn't want to sit across the table from her married friends, happy and healthy together, because it seemed to point out her loss. She knew her attitude was unreasonable and hoped it was temporary.

Closing her eyes, Janice wondered when it would end.

Irrationally, she wanted things to be as they had been before. She wanted to go to bed alongside her husband and wake up to find her world all right again. She wanted the pain to go away, her life to be back together. She wanted to feel loved again, to feel cherished. And she disliked herself for wanting to live in the past.

Maybe if she went out with David, walked among the people she knew so well, laughed a little and talked a bit, she'd feel more as if there was some meaning to her life. It seemed to Janice that she was drifting toward a nebulous goal that she hadn't chosen for herself, but rather one that had been thrust upon her. While she was determined to learn the business and perhaps even run Eber Insurance one day, a small voice inside often prodded her, asking, "Then what?"

Would a sense of accomplishment and the realization that she *could* do it be enough to make her happy?

Stefanie would soon marry and take up residence on the East Coast, where her husband-to-be was entrenched—which was as it should be. K.J. would step out into the world after graduation in a couple of years, and Janice wondered if small-town life would be her son's choice. So that left her basically alone in this big house, going to work daily in a profession that she needed to master but wasn't sure would truly ever excite her.

She wasn't necessarily stuck, though, Janice decided as she sat up. There were choices available to her. She just had to figure out what they were and what she honestly wanted. Keep the agency or sell it. Move away from Tyler perhaps, to a bigger city. Go back to college for her degree, get an apartment, travel.

Don't expect too much of yourself too soon, Anna had said to her on the phone the other day. Let yourself adjust. Yes, she would do that. She would get out among people a little more, starting this weekend.

But first things first, and she had to pass Friday's test. Resignedly, Janice picked up her book again.

AT PRECISELY NOON on Saturday, David stomped snow from his boots on Janice's front porch and rang the doorbell again. He waited somewhat impatiently but heard no footsteps. Walking to the windows, he peered in but could see no one moving about. He was right on time, yet Janice wasn't answering her door.

Perhaps she was in the back of the house. Walking along the narrow shoveled path to the backyard, he peeked in windows he passed to no avail. Her station wagon was parked in front of the closed garage, so she couldn't be far. As he rounded the edge of the house, he saw her at the far end of the lot.

She had on a heavy red jacket over dark slacks tucked into her boots, her hair blowing about her head in the lightly falling snow. Hands jammed in her pockets, she stood with her back to him, looking at what appeared to be a children's playhouse constructed some time ago. He walked toward her, letting his crunching footsteps announce his arrival.

Janice was too lost in her thoughts to hear his approach. She was seeing a long-ago summer day when Kurt had proudly shown her the little hut he'd made for the children, complete with miniature table and chairs. K.J., about three, and Stefanie, a big sister at age five, had been sitting inside happily sipping juice and munching on pretzels their father had provided for their first "tea party." Kurt had demonstrated how the shutters on each window really worked and then pointed out the piece of carpeting he'd put inside for them.

Blinking back tears, Janice wished the memory wasn't quite so sharp, quite so painful. Not really a handyman, Kurt had been so pleased at his first and only carpentry attempt. She'd hugged him then and praised his effort to the skies. Later, she'd even made little curtains for the windows, and the children had picked the color of the house, a garish blue. She and Kurt had painted it together, the kids helping with small brushes. Chipped remnants remained even now. Stefanie and K.J. had played inside that little house by the hour, inviting friends in, filling the yard with noise and laughter.

She'd been taking the trash out just now when one of the flopping shutters had caught her attention. So she'd wandered over and drifted into the past, something she did far too easily and often, Janice thought with a pang. She should have had Kurt dismantle the thing and haul it away years ago. But here it sat, another reminder of better days, days that would never be again.

For the first time since Kurt's death, she'd awakened this morning and not automatically reached out to the empty space in bed beside her. Her waking thoughts instead had been that David would soon be coming for her. She realized then that her sense of loss had begun to mellow into sweet memories of the good times they'd shared. But now she was disappointed to discover that even remembering the good times saddened her.

Hearing a sound, Janice turned and saw David only a few feet away, watching her with serious blue eyes. Swiping at a tear trailing down her cheek, she searched for a smile but came up empty. "Hi. I—I was just thinking I should have this torn down. Maybe use it for firewood." But the thought had her shivering.

David stepped closer. "The memories won't leave you alone, will they, Sunshine?"

That was it exactly. Dropping her gaze to the snow underfoot, Janice shook her head, wishing he hadn't caught her looking so damn pitiful.

Stepping behind her, David slid an arm around her waist and drew her back against his chest. "I know what that's like."

She heard the remnants of remembered pain in his voice and looked up at him. "I know you do. I'd hoped each day would be easier, but . . ."

"I guess we shouldn't blame ourselves for mourning the loss."

"No." She rubbed her cold hands together. "But how long does it go on? I think I'm fine, then I see something like this, and off I go again." Annoyed with herself, and knowing there was no good answer to her question, she looked up at him. "I'm sorry."

"Don't be."

"I'll be ready in a minute, as soon as I run in and fix my face." Hurriedly, she made her way to the house.

When she returned five minutes later, David opened his car door for her, noticing that her smile was once more in place and her gray eyes were dry, if a little too bright. He settled her inside and got behind the wheel, searching his mind for an upbeat subject.

"How are your children doing?" he asked as he headed toward town.

Janice angled her back toward the car door so she could look at him. She would set aside all sad thoughts for the rest of the day, she vowed. "You really want to know?" When he nodded, she decided to tell him the truth. "Stefanie calls me every Wednesday and Sunday, as if she's marked me on the calendar. She's very efficient. The notation probably reads, 'Check on Mom.' During her last call, we quarreled, so I don't know if she'll call tomorrow."

"Dare I ask what the quarrel was about?"

"Stefie is a lovely girl, but she has a lot of her father in her. Since Kurt's death, she's decided she wants to take over and run my life. She thinks I should sell the house—'it's way too big for you, Mom'—go back to college and get my degree, then move to the East Coast where things are really happening. As opposed to the stodgy old Midwest, where it's terribly dull."

David smiled. "Pretty firm in her beliefs, isn't she?"

"Oh, yes. Stefanie has her whole life mapped out. As soon as her fiancé passes the bar exam and gets connected with the firm of his choice, they'll plan their wedding, and not a day before. After they're married, they'll work in the city and buy an old house in the country to renovate. When it's finished, she'll get pregnant and quit her job. They'll have a boy and a girl and she'll stay home with them until they start school, because that's the only way to raise children. And they'll be gloriously happy."

David laughed out loud as he turned a corner, the heavy car holding the snowy road well. "Sounds like you know your daughter inside out."

"Maybe better than she knows herself. That whole plan to me is like reading a book when you already know how it's going to end. I've always been fairly cautious, but Stefanie's a fanatic. I hope it all works out for her, but I wouldn't count on it. Life has a way of throwing us zingers when we least expect them, altering all of our well-laid plans.''

"Doesn't it just? And how's K.J.? As organized as his sister?"

Janice let out a worried sigh even as she smiled. "He's quite disorganized, but such a sweetheart. He calls me spontaneously and often, always ending by telling me to keep my chin up."

David found he wanted to know more about the boy. "He's majoring in business, isn't he?"

"Yes. Kurt insisted on that. I think he had intentions of grooming his son to take over the agency."

"Is that what K.J. wants to do?"

"I think he's probably too young to decide yet. He could do worse than taking over Eber Insurance, don't you think?"

Stopping for a light, he turned to face her. "I think it's important to work at what you enjoy. The money will follow. The average man works forty years or more. If he's doing something he hates, that's a terrible waste of a life."

Janice was thoughtful a long moment. "You know, I think you're right. K.J.'s coming home for Easter. Maybe it's time we talked about his goals, his future."

"He's a really nice kid." They'd reached the outskirts of town, where the winter carnival was set up. David maneuvered the car into a makeshift parking area. Pocketing his keys, he turned to her.

In the sudden silence, Janice looked up and saw his eyes darken as he reached a hand to lightly touch the ends of her hair. Her pulse picked up its rhythm.

"You look lovely today," he said quietly.

Lovely? Had anyone ever called her lovely? If they had, it had been so long ago that she'd forgotten. Janice felt the heat rise to stain her cheeks and she shifted her gaze to her gloved hands.

David smiled. "I see you still blush when someone pays you a compliment. Do you remember the afternoon I took you home to meet my mother and sister? Mom said you had the most beautiful red hair she'd ever seen, and you blushed like fury."

She hadn't thought of Mrs. Markus in years. They'd popped into her small house on the outskirts of Madison and she'd given them warm apple pie and homemade cider. "I remember. You had a motorcycle and I rode behind you, hanging on for dear life."

"That beat-up old secondhand bike was all I could afford."

Janice tapped the Lincoln's dashboard. "You've come a long way."

"But I didn't have much back then and I desperately wanted to impress you."

"You did impress me," she said, knowing it was the truth. A football star, he'd been so tall and handsome. He still was.

"Not in a way that counted. I didn't have Kurt's self-assurance, or his money."

She frowned, wondering how they'd gotten started on this strange conversation. "Did you think it took money to impress me?"

David carefully removed a piece of lint from his jacket. "You married Kurt with his inheritance, his potential, his cocky confidence." His eyes rose to hers. "Why did you?"

She felt awkward explaining, but his intense look seemed to demand it. "Because I loved him. Because he . . . he . . ."

"Dazzled you? Swept you off your feet?"

"Something like that." Following her instincts, she laid a hand over his where it rested on his knee. "Why are you asking after all these years?"

He shrugged. "I just needed to know." Putting on a smile, he reached to open the car door. "We'd better go."

Janice let him help her out, then walked ahead of him, her footsteps disappearing in the powdery snow. She remembered snatches of other conversations she and David had had back then. He'd been more serious than most of her friends, certainly more than Kurt. He'd enjoyed long, probing talks, as if he needed to know what made people tick, how they thought. She'd liked that about him, but his questions unnerved her a little now. Perhaps it was because she had so few answers.

The land adjacent to Clyde Lawton's big clapboard farmhouse was set up for the bobsled run. David helped Janice around a huge mound of snow as they walked over to watch the races, which were just beginning. They stood back a little from the crowd, and Janice waved to several people on the opposite side of the track.

The snow fell steadily, but everyone was bundled up in thick coats, colorful scarves and heavy boots, so they didn't mind. Janice inhaled the crisp air tinged with the smoke of a nearby fire and the distinctive aroma of farm animals. Sliding her hands into her pockets, she felt a snowy gust toss her hair about and decided to enjoy the day.

David watched a young man with shaggy blond hair angle his sled around a slippery turn. "That's a rugged sport."

"Kurt used to compete in this event every year," Janice commented. "He took a couple of rough spills, but he jumped right back up."

"Did you compete, too?"

She shook her head. "I've never been terribly athletic. I like more sedentary activities—reading, music, plays."

That gave him an idea. "*The Phantom of the Opera*'s scheduled to return to Chicago in a couple of weeks. Would you like to go with me?"

A breeze lifted a lock of his dark hair as she turned to look up at him. In his eyes she could see remnants of the young man he'd once been, and it stirred a reluctant response in her. Yes, she wanted to go. Badly. But no, she would not. "David, I don't think it would be a good idea. Please don't misunderstand."

"No, it's all right."

She wondered if she could make him understand something she herself had trouble comprehending. "I'm just not ready to...to date again. I'm very often not good company. You saw what happened earlier. I get these unexpected crying jags and...well, I just need some time."

"I understand." He took her elbow. "There's Anna and Johnny. Let's go over and say hello."

She let him guide her across the field, but her steps were heavy. She'd disappointed him, though she hadn't meant to. Maybe coming out today had been a mistake.

But then Anna came to meet them and hugged her, and Johnny engaged David in a conversation on the merits of a land development opportunity he'd heard of, and she began to relax. The four of them strolled over to one of the large red-and-white-striped tents where hot drinks were being served. Sipping steaming coffee, Janice and Anna stood looking at the crowd.

"I ran into Britt Hansen earlier," Anna said. "Do you know her?"

"Only slightly," Janice answered. "She has a dairy farm around here, doesn't she?"

"Yes, not far. Her father was my cousin."

"Ah, yes. Britt's husband died last year. A farm accident, wasn't it?"

Swallowing a bite of doughnut, Anna nodded. "It was terrible. Britt was left with four young children. She's having a rough time managing the herd alone, but she'll come up with something. Britt will make it because she's not one to sit around feeling sorry for herself. She's a survivor."

Narrowing her eyes, Janice studied her friend. Subtle she was not. "Well, good for Britt. Tell me, dear lady, is there a message in this story? Something about widows getting off their duffs and getting on with life, involving themselves in new projects, and all that?"

Behind her glasses, Anna's eyes twinkled. "Now, would I go around tossing out such heavy-handed hints?" They both laughed. "Besides, I don't think I need to prod you. How'd you do on the test yesterday?"

She'd come out of class with a near-perfect score and the flush of accomplishment warming her cheeks, wishing she'd had someone special to share her minor victory with. But there'd been no one and she'd gone home to her empty house. "I passed with flying colors. Of course, I've got my nose buried in a book twelve hours a day, it seems."

"I'm proud of you." Pointedly, Anna glanced over her shoulder at David, who'd walked across the path to look over the horses with Johnny. "Has David been encouraging you?"

Janice nodded. "He's more supportive than any man I've ever known. Almost *too* encouraging, you know what I mean?"

Anna tossed her empty paper cup into a large tin barrel. "Aren't you looking for problems when there aren't any? Maybe he's just being a good friend." She glanced toward him again. "He's certainly an attractive man."

"Yes." Janice gazed through the open tent flap at David, who was running his hand along a brown mare's shiny coat, his blue eyes crinkling at the corners as he laughed at something Johnny was saying. A cap of white snowflakes lay on his dark head, an appealing contrast. "He called and asked if he could take me to the carnival today. I almost said no, but he's very persuasive. And he puts up with my moods, most of which aren't terribly sunny."

"It's good for you to get out," Anna commented. "And he seems like a nice man."

Suddenly, Janice didn't want Anna to have the wrong impression—that she had designs on David. "It's not a date, Anna. He's been advising me on how to invest the insurance money."

"Even if it was, would it be so terrible? You have no one to answer to, Janice."

Janice smiled at her friend and linked arms with her. "I know. But there's this guilty feeling, as if I'm betraying Kurt."

Anna sighed. "Time, my dear. These things take time." She drew Janice outdoors again, glancing up at the gray sky. "It looks like this snow won't quit for a while."

"It is, after all, a winter carnival," Janice said, then stopped in her tracks. "I wonder what those two are in such a deep conversation over?"

Anna turned to look and saw Edward Wocheck and Alyssa Baron with their heads together by the fence. She watched for a moment, then smiled. "Romance. I think it's in the air. George Phelps is out snowmobiling with Marge Peterson on the lake even as we speak."

Janice raised a surprised eyebrow. "Is George's divorce from Mary final?"

"I'm not sure."

"You work for the man. Doesn't he say?"

"George rarely talks about his personal life, though everyone knows what Mary's like. He's been quite distracted since he left her and took up with Marge. Understandable, I guess. Love makes a person a little dazed, wouldn't you say?"

"I wouldn't know," Janice commented dryly, then squeezed her friend's arm. "You're an incurable matchmaker, did you know that?"

"Not me. What do you say we talk those two men into a snowmobile ride? Are you game?"

Janice smiled. "Why not?"

THE DAY PASSED quickly in a swirl of activities. Janice and David took turns driving their snowmobile on the thick ice of the lake, swaying this way and that as they maneuvered around other vehicles out for a run. Afterward, they went to Marge's Diner along with half the town, it seemed, and filled up on corned beef and green beer. Janice introduced David to the people seated around them, a friendly bunch with cheeks red from the cold and smiles all around. Then, needing to walk off the heavy meal, the two of them high-stepped along a country road in an ever-increasing snowfall.

It was late afternoon by the time they stood beside a line of sleighs and carriages. "These remind me of the carriages you can rent in Central Park. Have you ever been to New York?" David asked as he helped her climb up.

"It's on my list for 'someday.'"

He stopped just short of offering to take her. He would steer clear of dragging her into the future with him, David decided as he settled the red plaid robe over their laps. "But this carriage you have to drive yourself."

"Not really," Jacob Beamish said as he came over and handed David the reins to a shiny black carriage harnessed to a placid gray horse. Jacob owned the horses, sleighs and carriages that he rented out each winter for rides to tourists and townsfolk. "Dolly here knows these roads better than most people. Just let her have her head. She knows the route real good."

"How long a ride is Dolly programmed for?" Janice asked as she watched Jacob adjust the canvas top over their heads. "This snow is still really coming down."

"Oh, pert' near an hour," Jacob answered. "But don't you worry none. You're safe as a babe with Dolly." With that, he gave a gentle swat to Dolly's backside and the gray mare took off down the snow-covered path, the bells on her harness jingling with each step.

"I'm surprised Jacob hasn't put plumes on his horses," Janice commented as she snuggled down.

"Do you get many tourists out this way in the winter?"

"A few ice fishermen and snowmobilers. Jacob rents out all sorts of winter equipment. He's a bit of a showman. Used to travel with the circus as a horse trainer. His wife's a former bareback rider. They retired here and this is how he keeps his hand in."

Picturing the rotund little farmer with his gray beard and infectious laugh, David smiled. "Show business must be hard to give up." Holding the reins loosely, he nonetheless kept his eye on Dolly. "Are you comfortable?" he asked Janice.

"Mmm." She was, comfortably full and comfortably tired from more outdoor physical exertion than she'd had in ages. David's shoulder tight up against hers was reassuring. Janice watched a clump of snow fall off the barren branches of a tree as they rounded the bend. The sky was growing increasingly dark, the snow falling without letup. The road stretched ahead flanked by a wooden fence on one side and open land on the other. The only sounds breaking the twilight silence were the clip-clopping of the horse's hooves in the snow and the musical tinkling of the bells.

In the intimacy of the covered carriage, she inhaled deeply and recognized a once-familiar smell. Could that be? "Do you still smoke a pipe?"

"Occasionally."

That was the scent she smelled on him, the one she remembered. The need to know more about the man he'd become persisted and she gave in to her curiosity. "David, tell me about your house."

Pleased that she was interested, he sat back. "It's north of Chicago in a suburb called Buffalo Grove. It's a wooded area, fairly isolated. The house is made of brick and Michigan fieldstone, with a cedar shake roof and lots of windows."

"You had it built?"

"Yes, when I left government work. I'd traveled all over at their expense and I'd saved quite a bit. I'd always wanted to design my own place and I finally did." As he warmed to his subject, his voice deepened. "The backyard slopes off into this thicket of woods. I built a redwood deck where I can sit and watch the animals. Squirrels, raccoons, wild rabbits, an occasional skunk. And the birds. Janice, you should see the birds."

Funny, but he didn't look like a man who'd be fascinated by birds. "Tell me."

"I've got half a dozen feeders all over the yard, and they come by the droves. Mourning doves that coo half the day. Chickadees and cardinals and blue jays. A few woodpeckers. And in spring, all around the house and near the edge of the woods there are wildflowers. Dark patches of violets, mayapples, delicate hepaticas. And lilac bushes in three shades of purple." He turned to her. "Their fragrance reminds me of you, your hair."

She didn't know how to respond to that, so she asked another question. "Do you sit on your deck often?"

"Not often enough, but every chance I get. Summer evenings, fireflies dance in the yard and crickets serenade from somewhere under the deck. Some mornings, this one fox squirrel with a bushy reddish tail hops right up on the deck railing. I keep a bowl of nuts—raw ones, in their shells—on the table. He sits there, bold as you please, cocking his head and waiting for me to hand him a treat."

"I thought squirrels were often rabid."

"They can be, but this little guy isn't. I usually place a nut about a foot from him and he marches over, grabs it with his front paws, pops it into his mouth and scurries off to bury it. In a few minutes, he's back for more."

"Greedy little guy."

"He is. One morning, I put two nuts down to see what he'd do. He crammed one in his mouth and, in his anxiety to get the other one in as well, he toppled off the railing onto the grass."

Janice laughed.

He turned to look at her in the reflected light from the snow. "There it is."

"What?"

"Your laugh. You used to laugh a lot when we were dating. I always loved your laugh."

Janice took in a shaky breath. "I guess I have been pretty glum lately. We all had more to laugh about in those days."

"We sure did. Do you remember the time I borrowed that sailboat and we took it out?"

"On Lake Winona. Neither of us knew much about sailing, as I recall. You ordered me around like a slave."

"There's a lot of work to sailing. I was afraid I'd make a mistake and we'd capsize. Then the water became real calm and we drifted for hours. Do you remember, Janice?"

She did, all too well. They'd eaten a picnic lunch, then stretched out in their swimsuits in the sun. The boat had bobbed around and they'd felt all alone far out from shore. He hadn't even kissed her that afternoon. They'd just held hands and talked.

Janice looked into his dark eyes and saw that they held a glimmer of something she couldn't quite identify. "I remember."

"I wanted so badly to kiss you that day," David confessed quietly.

It had been their first real date, she recalled, and she'd been curious about him, too. "I wouldn't have stopped you. Why didn't you?"

David shrugged. "I was trying to be sensible. And maybe I thought we wouldn't stop with one."

Averting her gaze, Janice thought that over.

"You were the sensible, cautious one, David. Not that I was wild."

"A young couple today probably wouldn't hold back," David added.

She thought of Stefanie and her Ross, living together for two years now. "No, they wouldn't."

"Do you ever wonder what might have happened if we'd kept on seeing each other, if things had turned out differently?"

She hadn't, really, not until now. She'd gone out with David only a few times and had been dating several others that fall. And she'd been so young, and free for the first time in her short life. Then Kurt had come on the scene and she'd forgotten everyone else.

Janice didn't want to hurt his feelings, but it had been David who'd stopped asking her out. She chose her words carefully. "When you stopped calling, I felt as though I didn't fit in with your future plans."

His fingers curled around hers as he reflected. "It wasn't altogether that. I hated having to just get by. No money, an uncertain future and so many obligations. You'd come from a wealthy background." He leaned in closer, until she turned toward him. "I was afraid to let myself care too much for you. Would you have waited until I made something of myself?"

She kept her gaze steady on his. "That's an unfair question to ask now, after all these years. Besides, the real question is, why did you think that what you had or didn't have in the way of money made a difference to me? I came from money, but I was never terribly interested in material things or in stockpiling wealth. What did I do to give you that impression?"

Slowly, he shook his head. "Nothing. It was all in my head. But I didn't know that then." Feeling the carriage jolt to a stop, David looked up and noticed that they were back where they'd started out. Bad timing, he thought. Or was it? "Looks like Dolly knows her way around, all right," he said as Jacob came toward them.

Nearly everyone had gone home except a few teenagers having a snowball fight near the barn. The wind had really picked up, Janice realized as she turned up the collar of her coat.

David flung aside the blanket covering. "I guess I'd better get you home. As it is, I'll have to dig my car out of a snowdrift."

Janice jumped down and landed with a whoosh into nearly a foot of new snow. While David paid Jacob, she frowned up into a murky sky.

How was David ever going to drive back to Chicago in a snowstorm?

CHAPTER SIX

JANICE STOOD in the shadowed warmth of the horse
barn with Mrs. Lawton while her husband, Clyde, and
Jacob Beamish helped David shovel out his car. As the
little farmer's wife droned on about the need for more
efficient snow removal service for their rural area,
Janice kept her eye on the accumulation through a
crack in the large weathered doors. How had this storm
developed into such a powerhouse so rapidly?

"I don't recollect listening to the weather report last
night," Mrs. Lawton said, answering Janice's unspo-
ken question, "so this really snuck up on me. It's pretty
late for a snowstorm, but then, we can have them right
through April. I just hope the power don't go out on
us. Could make for an awfully cold night."

Janice agreed as she hunched up her shoulders, bur-
rowing farther into her jacket. The barn door thunked
open with a reluctant groan. The three men stepped
inside, their clothes crusted with white.

"It's as clear as it's going to be," David told her,
shaking snow from his hair. "We'd better go quickly
though." He turned to Clyde and Jacob. "Thanks a
lot."

"I offered to put you both up for the night," Clyde explained to Janice, "but your man here wants to get going."

"I'm sure we'll be fine," Janice said as she stepped toward the door. But once outside, she wasn't as certain.

The wind had turned fierce, driving the snow in sheets that made it impossible to see more than a few feet ahead. With David's arm firmly around her, she trudged alongside him toward his big Lincoln, her head down and her face smarting. The temperature had dropped considerably, and the snow was quickly crusting in their hair and on their clothes.

It seemed they walked a mile, but squinting ahead through the snow, she saw the car's lights at last. David brushed the new accumulation off her door with his gloved hand and helped her inside. The motor was humming quietly and the heater was blasting away. She leaned into its welcoming warmth as he climbed in behind the wheel. Brushing snow from herself, she realized she was shaking.

She noticed through the windshield that the headlight beams shone only a few feet ahead. The swirling snow fought with the struggling wipers. She turned her worried gaze to David. "Do you think we can make it to my house?"

"It's a heavy car. I think we'll be all right." He pulled off his gloves, then reached over and did the same with hers. Vigorously, he rubbed her hands. "Are your feet all right, toes not numb?"

"Okay so far. You don't have chains on, do you?"

He shook his head. "I heard this morning that there'd be new snow, but no one predicted a storm like this. What a winter!" He peered through the window. "As soon as we get off this side road and onto the highway, we should be okay."

She shivered, wishing they hadn't taken the carriage ride, that they'd left sooner. "They won't be out with the plows or salting the roads until morning. They don't rush to do that around here, even on the highways."

David's big hand closed over hers. "I'll get you home safely."

If anyone could, it was David. She squeezed his hand in a vote of confidence. "I know you will."

There were some harrowing moments. Twice he nearly slid into what he knew had to be a snow-covered ditch alongside the road. He gripped the wheel and tried to keep to the center. They crept along, the only sound in the car the hum of the engine and their anxious breathing. Outside, the wind whistled and whipped and the blades thunked against the window. The car inched forward at a maddeningly slow pace.

The drive from the Lawton farm to Janice's street would ordinarily take ten minutes. After thirty, they still hadn't reached the turnoff road. She stared out the window, mesmerized by the dancing flakes dropping in such volume from the fathomless black sky. She'd watched storms like this before, but always from safely inside her home. Glancing at his profile, she saw that

David looked grim, his concentration intense. Hands clutched in her lap, she willed the car on to safety.

"Another fool out in this," David muttered as the headlights of an oncoming car became visible. Creeping along, he kept to the right as much as possible, hoping the Lincoln would hold the road and not slip off. Sluggishly, the vehicle passed on by, tossing up more snow against the side of the car.

Leaning forward, Janice squinted. "There's my street, to the left." She'd thought he might miss it in the unfamiliar white world.

He touched the brakes gingerly, afraid of sending them into a spin, then turned the wheel with caution. They skidded a short distance, but he was able to stop the motion and straighten the car. He let out a ragged breath. "Not much farther now."

He could just make out the house with its big porch as he pulled up in front of it. The wind had piled snowdrifts so high that the driveway that ran along the right side of Janice's house was nearly obliterated. Waist-deep snow covered the front walk and the porch steps weren't visible at all. "I think this is as close as I can get."

Janice strained to see. "I left the shovel by the side drive, but it's buried. I guess we'll just have to plow on through." She glanced at him as he shut off the engine. "At least we made it, thanks to you."

"I grew up driving in snow, but this was quite a challenge." He pulled his damp leather gloves back on.

"I'll get out and come around to your side and help you. I'm sure it's slippery under all that snow."

She didn't argue with him, anxious to get out of the car and into the house. When he opened her door, she took a deep breath, stepped out and felt him clutch her to his side with a strong grip. If he hadn't, she'd have fallen, Janice realized as her booted feet struggled to find purchase.

In moments, he had them walking up the lawn, but with some difficulty. The wind whipped the heavy, wet snow into their faces, making it difficult to see. Taking exaggerated, hip-high steps in the deep drifts was an arduous task. Cold and wet, they hunched forward and moved along at a snail's pace.

Where he thought the steps were, David brushed at the snow with his gloved hands, then kicked with his booted foot. It was a losing battle, he finally decided. He leaned close to her ear, the howling wind making it difficult to hear.

"It might be best if we go up on all fours. I'll make a path and you follow." He saw her nod and started up. It wasn't easy, but he finally felt the solid porch beneath his hands and scrambled up. Turning, he bent to help Janice.

With what felt like frozen fingers, she clutched at him as he pulled her upright. She paused a moment, fighting for her breath.

"Where's your key?" he asked into her ear.

"Coat pocket," she answered.

David pulled off a glove with his teeth, then brushed snow from Janice's jacket until he found her pocket. He wiggled his fingers inside and found the key. Holding her by the elbows, he sidestepped them both until they reached the door. It took two tries, but he managed to open the lock.

They all but fell inside, staggering a bit from relief and the weight of the snow on their clothes and boots. Janice groped for the light switch. "Oh, no," she groaned. "The power's out."

Leaning over, David shook the snow from his hair and wiped at the moisture on his face. "At least we're inside, out of the storm. We'll build a fire, get some candles lit. Do you have a flashlight I can use?"

Stomping her feet to get the circulation going, Janice tried to think. "Kitchen drawer." She pointed in the general direction of the kitchen.

David shrugged out of his jacket and took off his boots before going to the kitchen. It wasn't totally dark, since some light from the snowy reflection in the yard came in through the front windows. He groped around and finally found the flashlight in a drawer. He flipped the switch and was relieved that the batteries were good.

When he went back to Janice, he found she'd taken off her jacket and was sitting on a chair struggling with her boots, her wet hair plastered to her head. He bent to assist her and heard her grateful sigh. When he had the boots off, he placed them beside his by the front door, then turned to the fireplace. Gratefully he saw that not only was a fire laid, the wood storage box was full as well. He didn't relish the thought of having to go out back and search for the woodpile that was likely buried under several feet of snow.

It took but a few minutes before the fire was going well. In her stocking feet, Janice moved closer, rubbing her chilled hands. "The house hasn't cooled off too badly yet so the power's not been off long."

"Maybe they'll get it fixed quickly."

"Doubtful before morning." Roads all but impassable and the power off... Suddenly, she realized that meant David would have to spend the night. She raised wide eyes to his, trying to adjust to the thought.

He seemed to read her mind. "I could set out for Kelsey Boardinghouse."

Her good sense overrode her uneasiness. "Of course you won't. It's treacherous out there." She took in his wet hair, his damp slacks. At least his cable-knit sweater was dry. "I'll get us some towels. I'm going to change and then see if I can find something of K.J.'s that would fit you. You'll catch cold in those wet things."

"I don't want to be a bother," David said, standing with his back to the fire as he handed her the flashlight.

"You aren't. I'll be right back."

She returned in moments with a big, fluffy towel, which she thrust at him before she hurried off again. David rubbed his hair dry and wiped his face and hands. He was stripping off his wet socks when she came back downstairs with a towel wrapped around her head and wearing a yellow sweatshirt and matching pants, plus fur-lined slippers on her feet.

"These jogging pants should fit. K.J. doesn't own slippers, but I grabbed a pair of thick ski socks." She handed back the flashlight. "You can change in the downstairs bath, second door on the left. Just hang your wet things on the shower rod."

While he was gone, she used her towel to dry her hair and sat down on the brick hearth, finger-combing the strands into some kind of order. Finally, she took a deep breath and tried to relax.

A harrowing experience, potentially very dangerous, but it had worked out all right, thanks to David's strength and patience. She let herself absorb the heat as she tried to think of something they could eat or drink that would add heat. With the electric stove not working, there was little she could come up with other than brandy. Without the flashlight, she probably couldn't find it in the darkened dining room. Feeling on edge, she waited for David's return.

A glance at her watch told her it was only nine in the evening. Marooned in a shadowy house at night with a man who wasn't her husband... Janice swallowed around a lump in her throat. An attractive man, at that. The man who'd taught her to kiss.

Draping the towel around her neck, Janice sat staring into the flames, remembering. She'd been so young and so thrilled to be dating an upperclassman. She'd certainly been kissed before, but by boys she'd dated in high school, boys she'd known all her life. David, with his football physique, his probing gaze and quiet ways, had already been a man.

They'd been strolling away from a fall bonfire off campus near the lake on their second date when he'd pulled her into the shadows of an old tree and kissed her for the first time. Surprised, she'd been too nervous to respond.

"Is that the best you can do?" David had asked.

"I'm not very good at this," she recalled telling him. "I haven't had all that much practice." So very tall and handsome, he'd made her feel small and unsophisticated. She'd wanted so badly to impress him and had fallen short, embarrassing herself.

"I'll bet you're a quick study." Smiling down at her, he'd pulled her closer into the circle of his arms. "And I'm a very willing teacher. Now, open your mouth just a little and let yourself go."

She had, closing her eyes and letting his soft lips tease hers, his bold tongue seduce her, his big hands mold her to him. He'd been the first to give her a taste of that particular hunger, the sensual pleasure of being thigh to thigh and breast to breast with a mature man; the first to awaken restless needs deep inside her. In mere minutes, she'd been kissing him back, wanting more and still more.

When he'd lifted his head, she'd opened her eyes and seen that his were smoky with a passion even she in her innocence had recognized. The realization had frightened her and she'd trembled. But David had quickly calmed her fear.

"Don't worry, Sunshine," he'd said in that low, husky voice. "I'll never take you where you don't want to go."

True to his word, he hadn't pressed, then or after. Threading her fingers through her hair, Janice couldn't imagine why she was remembering all that now when...

"Well, what do you think?" David asked from the archway.

Glancing up, she smiled. K.J.'s gray sweats were a bit short on him, but he'd tugged the heavy socks up over his ankles to cover the gap. His black V-neck sweater was pulled down low as he stood with his arms spread and his palms open toward her. "It'll never make *GQ*, but at least you're dry."

"Right." He rubbed his arms, then slid his sleeves up toward his elbows.

"I was waiting for the flashlight so I could go look for the brandy. Might help to warm us up."

"Tell me where it is."

"In the dining room buffet. You'll find glasses there, too." She stood. "Meanwhile, I'll see if I can find some candles and place them around so we won't be bumping into the furniture." In the circle of light from the fireplace, she rummaged in drawers and came up with half a dozen. After lighting one from the fireplace, she took them into the kitchen and fixed them into several brass holders and ceramic candlesticks.

She was holding a candle end over the flame of another to soften it when a scalding drop of melted wax dripped over her hand. "Oh, damn," she muttered, peeling off the wax and sticking her burned finger in her mouth.

Coming up behind her, David set down the brandy-filled glasses and the flashlight and took her hand. "Let me see that."

"It's nothing, but I need an ice cube."

"Not ice. Don't you put butter on a burn?"

Swiveling to grab a cube from the freezer behind them, Janice shook her head. "No. The oil traps the heat in and the salt burns even more." Over the sink, she held the ice cube on her forefinger. "Ice draws out the heat and stops the pain."

"I suppose, raising children, you'd know more about first aid than I." The candlelight flickered across her features as she frowned at her burn. The snow had cleaned her face and she hadn't bothered to replace her makeup. Her hair lay in an appealing state of disarray, one errant lock curling onto her left cheek. He thought she was unbearably lovely and wished he didn't. It would just make spending the night alone with her more difficult.

"Aloe," Janice was saying. "The best thing is if you have an aloe plant. You cut off a piece, open it and place the sticky inside on the burn. Presto. It not only stops hurting in minutes, but before long it disappears entirely." She studied the minor problem. "I think I'll live." She turned to him and found her smile slipping a bit.

He was watching her quietly, his eyes turning smoky blue. Janice's breath caught in her throat.

David reached for her hand, turned it over and placed a soft kiss on the tip of her injured finger, then moved to place another on the sensitive skin of her palm, his warm lips lingering there. Raising his eyes to meet hers, he saw her mouth tremble open.

"David, I..."

"You're still getting hurt, aren't you, Sunshine?" he asked, a gentle smile on his face.

She remembered then another cool autumn day, bicycling with David on a path winding through a wooded park. She'd fallen and scraped her elbow. He'd helped her up and kissed the spot.

"I guess I am. Only it takes longer for the hurts to heal these days."

If there was a message in her words, he would heed it. "But everything heals, in time. You need to know that, to believe it."

"Everything? Are you so sure?"

Nodding, he picked up the brandy glasses and handed her one. "I am *very* sure. Listen to Dr. Dave." He tapped his glass to hers, deliberately lightening the mood. "Let's drink to speedy recoveries and new beginnings."

She *was* beginning her life over this year, Janice thought. Facing all sorts of new beginnings—her studies, the agency, adjusting to loneliness, and tonight,

learning to be alone with a man again. She saluted with
her glass and took a sip. The liquid heat slid down
slowly, smooth and silken. She shivered in reaction.

"You're still cold," David commented, misinterpreting. "Why don't you go sit on the couch in front
of the fire and I'll light the rest of these candles and
bring them in?"

She didn't bother to correct him. Removing the
afghan from the couch back, she wrapped herself in it,
stretching to put her feet on the coffee table, and sat
gazing into the crackling flames.

A close call, Janice thought, still able to feel his
mouth pressed to her palm. There was an awareness
between them that had apparently lain dormant all
these years. Both married to others and busy with separate lives, they hadn't thought of it. Until now, suddenly alone in the intimacy of a snowbound house. She
knew without a doubt that David felt it, too. Only his
sensitivity to her feelings had kept him from kissing her
just now.

And she'd wanted him to, she realized, as the dis-
appointment in her own reaction surfaced. Wanted to
flee from her troubled new life and her long, lonely
nights to the escape she knew she could find in his
arms. What was wrong with her? Closing her eyes, she
almost groaned aloud. She'd never been one to avoid
reality and evade problems, had she? She'd certainly
never been one to use people. Her attraction to David
centered around her need for comfort and no more.
Giving in to that wouldn't be fair to him.

Rubbing her forehead, she prayed for strength.

In a few minutes, he had the candlesticks placed around the room, leaving one burning in the kitchen. He threw another log on the fire and sat down beside her, propping his crossed feet inches from hers. Turning to Janice, he studied her a moment. "Are you all right?"

She sat up taller, forcing a smile, her mind racing for a way to keep them occupied. "Fine." Her eyes landed on a blue box on the hearth. "How about a game of Trivial Pursuit by candlelight?" That sounded safe enough.

Following her gaze, David went over and picked up the game. "You're on."

TWO HOURS LATER, they were still at it. "What does Friday call Robinson Crusoe?" Janice asked.

He pretended to think deeply. "Mr. Crusoe? No, wait, it's Rob. Or is it Robbie?" He waited for her smile. "All right, I give up."

"Master, silly." Janice put back the card, missed the answer to the next question, and then it was his turn again.

It occurred to David that concentrating on the trivial made the time pass quickly. It also made the more substantial things between them fade into the background, at least for the moment.

"All right, ex-football jock, here's one for you," Janice said. "What position does a footballer play if he's last in line in the I-formation?"

They were seated facing each other on the couch, each sitting cross-legged, an elbow propped on a bent knee. David grinned before he replied. "Halfback."

"Smarty-pants." Janice watched him roll the die and move his blue circular piece to land on green. She picked the next card, then beamed. "Aha! Science and nature—a bit tougher. What are Africa's fleet-footed bongo, bontebok and blesbok all varieties of?"

David scrunched up his face, pondering that one.

"Your travels didn't include Africa, I take it?"

"Actually, I have been there, but I didn't spend much time looking at the animals. Let's try the deer family."

"More like the antelope family."

"Deer and antelope. Pretty close. Do I get half a move?"

"'Fraid not, but nice try. My turn." She had only one more triangular pie to obtain in order to win. Janice threw the die and moved her piece. "Entertainment. My specialty. Shoot."

David read the pink question. "Where did all the flowers go?"

She smiled. "Ah, Peter, Paul and Mary. 'The young girls picked them, every one.'" She sighed. "I loved that song." Humming it, she rolled again. "Another pink one, and this one's for the pie. All right!"

David gave her a mock scowl. "Did you know you're supposed to let a guest win? Aren't you worried that my fragile male ego might be shattered if you beat me?"

Janice finished her brandy and stifled a yawn. "Not in the least. My question, if you please."

He frowned at the card. "This is too easy. What was the Beatles' last number-one hit single record?"

She gave a victory yelp. " 'The Long and Winding Road.' I win."

He laughed out loud at her pleasure, then sat staring at her. It suddenly struck him how seldom he'd felt like laughing over the past few years. And he couldn't remember the last time he'd spent several hours playing a board game. Janice was good for him, he decided. But was he good for her?

She leaned back against the cushions. "The Beatles. I wish I had a nickel for every time I listened to one of their songs, especially when I was younger."

"What's your favorite Beatles song?" he asked, watching the firelight streak her hair with red, wishing he had the right to reach out and run his fingers through the strands.

" 'Yesterday,' without a doubt." Tossing the afghan aside, she walked to the stereo. "Why don't I find that album and put it on? I know I have it and...oh, damn. I forgot we have no electricity."

David rose and walked to her in his stocking feet. "Who needs records?" Pulling her into dance position, he whirled her around, humming the song.

She giggled, whether from his silliness or the two brandies she'd consumed, she wasn't certain. "We can't dance on carpeting."

"Sure we can." He turned her, maneuvering her past the furniture. "'Yesterday,'" he sang softly, "'all my troubles seemed so far away.' Is that how it goes?"

Up close against his chest, feeling his heart beating in rhythm with hers, Janice sobered quickly. She looked up into eyes suddenly dark and aware once more.

"Help me out," David said. "I don't remember all the words."

"'Now I need a place to hide away,'" she sang, her voice low and husky. "'Oh, I believe in yesterday.'"

He stopped moving and her slippered foot landed on his sock, but neither of them smiled or moved. "Do you, Janice? Do you believe in yesterday?" He felt the pulse at her wrist scramble and knew she understood what he was asking. "Do you remember the time I walked you home after the bonfire, the first time we kissed, under that big maple tree that kept dropping its leaves all over us?"

So he, too, had been thinking back to those days. She should break the embrace right now, this very minute, Janice told herself. She was another man's wife, and even though that man was gone, he'd been dead only a few months. Yet she kept her eyes on David's, scarcely moving, hardly breathing.

"You told me you weren't very good at kissing. Do you remember that?"

Her voice, when she found it, was so soft he had to lean down to hear her. "Yes, I remember. I remember everything."

"So do I and the memories keep me awake nights. I didn't come looking for this, Janice, and I know you aren't ready for an involvement."

"No."

"But it would be foolish and dishonest to deny there is something between us." He waited the space of a long heartbeat, and when she didn't deny it, he became more assured that he wasn't alone in what he was feeling. He cupped the back of her neck and drew her nearer. "I need to know. Just one real kiss to see if the magic's still there."

"Just one," she whispered. She watched his head dip toward her and opened her mouth as he'd instructed her years ago. When his soft lips touched hers, her eyes drifted shut.

Hadn't she known, somewhere in the back of her mind, that this kiss was inevitable? Maybe as far back as the wintry day she'd looked up and seen him walking toward her after an absence of more than twenty years. Perhaps when she'd accepted his invitation to the winter carnival. Surely when the storm had stranded them together in intimate isolation. She'd known.

And the knowledge had both frightened and excited her.

Their explorations were timid at first, a gentle coming together, a breathless sense of remembrance. His lips moved against hers slowly, testing, letting the recollections mount.

He tasted the same, she thought with shocked disbelief. Like heady wine, like forbidden desire, an indefinably rich, male taste. Could that be? Could she truly be recalling such a thing? Impossible. Yet she knew it was so.

David drew back and watched her eyes flutter open, saw the astonished pleasure in their gray depths. He asked the silent question and read the answer in her unwavering gaze. They'd been foolish to think that one would be enough. He gathered her closer and felt her arms slide up his chest and encircle his neck.

This kiss was more impatient, the passion building as his tongue joined to mate with hers, and even their breathing seemed as one. His hands stroked her back, her slender rib cage through the heavy sweatshirt, and longed to creep under and touch bare flesh. But he did not, instead reveling in the feel of her breasts yielding against the wall of his chest.

His mouth seemed magical, Janice thought in a haze of sensation. Memories roared back in living color, of kissing him good-night at the back door of her dorm and in the last row of the old Gibraltar Theater, which was probably gone by now. They'd dated a mere half a dozen times twenty-five years ago, yet it suddenly seemed like only yesterday. Placing a hand on his shoulder and stepping back, she took a deep breath and reached inside for some remnants of strength.

"David, I'm not ready for... for where I think this might lead us."

"I know." He felt like a heel for rushing them into that kiss, yet exhilarated at the power of it. He'd wanted to know and now he did. The question was, what in hell did he want to do about it?

He'd never been a man who acted impulsively, nor one who would let his hormones lead him. He wanted Janice, but they were no longer kids. His renewed feelings for her were one thing, but altering his life to fit in a woman again was another. He was forty-six years old and he liked his life just fine the way it was. Most of the time. Didn't he?

Gently he cupped her chin, forcing her anxious eyes to meet his. "Don't worry. I'll never take you where you don't want to go."

She was able to offer a smile then, though it was a shaky one. "You used to say that when we dated."

"And?"

"And I believed you then as I believe you now."

"Thank you." He let her go and turned to add more wood to the fire, needing the mindless chore while he got himself under control.

It was nearly midnight, Janice realized as she sat down on the couch. She hadn't noticed until just this minute how chilly the house had become. The fire helped and so had the brandy, though she dared not have more of that. She could go upstairs to bed and offer him the guest room, but even with heavy blankets on the beds, it would be warmer here by the fireplace.

David turned, again seemingly reading her mind. "It's getting late. How about if I take that chair and you stretch out on the couch?"

"The couch is longer. You take that and I'll..."

"No. I'll be fine on the chair."

Not in the mood to argue, she went for bedding, returned and handed him a pillow and blanket. "Good night, then."

"See you in the morning."

She settled down under the afghan at the far end of the couch and tried not to notice him moving around in the chair, his long legs sticking out over the edge of the ottoman.

Listening to the fire snap and an occasional shifting of the logs, Janice reached for sleep that seemed to elude her. By the sounds of his movements, David was faring no better. After a while, she raised her head and peeked over at him.

She almost laughed out loud, he looked so uncomfortable with his legs dangling and his arms hanging, his head propped at an awkward angle. With a sigh, she sat up, hoping she wouldn't regret this. "David, come over here, please."

His head shot up. "What?"

"Bring your blanket and pillow and lie down at the other end of this couch. It's plenty long enough. You won't be able to move tomorrow if you spend the night in that chair."

This time, he didn't protest. He moved over and lay down, trying to keep his long legs from touching hers.

Janice bent her knees and pulled her legs up closer to her body. She watched him punch down the pillow and settle his head on it. "Okay now?"

"Mmm, fine."

She closed her eyes. It was the humanitarian thing to do, she told herself. He'd all but saved her life out there in the storm tonight. She owed him a decent night's sleep at least. Sharing a couch under these circumstances wasn't exactly like sleeping together. She tried to empty her mind, tried desperately not to relive the minutes in his arms when his mouth had been on hers, his breath mingling with hers.

CHAPTER SEVEN

HIS MOUTH WAS on hers, his breath mingling with hers. His arms were wound around her and his legs tangled with hers. And oh, it felt so good. She thought of nothing, no one, but him as she returned the kiss, arching closer, her tongue meeting his in a sensual duel.

It had been so long since she'd felt like this, wanted like this. Janice tightened her arms and...and awakened to find she was squeezing her pillow. Blinking, still wrapped in the dream, she lay on the couch, letting her heartbeat settle.

It had seemed so real, so warm and wonderful. David had... She popped her head up so quickly she felt a momentary rush of dizziness. David!

He lay on his side at his end of the couch, his head pillowed on one arm, the other arm dangling over the edge, almost touching the floor. One leg was bent at the knee, the other stretched out where it touched her own stockinged foot. He was snoring lightly and sound asleep. Releasing a nervous breath, Janice let her head fall back.

Why had she dreamed so vividly of kissing him? She'd not had sensuous dreams in years. What was wrong with her? It had to have been their dance, the kisses they'd shared last night, the warm familiarity of their evening that had triggered the response. Feeling the flush of guilt, she slowly eased out from under the afghan and got up, trying not to wake him.

She walked to his end and saw that he was still sleeping. Unable to resist, she studied him. There was something terribly vulnerable about a man who lay lost in sleep, unaware he was being watched. Those sensitive blue eyes were hidden beneath heavy lids fringed with dark lashes. His overnight growth of beard gave him a rakish look rather than an unkempt one. His mouth was slightly open, that mouth that she'd been dreaming of a few short minutes ago.

His blanket was tangled and all askew. He was long, loose-limbed, rawboned, his shoulders broad, his stomach still flat. He was moving into middle age with few noticeable changes from the young man whose body had once inspired more than one female fantasy. Turning from the memory, she left him.

Wandering to the front window, she saw that the fire had gone out, but that heat was flowing from the vents and the electricity was working once more. Vaguely, she wondered how long ago it had been restored. Protected by the porch, the picture window wasn't snow-covered, and she could see out. The sky was gray and heavy with clouds, but at least it was daylight. Wind-driven snow covered the porch, hiding the steps completely, and the yard was mounded high with artistic drifts.

She'd worried unnecessarily about her neighbors noticing that David's car had spent the night parked in front of her house. The spot where they'd left his Lincoln was piled high with snow, the front end unrecognizable from the back end. The wind was still blowing, though halfheartedly, but the snow had been reduced to a light sprinkle. Still, with no sun visible, she imagined it was probably quite cold.

Walking upstairs to her bathroom, Janice decided she'd feel better after a quick shower. In the mirror, she examined her face with a frown. She, too, was approaching middle age and, though she'd not thought about it much before, she studied her reflection now with a careful eye.

She had good skin with few wrinkles, except at the corners of her eyes, where she supposed they could be excused as laugh lines. The dark circles she'd had a month ago had all but disappeared. Her eyes still looked a little haunted, but not as badly. Stripping, she glanced at the rest of her body, concluding that she was a bit too thin. Her breasts, always the first place weight loss was noticeable, were smaller. Since she'd borne two children, her stomach wasn't nearly as firm as before.

With a sigh, she turned on the water and found that though it wasn't steaming, it was hot enough. There was no denying the marks of the years on her. Men, she guessed, managed to retain at least the illusion of youth more easily than women.

Stepping into the shower, Janice picked up the soap. Why was she thinking along these lines anyway? Inexplicably, she felt her eyes fill and she ducked under the spray, annoyed with her mental meanderings.

Guilt washed over her then, along with the cleansing water. How does one control one's thoughts? she asked herself as she shampooed her hair. She didn't *want* to feel like this, to be thinking of David in any way other than as a friend. She didn't *want* to forget she was Kurt's wife, Kurt's widow. Yet her mind wandered all too often.

Rinsing off both soap and shampoo, she shut off the water and grabbed a towel. She would get herself under control, Janice promised. She would stop all this daydreaming and night dreaming and return to the self she recognized. She would then perhaps be able to stop feeling so damn guilty one half of the time and lonely the other half.

After hanging up the towel, she blow-dried her hair, then went to her connecting bedroom to dress. Minutes later, wearing a new sweater and matching wool slacks in a soft shade of peach, she entered the kitchen and put on the coffee. She was just plugging in the pot when she heard a sound behind her and turned.

She couldn't prevent the smile. Despite his shadowy morning beard, David had the tousled look of a small boy awakened before he was ready to get up. Finding it hard to meet his eyes after her unsettling thoughts, she turned to pour juice for them. "Good morning," she said. "Coffee will be ready shortly."

Brushing back his hair, David stifled a yawn. "I take it the electricity's back on." He took the juice she handed him and drank thirstily.

"Yes, and the water's reasonably hot if you'd like a shower." It occurred to her that he didn't have fresh clothes. Kurt's things still hung in his closet, since she'd been unable to face packing them up. But she knew they'd never fit David, although her son's would. "K.J.'s room is at the top of the stairs. Please help yourself to whatever you need. I'm sure he wouldn't mind."

With a murmured thanks, he padded away.

Janice stood looking out the window. So he wasn't a morning person. Kurt hadn't been either, and through the years, she'd learned to more or less stay out of his way mornings, pouring his coffee and letting him be. She, on the other hand, usually awoke feeling full of energy and chatter. She would have to curb that again today, it would seem.

But only for today. Although the snowplows wouldn't be out as early as eight, they'd be along sooner or later. Then David would be on his way and she'd be alone again. Sipping her juice, Janice wondered how she felt about that.

Ambivalent at best. In the weeks she'd been alone, she'd gotten used to doing things her own way without checking with anyone else. She'd never experienced that before and had to admit to enjoying the freedom. But freedom had its drawbacks, loneliness being the primary one. Though David's presence in her house had given her a few unnerving moments, she'd noticed she'd slept better with someone nearby.

Was it as simple as having a warm body on the premises? Maybe she should get a dog, Janice thought as she poured her coffee. Comforting, loyal and usually undemanding, a dog could be a woman's best friend. Ah, but he wouldn't answer back when she talked to him, he wouldn't dance with her or call her Sunshine.

Janice heard the shower running in the hall bath. She would start breakfast in a few minutes. But, after they ate, then what? What would she do with David stranded here for hours yet, with those serious eyes studying her? Sipping her coffee, she decided it was probably going to be a long day.

THE SNOWPLOWS ARRIVED by late morning, but the digging-out process took most of the afternoon. However, by four the road had been cleared, David had his car cleaned off and running and he'd shoveled Janice's walk and very long driveway. Rolling his tired shoulders, he went inside, stomping snow from his boots, to warm up by the fire.

Janice had spent the afternoon making a hearty soup, and she served him a bowl after he'd changed into his own dry clothes. Comfortable with each other, they chatted about nothing important over cookies and milk.

Watching him reach for his third cookie, Janice noticed that he was looking out the window at the darkening sky. "Think we're in for more?" she asked.

"I hope not."

"You don't have to leave tonight. The roads might be better in the morning." She wasn't altogether certain that having him stay longer was such a good idea, but she felt it was the polite thing to offer.

"The man driving the snowplow said the highways were fine. I thank you, but I think I should head for home before too long." His blue eyes smiled into hers. "I think I've overstayed my welcome as it is."

"No, you haven't. I'm glad you were here." A little too glad.

"Thank you. So am I." Finishing, he stood. "I could help with the dishes...."

"No, that's all right." She walked with him to the door, fighting a sudden rush of melancholy at the thought of his leaving. Hating the confusion her feelings always seemed to be in lately, she watched him tug on his boots, then reach for his coat.

With his jacket hanging open, he turned to her. Why was it every time he had to leave Janice, he struggled with a desire to stay? Something he'd have to get over, David told himself. The attraction was there, but Janice needed time to adjust to the many recent changes in her life. And he had to adjust to suddenly wanting her again after all these years.

"Thanks for everything," he wound up saying, the stock phrase sounding awkard to his ears.

Arms folded across her chest, she nodded.

"Good luck with your studies."

"Thanks." Why were they behaving like two polite strangers after the intimate hours they'd shared?

"Well, I'll call you."

"All right." She saw his hand curl around the doorknob, yet he hesitated. Emotions in a whirl, she swallowed hard. She couldn't let him go like this. "David?"

He turned, his eyes filled with a question. And with need. "Yes?"

"Come here." She opened her arms and he stepped into them, his hands circling to her back as he drew her inside the folds of his jacket.

His heart turned over at the look in her gray eyes. She didn't want him to leave any more than he wanted to go. Realizing that, he bent his head and took her mouth.

She opened her lips under his, inviting a more intimate kiss, her hands bunching in his sweater at his back. Drawing in a deep breath, she recognized his special taste as his lips moved over hers. And she was suddenly alive again, aware of his heart pounding against hers again, conscious of the blood rushing through her veins again.

David's kiss was like no other—more exciting, more breathtaking. No one had ever made her feel so desirable, so wanted, so filled with restless needs.

She was so soft under his hands, her body molding to his, pliable and shuddering all at the same time. The kiss became bolder, flavored with memories. Of another time, another place, the years between forgotten. He took and she gave, then they reversed that, each feeding the other's needs. When David drew back, he wasn't surprised to see that he was trembling.

"I tried to leave without touching you again," he told her, his breathing ragged.

"I tried to let you. I couldn't."

A breath away, he kissed her again. "You taste so good, so damn *familiar*." How could that be, after all these years?

She tried a smile. "I've thought the same about you." With a reluctant sigh, Janice stepped back, sinking down from her tiptoes. "I don't quite know what to do with the way you make me feel. I've never..." She groped for words.

"Neither have I." His fingers trailed down her smooth cheek. "This has caught us both by surprise."

She ran a hand through her hair. "I have these classes and..."

"And I have a trip coming up sometime next week. My swing up north to visit clients. I'd planned to stop to see my sister and her daughter in New York afterward."

Yes, that would give them each some time. Time to sort out their feelings. "When you return...you'll call me?"

"Yes." He touched his mouth to hers once more, very tenderly, lingering a bit longer than he'd intended. If he didn't leave now, he wouldn't at all, David realized. He turned and opened the door. "Bye for now."

"Bye." The window on the storm door filled with steam. Janice dabbed at the cloudy vision as she peered out, watching David hurry along to his car. He climbed inside, grabbed a brush, climbed out again and began clearing the windshield. Finally, he slid into his seat and pulled away.

On a shaky breath, Janice closed the door and leaned back against it. She'd fought this feeling for weeks now, avoiding the thought, struggling against the attraction. But it wasn't any use.

She wanted David Markus.

But was that wanting based on a solid feeling, a longing to renew a past relationship that had never gotten off the ground, or on a sudden new need? Pushing away from the door, Janice walked back to the kitchen to straighten things up. Time was the only thing that would help her decide. She would do the dishes and beef up the fire and find her insurance books. She would study and pass those tests if it was the last thing she ever accomplished.

And when she'd done all that, then she'd take the time to sort out her feelings about David Markus.

JANICE WALKED out of the red-brick building into the sunshine of a mid-April afternoon and realized she felt glorious. She smiled into Tom Sikes's myopic eyes. "Thanks for all your help," she said warmly.

"I did very little today, Janice," Tom answered. "You're the one that won them over."

She moved into a full-blown grin. "I did, didn't I?"

"Yes, indeed. Are you coming back to the office?"

Janice shook her head. "I think I'll go on home. I've been neglecting a lot of things around the house lately. But I'll be in tomorrow."

"Good. See you then. And again, congratulations." With a wave, Tom walked toward his car.

Janice turned and made her way to her new Capri XR2 convertible and decided it was a perfect day to drive with the top down. As she climbed behind the wheel, she couldn't stop smiling.

She really had done it.

She'd convinced the board of directors of Raystar Corporation, which owned several commercial properties Eber Insurance had insured for years, that she was not only capable of filling Kurt's shoes, but that the firm was moving in the right direction. Her presentation had shown the directors that the agency was fiscally sound and that, with Janice at the helm, they'd made contact with several new underwriters and now offered an even broader base of coverage from which Raystar could choose. Tom had come along to back her up, but she'd done most of the talking. When the vote had been taken as she and Tom waited anxiously in the reception area, it had been unanimously in favor of renewing with Eber Insurance, they'd been told.

Leaving the parking area, Janice headed back to Tyler. She hadn't felt this good, this proud, in far too long. Months of study and hard work had paid off, she thought with pleasure as she swung out into traffic. She'd attended the classes, passed the required tests and all the state exams. She'd spent hours at the agency, meeting with Tom and the sales staff, finally deciding to let two producers go for not carrying their fair share of the load. She'd placed ads, interviewed endlessly and ultimately hired two young women recently graduated from college. They were both intelligent, ambitious and aggressive. Janice was pleased with their performance so far.

Kurt had never felt women did well in sales work, and though Janice had disagreed, she'd never expressed her feelings. That perhaps had been a mistake. But she'd made a lot of mistakes in her relationship with Kurt, she was discovering.

She should have insisted she be treated equally early in their marriage, and perhaps then he would have considered her a peer as well as a wife. But she'd been too awestruck by him in the beginning and too busy raising their children afterward. The fault had been more hers than his for, used to a dominant father, she'd readily accepted a dominating husband.

Ah, but that was then and this was now. Stefanie and Ross had flown in for a visit over Easter, and her daughter had been astounded and pleased at the change in her mother. There was one woman who would have an equal marriage from the beginning, Janice thought, envying Stefanie's self-assurance. But she was gaining some of her own.

She'd had a lot of decisions to make in the three months since Kurt's death. Once she started, she'd found she rather enjoyed the challenges. She'd paid off the bills, a little startled that there wasn't as much money as she'd thought there would be. But she was all right and the company was doing well, so her future wasn't in the least shaky.

Her hair flying in a warm spring breeze, she passed a slow-moving van, loving the feel of the first car she'd ever picked out all by herself. She'd turned in her station wagon and sold Kurt's beloved Mercedes to buy this snazzy red convertible, feeling a little like the butterfly who'd emerged from its cocoon. Her decision wasn't totally frivolous, but it was a bit unlike the old Janice. She'd hesitated to show the car to Anna and Alyssa, thinking they'd be critical of her choice. But they'd surprised Janice by cheering her on.

K.J. had surprised her, too. He'd come home for spring break and, though she'd been deep in her studies, she'd been so glad to see him. Sons, she'd discovered, didn't dash home from college to spend weekends with their families the way daughters did. They'd talked, and she'd explained that she wanted to keep the company going so one day he could take over and have a going concern to build from. Oddly, he hadn't seemed enthusiastic at all, and when she asked him why, he'd broken down and told her he really wanted a career in art—political cartoons, to be exact.

Of course, Janice had known for years that her son loved to draw. His room was filled with sketches and charcoal drawings. But she'd considered his interest more a hobby than a career choice.

When she'd shown a marked interest, he'd brought out several of his recent cartoons, and she'd been pleasantly surprised at his evident talent. K.J. had really opened up then, confiding that he'd been fearful of dashing his father's dream of his taking over Eber Insurance, so he hadn't mentioned his change of heart earlier. And he hadn't known where his mother stood on the subject, either.

Janice had hugged him then and told him she would support his career choice a hundred percent. No one knew better than she how crushing it could be to be a square peg being shoved into a round hole. Even with her victory today at Raystar, she was pleased at how far she'd come, but in the back of her mind was the thought that the insurance business wasn't really for her. She and K.J. had left it that they would discuss his future more thoroughly when he came home from college for the summer.

The summer. It was around the corner. Spring had sneaked up on her and already the days were warmer and the flowers starting to bud after several weeks of rain. David had told her just yesterday that he'd been out weeding the flower beds in his backyard.

David. Again, Janice smiled, thinking of the man who'd become more and more important over the past months. He'd returned to Tyler several times since the night of the snowstorm. Once he'd been passing through on his way to visit a client and they'd only been able to share a quick lunch. Another time he'd driven up for a leisurely dinner at a country inn he'd discovered on one of his trips.

One Sunday, he'd arrived and taken her out to breakfast, and then they'd gone for a long drive in the country. He'd insisted she stop working long enough to have a picnic by the lake, and one Friday night they'd gone to a play. Wonderful hours spent together, and each time, they'd spoken more with their eyes than their lips.

Then there'd been the phone calls. They'd talked like old friends, several evenings for more than two hours. She'd shared her day with him and he'd enthusiastically congratulated each little success she'd achieved. It was wonderful having someone in her corner cheering her on. One particularly lonely night, she'd called him, but he hadn't been home. Later, she'd been glad, for she'd ached with the need to see him and might have said something foolish.

And he'd sent her gifts. Small things that nevertheless meant a great deal. A book she'd mentioned wanting to read, a box of fresh pears from a client who shipped fruit, candy wrapped in gold foil. And, at unexpected moments, a single yellow rose.

The very thought of him, the sound of his name, warmed her. She was woman enough to realize she was beginning to care far too much—and romantic enough to be unable to stop herself. David seemed perfect, sensitive and caring and supportive. Oddly, it was that very perfection that bothered her. He never disagreed,

criticized or argued. She and Kurt had seldom argued
because, early on, she'd gotten into the habit of giving
in to him. But with David, he seemed to agree before
she even stated a preference. It was beginning to worry
her.

Chastising herself for seeing a problem when probably none existed, Janice pulled into her drive and
checked her watch. David should be home by now.
She'd call and share her victory news with him, then get
busy with a list of household chores she'd put off for
far too long.

LEANING BACK in the desk chair, Janice rolled her tired
shoulders and sighed. She'd gone grocery shopping and
done the laundry, then had a quick salad for dinner.
Still keyed up, she'd brought her coffee into the den.
She decided to balance her checkbook, something she
hadn't gotten to for a couple of months, then take a
long, leisurely bath.

Taking a bracing sip of coffee, she leaned forward to
mark off the checks. Finishing ten minutes later, she
started to add up the outstanding checks. But the add-
ing machine was out of tape. She opened the middle
drawer, searching for the extra rolls she was certain
Kurt had kept on hand.

A quick look and she came up empty-handed. The
top right-hand drawer didn't have them either. She still
hadn't inspected the entire desk since Kurt's death,
another task she'd kept putting off. Frowning, she
pulled out the second drawer on the right, shoving her

hand to the rear, rummaging about. She withdrew only a long white envelope. About to set it aside, she turned it over instead. One word was written on it in Kurt's bold printing: Chicago.

Curious now, Janice opened the envelope and removed the first bundle bound with a rubber band. The canceled checks from that separate account Kurt had had, all made out to Diane Flynn. She studied the handwriting, recognizing it definitely as Kurt's. They were for various amounts, none under three hundred dollars. Turning one over, she saw the endorsement, a slanted, somewhat childish signature. And the stamp from a bank in Chicago.

Who was Diane Flynn and why had Kurt been making payments to her, payments he'd kept hidden from his wife?

Reaching into the envelope, Janice removed a second packet of what appeared to be receipts paper-clipped together. Unfastening them, she browsed through. There were several dozen, all made out to Kurt Eber, all for more than five hundred dollars, with consecutive monthly dates going back three years. In the corner of each was scrawled an odd notation of a money-order number. Or so it read.

The receipts were imprinted with a small logo in one corner and the name *Cambridge Apartments—Chicago,* then the address below. They were all signed by someone named Raymond Hauser. Leaning back in the swivel chair, Janice grew thoughtful.

Three years of receipts from a Chicago apartment building in Kurt's name. Why had Kurt kept an apartment in Chicago? And if he had, why had he never mentioned it? All paid for evidently by money order. Why not by company check or that separate checking account?

Now that she thought about it, in going through his past expenses for the filing of her income tax just recently, she hadn't run across any hotel receipts for his trips to Chicago, although there'd been some from other cities he'd visited. He certainly hadn't spent enough time in the Chicago area to warrant renting an apartment by the month. How very odd.

Riffling through the stack, she found a folded sheet at the back of the pile. As she opened it, a small receipt fell out. It was from Meyers Jewelry, a store she'd never heard of. Merchandise for more than nine hundred dollars, paid for in cash. The date was three years ago and what the merchandise was wasn't spelled out. Beginning to tense up, Janice unfolded the sheet and looked at it.

This receipt was for medical services rendered by a Dr. Raoul Hernandez, listing his Chicago address. Fifteen hundred dollars in cash. It was a carbon copy so the date wasn't clear, though it looked to be two years ago. Tossing the stack onto the desk, Janice swung her gaze out the window at the darkening twilight.

Why had Kurt paid for medical services in cash when they had very good medical insurance coverage? She tried to think back to two years ago, but could recall no incident where Kurt had been injured, away or at home. Or even sick with a cold. He'd always been very healthy, at least on the surface. Could he have had a problem he hadn't told her about?

It seemed unlikely, since during those two years, he'd jogged, played tennis, handball—any number of strenuous activities. Surely if he'd had trouble that long ago, he'd have slowed down or she'd have noticed some other sign. Why had he kept the canceled checks cashed by this Diane Flynn in the same envelope as the apartment receipts? What was Kurt's connection to this mysterious Diane Flynn? Janice rubbed at her forehead, trying to come up with a reasonable explanation.

The next time she looked up, she saw by the wall clock that it was nearly eight. No longer in the mood to finish balancing her checkbook, she shoved the bank statement into the top drawer. She stuffed the canceled checks and receipts back into the envelope and thoughtfully set it on top of the desk.

Should she call and ask David if he was familiar with the Cambridge Apartments and if Kurt had ever mentioned renting one? Why not? It couldn't hurt and it might save her additional worry if he did know something. Besides, she'd wanted to tell him about her presentation.

As always, when she heard his voice, she found herself enjoying a feeling of warmth. "I wasn't sure you'd be home," she said.

"I knocked off early today. There's so much yard work to be done that I'll probably stay home tomorrow as well. So tell me, how'd it go?"

Smiling, she told him in minute detail about Raystar's reaction. "Can you believe it?" she finished, out of breath.

"Of course, I can. You're good and they realized it. But I've known that for some time."

The warmth spread. "Have you now?" Remembering what she'd called about, she decided to plunge right in. "David, are you familiar with Cambridge Apartments in Chicago?"

Seated outside on his redwood deck, cradling his portable phone, David felt a jolt of apprehension. "I think they're on the northwest side of town. Why?"

She told him about the receipts she'd found earlier. "Did you ever hear Kurt mention renting one of those apartments?"

He could answer that one honestly, but he knew there might be tougher questions coming. "No, I can't say I did." He'd known about *an* apartment, but he'd never heard the name. Kurt had usually met him at a restaurant.

Janice toyed with the envelope of receipts. "Do you recall Kurt ever becoming ill in Chicago, needing a doctor perhaps? Not recently, but a couple of years ago?"

Another easy question. Leaning forward, David tapped his pipe on the railing. "No. If he was ill here, he never mentioned it to me. Why?"

"I also found a receipt from a doctor for fifteen hundred dollars. As you know from going through the files, we've had good health insurance coverage for years." Janice found herself tensing again. "There was also a receipt for several hundred dollars for jewelry purchased in Chicago."

David stared up at the stars twinkling in the evening sky and felt a chilly wind blow across his face. "Maybe he bought you a bracelet or something else and you've forgotten."

"Kurt wasn't one to spend money on jewelry. Besides my wedding ring, I have a necklace that belonged to his mother plus a few pieces of good jewelry from my family. The rest is costume."

"Then I don't know." He didn't, but he could damn well guess, and he wished that Kurt, if he had to have secrets from his wife, had covered his tracks better.

Janice decided to ask the big question. "Do you know a Diane Flynn in Chicago?"

"No." Technically speaking, the way she'd worded the question, he wasn't lying. He didn't *know* Diane Flynn, though he certainly did know of her.

The nightmare he'd worried about since the day of Kurt's funeral was here. How had she found out about Diane Flynn? "Should I know her?"

"I just thought you might, since she evidently lives in Chicago. Of course, I realize it's a big city." She closed her eyes briefly. She'd begun this and now felt the need to finish it. Reluctantly, she told David about finding Kurt's separate checkbook, and then today, the canceled checks in the same envelope as the rent receipts. "What do you make of it?"

She was a bright woman, David was well aware, and getting closer to an ugly truth he'd just as soon have kept from her. If he told her what he knew, it would undoubtedly spoil her memories of her dead husband and upset her irreparably. Maybe the best thing would be to hedge a bit, to give her more time to grow stronger. Or was he just a coward?

Not liking that thought, he shifted gears. "Do you think Kurt was having an affair with this woman? Is that why you're asking all these questions?"

Janice brushed a lock of hair from her cheek distractedly. "I don't know what to think, but that has occurred to me. A special checking account, money-order payments, receipts for cash. Certainly he was keeping something from me, something I'm not altogether sure I want to know."

She seemed to want to hide from the truth, and for now he would let her. She might be angry with him later, if she ever discovered everything, but he'd risk it, David decided. He simply couldn't blurt it all out, couldn't hurt her like that. Maybe she'd drop the whole mess. He wasn't protecting his dead friend—had never done that when Kurt had been alive. Even then, he'd kept silent to keep from hurting Janice.

Disliking the situation and furious with Kurt for putting him in it, David opted for a half-truth. "Kurt didn't seem the type to have a mistress." That was one thing that had puzzled David, until the day he'd asked Kurt about why he'd taken up with Diane Flynn.

There was an edge to his voice and Janice wondered at the cause. "Is there a type, David?" She let out a sigh. "I wish I'd never looked into that envelope."

He tried to sound casual. "Maybe the best thing you could do is to forget it. Sometimes it's best to..."

"Let sleeping dogs lie. Yes, Alyssa's already given me the same advice."

"You discussed this with her?"

"Not all of it, since I found the apartment receipts only today. Her husband died quite a few years ago and she has this gut feeling that he'd been unfaithful to her."

"But she doesn't know for certain. And since that's the case, I believe it's best not to dwell on it, but rather to try to forget your suspicions. What can be accomplished after the fact, after the man's dead?"

She was surprised he didn't see her reasons. "Betrayal is very difficult to live with. Once you lose trust in a man, you may never be able to trust another."

Was there a hidden message in her words? he wondered. "I don't agree. There's a new beginning with another man, a new chance to learn to trust, and honor that trust. I say let it go."

Janice released a shaky breath. "Easier said than done. I'll have to think about this." Though she'd introduced it, she now badly wanted to change the subject. "So tell me, where are you? In your hot tub?" The hot tub had become a standing joke with them, mentioned in most of their calls, though picturing David in it aroused more than her sense of humor.

David laughed, glad to switch the conversation to a brighter topic. "No, but I'm going to get you in my hot tub yet one of these days."

"You just might at that." Struggling through a yawn, she decided that bath she'd been thinking about held a lot of appeal. "I think I'll make it an early night. Talk with you soon?"

"You bet. Good night, Sunshine."

Janice hung up with a smile and sat staring at her hands on the desktop. She'd splurged and had a manicure before going to the presentation today and was pleased at the professional look, the pale pink polish a nice touch. For a long moment, she studied her wide gold wedding band. Finally, she came to a decision. It was time. Slowly, she slipped the ring off and placed it in the top drawer.

She wished she could as easily set aside the uncomfortable feeling that Kurt had kept things from her deliberately, things that would have torn at the fabric of their marriage. Things that were now threatening to shatter memories that she cherished. But she was sick and tired of hiding her head, of ignoring obvious signs. If she couldn't face the truth, what kind of woman was she?

Arriving at decisions quickly was becoming easier with practice, Janice thought as she stood. In the morning, she would call Tom and tell him she had something to take care of and wouldn't be in. Then she would head for Chicago where, hopefully, she'd find some answers to questions that had been plaguing her for weeks.

Turning out the lights, she started up the stairs, hoping she wasn't about to grab a tiger by the tail.

CHAPTER EIGHT

AS JANICE HEADED toward Interstate 94 in her bright red Capri, she scarcely noticed the budding wildflowers coming to life along the country road. Her mind was on her mission and her destination was Chicago.

It could very well be that she was making a big mistake or going on a wild-goose chase, she thought with a sigh. But she had to find out the truth so she could put her doubts to rest. She had to find Diane Flynn.

This morning, she'd called Chicago information to see if she could get a phone number for Diane Flynn at the Cambridge Apartments. She'd been told that there was no listing for a D. Flynn at that address. Dr. Hernandez was no longer practicing medicine in the Chicago area, she'd discovered through several more calls. And the jewelry store listed on the sales slip didn't keep receipts more than a year old unless they were on charge accounts, the manager had informed her. So many dead ends.

Janice felt she had no choice. She had to go in person, to give it her best shot before she could lay it to rest. If, in fact, she could. The whole thing was like a dangling loose end, bothering her in her quiet moments, the questions nagging at her.

After their unsettling conversation last night, she'd not told David she was driving down today. If it turned out to be nothing, she'd tell him, and together they'd laugh it off. In a way, her relationship with David was another reason she needed to do this. She firmly believed that she had to put everything in her past behind her in order to be truly free to love again. And she badly wanted that unconditional freedom.

Swinging onto I-94, Janice pushed the button to raise the window she'd opened earlier. It was a cool though sunny day so she'd worn a suit, beige-and-blue plaid with a navy silk blouse, and high-heeled pumps. David was so tall that she enjoyed wearing heels with him. And it was in the back of her mind that, finished with her hunt-and-search mission today, she just might surprise him with a visit and persuade him to go out to dinner.

Janice shot around a lumbering old truck, then pulled back into the right lane, her eye on the mirror. It was altogether too easy in this fast little car to forget the speed limits. She set the cruise control and, for the next hour and a half, concentrated on the heavy Friday morning traffic and tried not to let her concern over Diane Flynn distract her.

THE CAMBRIDGE APARTMENTS, as she'd learned earlier through her calls, were on the northwest side of Chicago, in an area known as Irving Park. It was not a bad address, but not in an expensive neighborhood, either. Janice pulled into the fenced parking lot and studied the three-story red-brick building. Older, but well maintained. She got out of the car and went into the small entryway.

No one named Diane Flynn was listed on the two dozen or so mailboxes or doorbells. She pushed the superintendent's buzzer.

"Yeah?" came the static-laden reply.

"I need to talk with you," she answered. "My name is Janice Eber."

"We got no vacancies."

'I don't want to rent an apartment. I'm looking for one of your tenants. Diane Flynn."

A moment's hesitation, then he came back on. "Wait there."

She did and finally the heavy door opened. The man was in his sixties, quite thin, his work pants hanging on his bony frame, his lean face pale and unhealthy looking. Frowning, he motioned her inside the lobby.

The floor tile was old but clean and polished, the walls freshly painted and the two plants flanking the elevator fake. She turned to the superintendent. "Would you be Raymond Hauser?" Janice asked.

"Yup. Superintendent. Over here." He indicated a tiny alcove office and she followed him over. "You looking for Diane Flynn? She's not here."

"But she did occupy one of your apartments?"

Raymond removed a handkerchief from his back pocket and blew his nose loudly. "Damn allergies." He sniffed and stuffed the handkerchief away. "She lived here about three years, I guess. Left along about February."

Janice withdrew the packet of receipts from her purse and held them out to the man. "These receipts are signed by you and made out to Kurt Eber. Do you know him?"

Raymond studied his own signature a few seconds. "Met him when he rented the apartment a while back I saw him a couple times after. He came and went."

"Then this Diane Flynn lived in the apartment alone?"

The man wiped at his nose with the back of his skinny hand. "I don't pay much attention. Long as the tenants pay on time and don't cause no trouble, I mind my own business. I insist on cash 'cause the owners had trouble in the past with bounced checks. All I know is the man sent his money orders to me regularly and the woman lived here." Raymond sent her a suspicious look. "Why you want to find her, anyhow?"

She'd rehearsed her answer, hoping to gain the superintendent's cooperation as she put on a friendly smile. "She hasn't done anything wrong, that I know of. I just want to talk to her. Did she leave a forwarding address?"

Raymond moved behind the metal desk, opened the top drawer and pulled out a small bundle of mail held together with a red rubber band. On top was a piece of paper with a scrawled address. "I been meaning to send this mail to her. Just didn't get around to it." He tapped a finger to the paper. "This here's where she's living, I guess. You going to go see her?"

"Yes."

"You mind taking this to her? Save me mailing it, you know."

Janice accepted the bundle. "I'd be happy to." Glancing down at the forwarding address the woman left, she frowned. "Do you know where this street is located?"

He squinted at the paper. "Down toward town, off Addison probably. Kind of a rough neighborhood around there. I'd be careful, if I was you." He walked back to the lobby and tugged open the door, holding it for her.

"Thank you, Mr. Hauser." Back in her car, Janice looked over the packet of Diane Flynn's mail. A shut-off notice from the electric company, the postmark February. Something that looked like a doctor's bill, but it wasn't from Dr. Hernandez. The rest was junk mail.

Mr. Hauser had said he insisted on cash, which explained why Kurt had gotten money orders. But why had he been paying Diane Flynn's rent?

Trying to keep her mind from the obvious conclusion until and if she had proof, she picked up the map she'd left on the passenger seat and pinpointed the street. A rough neighborhood. Wonderful. Hoping the traffic in town wouldn't be too heavy, Janice set out.

It took her some time to locate the building. If the other structure was old, this one was ancient. An ethnic mixture of children were playing ball in the street as she eased into a parking space, carefully locking the doors as she got out. No security buzzer system on this lobby door. Janice walked in and located the mailboxes. Diane Flynn's apartment was on the second floor.

No elevator, either. Janice climbed the stairs, noting the graffiti on the walls. Cooking odors heavy with cabbage and the smell of stale smoke assaulted her nose as she reached the hall. Walking on the threadbare carpeting, she checked the numbers, looking for 210. Loud rock music blared from behind one closed door and the wailing of a baby could be heard from around the corner. Then she was in front of 210.

No doorbell. Swallowing, Janice raised a less-than-steady hand and knocked twice. She waited and was about to knock again when the door inched open, revealing a guard chain. The blond head of a woman appeared, her eyes questioning.

"Yes?" she asked.

"Are you Diane Flynn?" Janice asked.

"Yes. Who are you?"

"Janice Eber." She held out the bundle. "The superintendent at Cambridge Apartments asked me to drop off your mail. Do you have a minute to talk to me?"

The blue eyes inspected her thoroughly. "Okay." She closed the door, slid back the chain and allowed Janice into the room.

Shabby was the kindest word she could come up with, Janice thought. The furniture wasn't too bad, but cheaply constructed. The painted walls were a dingy beige and the carpeting on a par with the runner in the hall. But the place was neat. She turned to Diane and handed her the packet of mail.

Diane took it, glancing at the envelopes without much interest, then waved toward a brown corduroy couch. "You want to sit down?"

"Thank you." Trying to gather her thoughts now that she was face-to-face with the woman, Janice sat.

Diane looked to be no older than thirty, possibly younger. She wore faded blue jeans and a short-sleeved sweatshirt along with tennis shoes, holes at the toes of both. Her blond hair fell past her shoulders and she shook it back as she sat down in a maple rocker opposite Janice.

Her wide blue eyes studied Janice's outfit with a hint of envy and she smiled shyly. "I didn't know Kurt had a sister. He told me he was an only child."

A sister? Janice crossed her legs and folded her hands together nervously. "He was."

"Oh. Then who are you?"

She'd known. Hadn't she known somehow that this was the sort of conversation they'd be having? Janice swallowed hard before answering. "His widow."

"Widow? Kurt wasn't married."

"Yes, he was. To me."

It took a moment to register. Diane's eyes filled at the realization, then fluttered shut as her head bent and her slim shoulders drooped. "I had a feeling something terrible was wrong when he didn't come back for so long." She raised a clenched hand to her trembling lips. "How...how did he die?"

"A very sudden heart attack, in mid-January."

"Oh, God."

Oh, God. Janice's thoughts echoed the woman's. A part of her wanted to reach out and comfort Diane in her shock at the news; another part wanted to run away, to not listen to the story she'd come to hear. Hadn't this thought been hovering in the back of her mind ever since she'd discovered Kurt's secret checkbook? He'd obviously had a relationship of some sort with this young woman. Janice struggled to accept that while Diane wiped at her tears.

"How long had you known Kurt?" Janice asked finally.

Diane drew her legs up under her on the chair, her eyes still bright with tears. "I met him four years ago. I even remember the date—August 12th. I had to work a double shift that day and I was really tired."

Janice knew she would have to go slowly here. She remembered Kurt's charming ways, his likability. This child/woman was young and naive. If there was fault here, it likely wasn't Diane's alone, she thought, wrestling with a rush of anger. "Where did you work?"

"At the Hotel Carlisle. In the coffee shop. Waitressing. He used to stay there on his trips into town. He was so nice. A big tipper, you know. Never rude or a big flirt like some of those traveling salesman. A real gentleman."

Janice felt a heaviness in her chest as she nodded. "Yes, I always thought so, too."

Diane's eyes overflowed as she looked at the woman on her couch. "I didn't know he was married. Honest I didn't. He told me he'd never married, that I was the first woman he... Oh, God!" She buried her face in her hands, finally giving in to her tears.

She shouldn't have come. Janice leaned back, her hands moving to her elbows, hugging herself as she fought for control. David had been right and so had Alyssa. She should have let sleeping dogs lie. Discovering the truth only caused pain.

"I found a checkbook register in Kurt's desk listing checks made out to you over a period of several years. Then I found rent receipts from the Cambridge Apartments."

Diane nodded. "We lived there until February. When Kurt stopped coming home, I knew something was wrong, but I didn't know how to find him. See, he'd told me to never call him at work, that I could get him fired if I did. But the next month's rent was coming due and I'd run out of money. So I called Metropolitan Insurance."

"Is that where he'd told you he worked?"

"Yes, as a traveling salesman. But they'd never heard of him." She sniffled and shook her head. "I didn't know what to do. So I moved out of there and found this place." She looked around at the run-down room. "It's all I can afford right now. I was lucky they took me back at the Carlisle. I work the evening shift. It pays more."

Janice had questions, so many questions. She leaned forward. "When you first met Kurt at the Carlisle coffee shop, you started dating, I take it."

Diane smiled in remembrance. "Yeah. He'd wait for my shift to end and we'd go for a walk. Sometimes a movie. He told me he was lonely traveling so much. Finally one night he asked me up to his room. We fell in love, you know. I wasn't a virgin, but I hadn't been with many guys. I was only twenty-two."

Twenty-two just four years ago and Kurt had been forty-two then. Dear God, what had he been thinking of? Lonely and in love, this woman was saying. This woman who was only slightly older than Kurt's daughter. And his wife hadn't suspected a thing. Janice choked back her rising nausea. "Go on."

Diane shrugged. "After a while, we got tired of sneaking around. The management didn't like the waitresses seeing hotel guests after hours. So one day Kurt came in all excited. He'd rented us this apartment."

"In the Cambridge building."

She nodded. "It was nicer than any place I'd ever lived. My folks drank, you know. I left home, dropped out of school at sixteen and I never had much. But Kurt made up for all that. We picked out our furniture together." For a moment, she looked dreamy. "We had so much fun, you know?"

Janice struggled with a variety of emotions. Anger, hurt, a deep sense of betrayal. And the big question. How had she failed Kurt that he'd needed this woman? "So then you lived together at Cambridge Apartments?"

"Sort of, but Kurt wasn't there much because of his traveling job. He was such a hard worker, you know. I always told him he worked too many hours. And then there was his mother. He had to look after her."

"His mother?"

"Yeah. She lives in some small town in Wisconsin. Kurt had to spend time with her. Holidays and weekends and that. She's up there in years and not well. Does she know Kurt died?"

Janice let out a deep breath. "Diane, Kurt's parents were from Boston and they both died when Kurt was still in college." She watched that sink in. "Yes, he lied to you, too."

Diane clouded up again. "I can't believe he lied. Not Kurt. He was such a *good* man."

Obviously, this poor, sad woman had believed everything Kurt had told her. She'd needed to believe him, so she had. Janice understood perfectly. She'd done the same. Two foolish, trusting women.

She swung her eyes toward the window, streaked with the winter's accumulation of grime. Well, she'd found what she'd been looking for. Now she'd have to live with the truth.

"Mommy."

Janice turned at the sound of the small voice. A little boy stood in the archway, rubbing his eyes sleepily. He wore only a T-shirt and training pants.

"Come here, Sammy," Diane said, holding out her arms.

As realization slammed into Janice, she gasped out loud, unable to prevent her response. The child climbed onto his mother's lap. He had dark curly hair and, from the safety of the arms that held him, he stared back at the visitor with solemn brown eyes as he popped a thumb into his mouth.

"This is my son, Samuel," Diane said, her voice suddenly protective and more than a little defensive.

"How... how old is he?"

"Two this last April."

Two. She had pictures at home in her photo album of Kurt, Jr. at this age, Janice thought, pictures that could easily have been mistaken for this boy. "Kurt's father's name was Samuel," she said, surprised she was able to speak.

"He told me that."

Janice rubbed her forehead with a shaky hand. "I'm sorry. This has been quite a shock." When she'd found the canceled checks and receipts, she'd suspected Kurt might have been having an affair. But a child! She'd never dreamed of a child.

Fighting a burgeoning rage, Janice rose and walked to stand facing the window, needing a moment to compose herself.

She'd badly wanted more children, but Kurt had said that the expense of raising two was plenty. After K.J. had been born, she'd allowed him to talk her into having her tubes tied. And yet he'd fathered a son he'd kept hidden from her in Chicago. Janice didn't know which betrayal hurt the most, learning he'd had a mistress or discovering he'd had an illegitimate child.

"Do...do you have children?" Diane asked hesitantly.

Janice swung around slowly. "Our daughter's twenty-two and Kurt, Jr. is twenty." Anger at her dead husband replaced some of the hurt she'd been living with as she studied the other woman he'd also deceived. "Did you plan this child?"

"No, but Kurt was so happy when he learned I was pregnant. He was with me when I delivered, even watched."

The woman wasn't trying to hurt her, Janice had to remind herself. But she was managing all the same. Kurt hadn't been in town for either of her births. Janice pressed a fist into the knot that had formed in her stomach, hoping her breakfast coffee wouldn't reappear. "Where did you deliver?"

"At a clinic near the apartment. Some Hispanic doctor."

It was all falling together. "Dr. Raoul Hernandez?"

"Sounds right. Why? Do you know him?"

Janice shook her head. "I found the receipt. Also another, for a piece of jewelry back some time ago."

Diane's thin face broke into a smile as she pulled a chain free of her T-shirt. On the end dangled a gold heart. "For this, probably. Kurt said we couldn't be married while his mother was alive. She depended on him too much. So he gave me this and said it would be the same as a wedding ring." Dropping the chain, she clutched her child closer and began to rock. "Why did he lie to us?"

Why, indeed. "I don't know, Diane. I honestly don't know."

"Mommy," Sammy said, "cookie?"

"Sure, sweetheart." Diane rose and set the boy in the chair. "Can I get you a cup of coffee or something?" she asked, looking over at Janice.

"No, thank you." She sat still, utterly stunned, trying to absorb the news that this boy solemnly watching her was Kurt's son. *Why? Damn it, Kurt, why?* She'd been a good wife, loyal, faithful, trusting. Too damn trusting.

Diane returned, handing her son a cookie. Awkwardly, she sat down on the far edge of the couch and turned toward Janice. "My dad used to run around on my mom. But I always thought it was because he drank. I don't know what makes a man want more than one woman in his life. I only wanted Kurt. And now...now he's gone forever."

Gone and good riddance, Janice thought viciously, then closed her eyes on the thought. She'd spent months mourning a man who, she was discovering, had been a stranger. For years she'd lived with a man who'd been living a double life, living a lie. *How could you do this to me, Kurt?*

Janice watched the little boy chew on his cookie. "Who takes care of him while you work?"

"I had to hire a sitter. A teenage girl comes in after school. I don't leave until four, so it works out." She ruffled the child's dark hair. "And you're a good boy, right, Sammy?"

Sammy smiled and nodded.

Janice felt her heart twist as she recognized Kurt's lopsided grin. *Damn you, Kurt!* Her head was pounding and her stomach burned. Unsteadily, as if recovering from a long illness, she rose to her feet. "I have to go."

Diane got up too, her stance hesitant. "You don't hate me, do you?"

For a long moment, Janice stared at Sammy, then at Diane. Victims. All three of them were victims. "No, I don't hate you. I wish you luck, Diane."

Diane moved to pull back the chain. "Yeah, you too, Mrs. Eber."

Eyes filled with anguish and indecision, Janice looked into the woman's youthful face. What were her chances, waitressing nights, and without even a high school diploma, of ever getting out of this neighborhood? What would become of her son—Kurt's son?

It wasn't her problem. Clutching her handbag, she walked out. "Goodbye, Diane."

Passing a tall teenager with a large tattoo on his forearm, Janice hurried along the hallway and down the steps. She badly wanted to be out of this depressing building, away from this dismal neighborhood, far from pathetic Diane Flynn and her somber-eyed son.

Her hands were shaking so she could scarcely unlock her car door. Safely inside, she started the engine and quickly shot out into the now-empty street.

She drove then, paying little attention to where she was going, needing to put miles between her and the scene she'd just left. She held the wheel in a damp grip, her mind replaying all she'd heard. It wasn't the traffic she saw but a dark-eyed, curly-headed boy of two who sat cuddled in his mother's lap.

Kurt had wanted Diane's baby, but he'd made sure his wife wouldn't have any more. Kurt had watched as Sammy had entered the world, but he hadn't been available when Janice had delivered. Kurt hadn't figured on dying quite so soon. But he had, shocking them all, changing so many lives. He'd left Stefanie and K.J. fatherless. He'd left Janice, at first a grieving widow and now bitter with betrayal. And he'd left his second family to fend for themselves—a small child and an uneducated woman.

She remembered that Kurt had seemed to spend more time in Chicago than in other cities in recent years. He'd told her his business was expanding to the point where he'd opened a branch office there experimentally. She hadn't thought to question him or ask why. She'd believed him.

Stupid, gullible, naive. She'd been all those and more. Kurt hadn't just had an affair, bad as that was.

He'd treated Diane like a wife, going furniture shopping with her, having a child with her. Meanwhile, back in Tyler, his dumb wife had tended her flowers, washed his clothes and planned special dinners on his return.

Stomach roiling, Janice looked up and found herself at an expressway crossroads. One sign pointed toward the northwest and Buffalo Grove. Turning in that direction, she decided to visit David. She badly needed someone to help her cope with all this.

WHEN HE DIDN'T ANSWER the doorbell right away, Janice almost got cold feet. Perhaps dropping in on David wasn't such a hot idea. What if he was entertaining another woman? On this day of days, nothing would surprise her. He really wasn't tied to her in any tangible way. She was probably overreacting, she knew, but she wasn't feeling terribly charitable toward the male of the species just now.

According to her watch, it was four. He'd told her last evening that he intended to do a few minor repairs around the house today. Had he changed his mind and decided to go into town, perhaps to his office? Again, she checked the slip of paper she'd written David's address on this morning. The same as the brass numbers on the door.

The rustic house he'd described perfectly was before her, looking very much as he'd depicted it. Constructed of brick with fieldstone trim and a cedar shake roof, he'd said. And beautiful leaded-glass windows that she was certain he'd had to have custom-made since they weren't commonly produced any longer.

Think about the house, Janice commanded herself as she pressed the doorbell again. Better that than Diane and Sammy. If he didn't answer in another minute, she would—

The door swung open and David, a hammer in one hand and a meerschaum pipe stuck between his lips, stood there. Astonishment turned to pleasure as he smiled down at her and removed the pipe. "Hey, Sunshine. What a nice surprise." He drew her inside and pulled her into a hug. "What brings you so unexpectedly to my neck of the woods?"

"David, just hold me a minute, would you please?" She gripped the material of his denim shirt, burying her face in his warm throat, needing to feel him close.

Sensing her tension though he hadn't seen signs of it on her face, he caressed her back and placed a kiss in her hair. She wasn't crying, but she was trembling. He could think of only one thing that would upset her this much, and he hoped he was wrong.

Taking a deep breath, Janice withdrew and tried for a smile, averting her eyes. "I hope you don't mind my dropping in like this."

Setting his pipe in a nearby ashtray, David smiled. "Are you kidding? I'm thrilled." She looked as if she needed a little time to collect herself. "Would you like to see the house?"

"I'd love to." She placed a trembling hand in his, grateful for his understanding. She knew she wasn't fooling David, but she'd take the few minutes and hope her nerves would settle.

Walking with him, she admired the plank flooring, the cathedral ceilings, the full-wall fireplace in the great room opposite a wall of windows looking out on the wooded yard. The kitchen was a woman's dream, the bedrooms all large, the master suite huge and inviting with its hot tub, the one he'd joked about getting her into soon.

They wound up on the redwood deck with its peaceful view of the sloping lawn and the privacy afforded by the seemingly haphazard placement of mature bushes and shrubs. "It's truly lovely here," Janice commented.

Watching her, David decided she was quite good at pulling herself together. She was still pale, still a little shaky, but improving. At least she'd come to him. He'd suspected that one day they'd be having this scene and, truth be known, he'd be glad to get it behind them.

"I was out there working on building a rose trellis when I thought I heard the doorbell." Gesturing with the hammer he'd been using as a pointer, he set it down on the table and touched her arm. "Can I get you something? A drink?"

Janice gave a short, bitter laugh. "A drink in my present mood would knock me right out. Or send me into the weepies. I don't think you want either of those." She rubbed her arms, feeling a sudden chill in the cool shade of the covered deck. "Have you any coffee?"

"Coming right up. You want to stay out here or come in?"

"Out here." She heard him go inside, leaving the sliding glass door open, while her eyes drifted to a bushy-tailed squirrel cocking his head at her from the base of an old maple tree. Was that the little fellow David had told her was often bold enough to hop right up on the deck and beg for treats?

Janice noticed a bowl of assorted nuts on the redwood table. Taking one, she got up to lean over the railing, holding it high enough to get the squirrel's attention. Then she set it on the ledge and sat back to watch.

The squirrel came a little closer, his head turning this way and that as he checked things out. It didn't take him long to scurry onto the deck, then scamper up and pause on the railing. He looked at the treat longingly, then at the newcomer watching him before looking back to the nut still out of his reach. His little nose twitched comically. Janice laughed out loud.

"Fresh coffee ready in a minute," David said as he came out, taking the chair beside her and smiling at the squirrel. "I see you've met Sammy."

She jerked her head toward him as the blood suddenly drained from her face and her laughter died.

"What is it?" David asked.

She shook her head as the momentary dizziness passed. "Nothing, really."

The squirrel, realizing the people were occupied, grabbed the nut, turned around and raced out of sight. Neither of them noticed.

David leaned forward and took her hands in his, noticing how cold they were. "Tell me what's happened."

"I . . . I found Diane Flynn today."

He'd guessed as much. He'd have given a lot to spare her this, but he remembered how determined she'd sounded when they'd talked. Still, he hadn't thought she'd set out the very next day. "I'm sorry you had to go through that."

Slowly, she raised her head to look at him. "You knew all along, didn't you?"

She deserved the truth. "I knew about her quite some time ago, yes."

"And you didn't tell me."

He held her fingers in a loose grip, his thumb caressing the soft skin of her hand. "I thought about telling you last night. But I decided not to, hoping you'd drop the whole thing. Learning about Diane has only hurt you. I told you then how I feel. The man's dead. What can you do about it now?"

"About Kurt? You're right. Nothing. But what about his son?"

David frowned. "His son?"

"Yes, his and Diane's son. Sammy. Named after Kurt's father."

Good God! Small wonder she'd paled when she'd heard what he'd named the squirrel. "Janice, I didn't know about a son."

She studied his face and decided to believe him. Leaning back, she let out a whoosh of air. "He's two years old, with dark hair and eyes. Looks just like Kurt. And K.J." Choking back a sob, Janice swung anguished eyes to his. "Why, David? Why did Kurt need another woman in his life? Why weren't his other two children and I enough for him?"

He angled his chair closer so he could slide his arm around her, and pulled her to him. "I wish I could give you an acceptable answer."

She would not cry. *She would not.* "I wish you could, too." After a moment, she broke away. "When he told you about her, what did he say?"

She needed to talk it out, to know all of it. "It was a long time ago, three or four years, I'd guess. He called to say he was in town and asked me to meet him for lunch one day. He told me he'd met this great little gal. She was young—"

"Yes," Janice interrupted. "She was twenty-two at the time and Kurt was forty-two."

David nodded, sharing her anger. "And he said he was planning to help her out, to find her a better apartment because she'd been having a rough time of it. I thought that was odd, but he never mentioned sharing the place with her."

How charitable of him. "Did you ever meet her?"

"No. He only told me her name and a bit of her background."

"Then you didn't know about their little love nest in the Cambridge Apartments?"

He shook his head, thinking she was entitled to some bitterness. "I knew he'd set Diane up in an apartment, but I didn't ask where. For what it's worth, I didn't approve of what he was doing and I told him so."

"And what did he say?"

There was no kind way to say it, though he searched his mind for one. He hadn't been there for Eleanor. He had to be strong for Janice, a woman he knew he'd cared for, for a long while. "He basically said that this thing between them just happened, that he hadn't planned on getting involved. He told me that he cared for both of you and he'd see to it that neither one found out about the other so no one would get hurt."

"Well, that's one plan of good old Kurt's that didn't quite work out. We've *both* been hurt." Unable to sit still, Janice rose and walked to the far end of the deck. Blinking back the tears, she tried to focus on the forsythia about to bloom in the far corner of David's yard.

He came up behind her, sliding his arms along hers. "I'm so sorry you're hurting."

Janice struggled through a shudder. "I feel so betrayed, David. And I feel so stupid that I didn't notice anything. He was seeing her for four long years, all the while coming home to me and pretending I was the only woman in his life. Damn him!''

David couldn't have agreed more. He held her gently, rubbing his hands along her arms.

Janice turned in his arms to look into his eyes. "I know you suffered a terrible loss when Eleanor and the baby died. And you still have lingering guilt. But this anger I feel over Kurt's betrayal is a hundred times worse than the grief I felt at his death.''

They stood inches apart. ''I know.''

A trembling sigh escaped from her. ''It would seem you and I are a couple of the walking wounded.''

''My mother always says that it isn't what happens to you that matters. It's how you handle it. You and I are survivors, Janice. We'll make it.''

''Will we?'' She swayed toward him. ''Make love with me, David. Help me forget.''

Without another word, he scooped her into his arms and carried her upstairs.

CHAPTER NINE

IN DAVID'S BEDROOM, they stood facing each other. He could tell Janice was nervous, although the suggestion had been hers. He would try to ease her mind. David knew the act of love offered different things at different times, passion being only one. Comfort was also a part of loving. He hadn't understood that with Eleanor, so often hadn't been there for her. He'd learned from that mistake.

He touched her cheek. "Countless times, I've fantasized about making love with you here."

Her thoughts had taken that path, too, more than once, but she was unsure of whether to admit it or not. Did men realize that women thought about things like that? It was so long since she'd spoken of such things with a man that she didn't know how much to say, or how little. Perhaps her actions would speak louder than any words she could come up with. Janice reached for his kiss.

His mouth was soft and yet firm on hers and she could taste the pipe tobacco on his tongue. No shy response this, but the response of a man of passion whose hands molded her unresisting body to his. And

Janice let herself go with it. This was what she needed, to lose herself in David, to feel and not think.

She was here, in his arms, where he'd pictured her so often these past months. David shifted to kiss her face, her throat, then back to her mouth, waiting eagerly for his return. She swayed with him, her hands stroking his back, a soft sigh drifting from her parted lips as he eased back to look at her.

There was no need to rush, David reminded himself. It had been twenty-three years since that autumn interlude when he'd dated a shy young coed. He was even more attracted to the woman she'd become. "You smell like sunshine," he whispered into her hair, into the sweet folds of her ear as he kissed that spot, too.

Janice shuddered as his warm breath rushed into her ear. "Can't be," she answered, her voice thick. "I haven't been in the sun."

"I see only sunshine, smell only sunshine." His mouth captured hers again and he arranged her curves against the harder lines of his body, letting himself enjoy being close to her. As he released her, he felt her tremble and smiled down at her. "Let's think of this as a new beginning for us," he said as he helped her remove her suit jacket and set it on the chair.

Yes. She wanted badly to put the past aside and begin again. "Us. I like the sound of that."

"Maybe it should have been us from the start."

"Maybe." Maybe David wouldn't have hurt her the way Kurt had, wouldn't have betrayed his marriage vows.

David took her hands into his. "I never really forgot you, Sunshine. I just put you in a separate compartment of my mind because I thought you were happily married."

"I thought so, too." There was a catch in her voice.

David studied their entwined fingers. "I think Kurt always knew I had a thing for you."

His admission made her raise her eyes to his. "*Did* you have a thing for me?"

"Yes. I pulled back from you then because I knew I could easily fall in love with you and I wasn't ready for that kind of commitment. But I am now. I love you, Janice."

She felt her heart turn over. "Oh, David. I don't want you to say anything you don't honestly mean."

"I won't." His arms went around her, feeling her soft breasts yield against the wall of his chest.

Standing this close to him, Janice found her senses beginning to swim and her knees beginning to weaken. Her troubled thoughts faded and she could think only of this man and this moment. "I had no intention of getting involved again, much less so soon. But since you walked back into my life, I can't seem to stop thinking of you. I feel a little like an inexperienced teenager admitting this, but I'm utterly stunned at the way you make me feel."

His lips curled into a smile. "I'll bet you say that to all the guys."

"The truth is, I've never said that to anyone."

He took her mouth then, her warm and captivating mouth, which sent delicious thrills throughout his system. The more he tasted, the more he wanted. Drawing back, he was surprised as always that she could make him ache so quickly.

But he'd promised himself he'd go slowly. He knew that coming to him like this was a big step for Janice. He would give her the time to adjust to her decision.

He saw her fight a shiver and dropped his arms from her. "It gets cool here by nightfall. I'll light a fire." He walked to the corner fireplace he so seldom used and bent to open the screen.

Janice drew in a badly needed breath and glanced at David's bed. And what a bed it was. King-size, four-poster with a beautiful navy-and-gold geometrically patterned spread. She walked across the room to where the balcony doors were slightly ajar. The evening air, ripe with the scent of spring, mingled with the aroma of wood smoke as David lit a match to the fire.

Finishing, he dusted off his hands and strolled up behind Janice as she stood looking out onto the quiet scene. His hands crept around her, covering hers as she hugged herself.

From the vantage point of the second floor, she could see the woods spreading beyond his yard, and in the distance, the setting sun was streaking the darkening sky with ribbons of orange and gold. "Beautiful, isn't it?"

"You're beautiful," he said, placing his lips on the soft silk of her neck.

Janice shook her head. "No, and I regret that I'm not, for you. If not beautiful, when we first dated, at least I was young."

He burrowed his face into her hair. "You were beautiful then and you're beautiful now."

She was grateful he thought so, though she knew she wasn't. Then she felt his hands move to the row of buttons at her back. Her heart lurched as he slid the blouse from her shoulders.

Her breathing became erratic as he unclasped her bra, ran his hands around her rib cage, then cupped her breasts, one in each hand. Closing her eyes, Janice leaned back against him, unable to prevent a soft moan from escaping. She was certain he could hear her heart thudding as he stroked her slowly, lovingly.

Needing more, she turned around, her fingers fumbling to open his shirt while he unzipped her skirt. She let it drift to the carpet, followed by her slip. At last she pressed close to his chest, closing her eyes at the sensual feel of the soft hair cushioning her breasts. Rising on tiptoe, she was awash in a rush of feeling as her mouth sought his.

And suddenly, for Janice, it was a lazy afternoon again and they'd taken a sailboat out onto the lake. With the heat of an Indian-summer sun spilling down on them, they'd lain on the warm planks and held hands, indulging their youthful longings. They'd swayed with the movements of the water and rocked with the wonder of being free and alive and young. They weren't so very young now, but it didn't seem to matter, Janice realized as she drew back to look into David's dark eyes.

"I want you so much," he said. "So very much."

His words were like a balm, healing all the cold, lonely places inside of her. She would let him lead the way, and she would follow, knowing that David would never take her where she didn't want to go.

The firelight cast soft shadows on her golden skin as he gazed into her eyes, pewter gray with anticipation. He dipped his head to touch his lips to her shoulder.

The thought of being without the protection of most of her clothes while he was fully dressed unnerved her. Her hands shook as they pushed his shirt from his shoulders, then settled at his waist, hesitant, uncertain. Her heart had suddenly shifted to her throat as her eyes rose to his.

"Touch me, please," he said. "I've waited so long."

She saw that he was as tense as she, and the knowledge allowed her to relax fractionally. Slowly, with her eyes on his, she trailed her hand down and caressed him intimately for the first time. She heard him draw in a sharp breath, then she stroked him and he closed his eyes on a sigh.

It was going to be good, Janice thought, feeling him pulse beneath her fingers. Less frightened and more aroused, she trembled as he helped to ease the rest of her clothes off.

David walked her over to the bed and pulled back the spread before removing his clothes. Not in the least self-conscious, he stood before her, his eyes inspecting what his imagination had conjured up repeatedly. And he smiled approvingly.

His own lack of modesty calmed her, and Janice lay down on the bed, waiting. Waiting for her lover.

Joining her, David kissed all the secret places he'd been longing to explore during the past weeks. He'd dreamed, dreamed more than once of touching his mouth to her breasts, of skimming his fingers along her slender thighs, of being free to linger and examine. Now, he did so without hesitation.

He'd have been a shy lover back in college if they'd have gotten together, David knew, but the years had given him confidence in the bedroom. As his hands moved over her, followed by his mouth, he heard her soft sounds of pleasure, and he felt good. So very good.

Caught up in passion, Janice quickly lost the last of her inhibitions and let her seeking hands learn him, her restive mouth taste him. Impatience skittered along sensitive skin, his and hers; they'd waited too long to go too slowly.

Rising on an elbow, David asked, "About birth control?"

Janice closed her eyes, trying not to react, trying not to recall the man who'd seen to it that she couldn't conceive. She would not allow the memory to spoil this special moment. "It's all right. I had some surgery a while back."

He joined with her then, slowly, prolonging the enjoyment. After all these years, lovers at last. Eyes locked with hers, he didn't need to say the words aloud, for he was able to read the same message in hers. Perfectly in tune, they began to move together.

So beautiful to watch, he thought, the light flush on her lovely face, the concentration of her eyes on his, the marvelous way her body fit to his. Never had it been like this before. Never had he doubted that it could be this way with this one woman.

Love makes the difference, David decided.

So incredible to be here with him, she thought, watching beads of sweat appear on his forehead as he found the rhythm. Never had she dreamed she'd find this kind of passion. Never had she dared hope she'd find this strong love.

Love made the difference, Janice acknowledged, but she couldn't say the words.

Knowing she was almost there, he smiled into eyes half-closed. "I love you, Sunshine," he whispered.

But she scarcely heard, for just then she was breaking free, closing her eyes on a pleasure so intense that tears rolled down her cheeks unnoticed. For a long moment, David watched her. Then, with a final thrust, he joined her in a blissful shattering.

"YOU MUST THINK me terribly backward, but this is my first time in a hot tub," Janice said as she stretched her arms along the tiled edge.

"I've become an addict. It's a rare evening that I don't get in, even if just for a few minutes." Seated next to her, he watched the bubbles swarm around her breasts and the steam rise to float up toward the ceiling. She was finally relaxing.

In his big, four-poster bed he'd made love to her slowly, tenderly, a second time. She'd been hurt and needed to heal, to recover from the shock. He'd tried to let her know how much he valued her, how much he loved her. With soft kisses and sweet words, he'd worshiped her. He'd taken his time, lingering over each special place he'd longed to caress, each tiny spot he'd searched out to stroke, each pulse point he'd nuzzled with patient lips.

And she'd come to life again, opening like a flower, the pain leaving her huge gray eyes, replaced by a hunger reflected in his own. She'd reached for him finally, and this time their coming together had been a bonding of spirit as well as body, a renewal of self-worth. Afterward, they'd been reluctant to move apart, lying a while still joined, their eyes communicating what their lips had yet to say.

Now, as David watched her lean back and stretch out her slender legs, he hoped the swirling water would complete the task of chasing away the kinks from her body and the hurt from her eyes.

"How ingenious of you to have a skylight put in," Janice commented as she stared upward at the night sky.

David hit the button to slow the bubbles. "You can sit here and count the stars." He reached over and laced his fingers with hers. "I've dreamed of having you here so often."

She raised her head and smiled at him lazily. She would keep thoughts of reality at bay a bit longer. "My dreams are built around you, too, these days."

"Are they wild and sexy dreams?"

"I'm not sure I remember how to dream wild dreams."

"Let me refresh your memory." Angling around, David shifted to face her and straddled her knees, bracing his arms on the tub's edge, his body supported by the ebullient water. Brushing against her suggestively, he smiled into her eyes. "Feel anything?"

"Mmm, you seem to have revived my interest in sensual fantasies." She brought her hands to rest on the smooth skin of his shoulders. "I thought I was through with all that."

"You're far too young to be through with any of that." He nuzzled her damp neck. "I intend to remind you regularly and often that you're a woman, a very beautiful woman, a very desirable woman." He touched his mouth to hers, the kiss filled with promise.

Janice knew he was saying all the right things to make up for the pain he knew she'd suffered. She wanted to believe him, yet she was wary. Where once she'd believed a man without hesitation, now she would question everything. Kurt's legacy, she thought with a rush of bitterness.

She touched David's cheek. It wasn't fair to this good man that she had that lingering load to carry.

Maybe in time, she would get over her husband's betrayal. Meanwhile, there was David. "You're so good to me," she whispered.

"Marry me, Janice," David said softly. "I want us to be together."

She just stared at him, the moments stretching into a full minute. Her eyes filled involuntarily, until finally she pulled him closer so his cheek rested against hers. "Ah, David. I can't make that kind of decision right now."

"I realize you've had a terrible shock. You're hurt and confused. You need time to get over this blow." He craned his neck back so he could see her face. "You do care for me, don't you?"

Janice blinked, annoyed that the tears were falling after all. She hated having her emotions so out of control. "You know I do. It's just that I guess I need some time to sort things out. I don't want to come to you dragging around all this excess baggage. Resentment and anger and distrust." She brushed her damp hair from her face. "I hate what Kurt's done to me, hate the woman I'm turning into. Maybe you'd better reconsider."

"I love the woman you are. I knew that, if you learned about Diane, it would take you a while to get over the knowledge. It's only natural." He sat down beside her, sliding an arm across her shoulders. "And that was before I knew about the boy."

Ah, yes. The boy. But she didn't want to think about the boy. Or his mother. She wanted to forget them for a little while longer. At least for the rest of tonight.

He was holding her loosely, so she had no trouble slipping out of his arms. Catching him by surprise, she pulled him forward and ducked him under the water. While he found a foothole and came up, shaking water from his hair, she scooted to the other side, trying to smother a giggle. This was more like it. Who could think dark thoughts during horseplay?

As she'd known he would, he came after her, this time pulling her under with him. She surfaced near the edge of the tub, grinning and watching for him to reappear. Laughter mixed with lovemaking. Janice had never known it could be quite like this. David came up with a splash, his laugh ringing out in the steamy room as he groped around and found her.

He wiped at his face, blinking till he could see better, then yanked her to him. Very close. The laughter faded, the answering smile slipped away. Slick hands slid slowly over water-softened skin as they stared into each other's eyes, recognizing their mutual need. When his mouth touched hers, Janice felt the heat inside her expand and grow.

The kiss went from tender to passionate quickly, as they discovered they hadn't had nearly enough of each other. David shut off the jets, then stepped out and helped Janice up. He grabbed a big towel and wrapped her in it before picking her up and carrying her to the bed they'd risen from just an hour ago.

"I'm still wet," she murmured against his shoulder as he laid her down as gently as he would a child.

"I'll dry you." And he did, somewhat haphazardly, before he was distracted by the sweet curve of her breast, which cried out for a kiss. Then he was lost in her softness, in her intoxicating scent, in the taste of her satiny skin.

Delighted to see she was as eager as he, as aroused as he, David stretched her arms above her head, touching his palms to hers as he joined with her, all the while watching her face. She arched to meet his first thrust and closed her eyes.

But he needed something, wanted something only she could give him. "Janice, look at me," he said, his face inches above her own.

She did, searching his blue eyes, wondering why he'd stopped.

"Do you know who's making love with you?" His voice was strained, his expression tense.

Then she understood. He, too, had his insecurities and needed reassurance. "Yes," she said firmly. "David. David is making love with me. And it feels wonderful."

His face relaxed then and he began to move, slowly at first, then more quickly, more surely, more deeply. Their eyes stayed open and focused on each other, sharing the journey. David felt her heart beating against his, felt his breath mingling with hers. Pacing himself, he watched her climb. Finally, as her eyes drifted closed, his did also and they shared the explosion.

HOW WAS IT POSSIBLE that in one weekend, her life had changed radically again? Janice thought as her convertible hummed along the tollway heading back to Wisconsin. It was early Sunday evening and she was exhausted. She'd learned of a betrayal and taken a lover. Not your usual weekend.

Physically, her body felt wonderfully satisfied. Emotionally, she was a wreck.

She and David had spent nearly the whole time since her arrival late Friday afternoon—forty-eight hours—secluded in his wonderful house. Many of the hours, waking and sleeping, had been spent in bed, something she hadn't done since her honeymoon, brief as that had been.

They'd talked, sharing stories of their childhood, her children, his travels. And David had spoken of his marriage and the death of so many of his dreams when his family had been killed. Covered only by a sheet, wrapped in each other's arms, they'd talked from the heart, learning each other.

Janice had made a concerted effort to not think beyond those four walls for those two days, knowing there'd be many hours for that later. And she'd been enormously pleased that she not only cared deeply for David, but that she liked him as well. Liked his softspoken ways, his compassion, his sense of humor. Liked the way he made her feel.

And, inevitably, they'd turned to each other again and again, needing to explore this new passion that smoldered beneath the surface and colored everything they did. David was a wonderful lover, inventive and patient, taking her to heights she'd not thought possible.

And he was agreeable, almost to the point of irritation. What an odd thought, Janice decided as she eased up on the gas pedal. It was just that, in all her life, she'd never known a man who seemed so attuned to her every need. Whatever she wanted to eat, he fixed. What she felt like doing, they did. So much so that she began to suspect the motives behind so much amiability.

He'd brought up the subject of marriage again, though he'd said he wouldn't push. Janice had to admit that the thought had crept into her consciousness during the past months, and she'd wondered what marriage to David would be like. Physically satisfying, of that she was now certain.

Yet surely he couldn't be congenial day in and day out, could he? It was as if he veered away from the slightest hint of dissension. When she'd pointed that out to him, he'd merely answered that he wanted to make her happy. Something to think about.

Just before she left, he'd grilled steaks for them and served her a wonderful early dinner. She'd had trouble leaving, not just because she wanted to stay with him, but because she knew that, left alone again, she'd have to face the realities of Kurt's betrayal.

Easing into the passing lane, Janice swung around a large touring bus, finding that her hands were clutching the wheel tightly at the very thought of the man who'd once been the center of her world. She obviously had not been the center of his for some time now, if ever.

It hurt. Lord, but it hurt. Flexing her fingers, she tried to make herself relax. But her mind dredged up the picture of that dark-eyed two-year-old sitting on his mother's lap. How could Diane have believed such a contrived explanation of why Kurt couldn't marry her—that he had a sick mother?

Janice let out a ragged sigh. No, that wasn't it. Diane hadn't questioned him because she'd badly needed to believe. As Janice herself had done. Never in all those years had she asked Kurt a single question about his comings and goings, never had she suspected him of a single wrong move. *Fool!* she chastised herself.

Diane was worse off than she was, living in that shabby place with a low-income job, a limited future and a child to raise. Well, she deserved her fate for being so trusting, for stealing another woman's husband.

But that didn't ring true, either, Janice thought as she pressed a fist into her stomach, hoping to ease the heaviness there. Try as she would, she couldn't hate that pitiful young woman. She hadn't stolen Kurt. He'd gone willingly. He'd found them an apartment and gone furniture shopping with her. He'd been the experienced one and he'd gotten a woman half his age pregnant. No, she couldn't hate Diane. But she could hate Kurt.

And she did.

With an eye on her rearview mirror, Janice stepped down on the gas pedal, anxious to get home. But when she pulled into her own drive an hour later and hurried inside, she found herself feeling like a stranger in her own home.

The house was dark, though it was only eight. The rooms she'd decorated with such a loving touch mocked her silently. Everywhere she looked, memories, now tarnished, waited to jump out at her, wrenching her in their silken grip. Kurt had sat on that couch with her, eaten at the dining room table with her, slept in that bed upstairs with her.

And all the while, his mind had been on another woman.

"Oh, God," she moaned, sinking into a chair. *Why, Kurt? Damn you, why?*

CHAPTER TEN

JANICE GRABBED hold of the seams with both hands and pulled the mattress slowly but surely out of her bedroom and into the upstairs hallway. Huffing a bit from the effort, she hauled the heavy thing free of the doorway and propped it against the wall, then stopped for a moment to catch her breath.

Everything was out now and she was ready to redecorate.

It was Monday morning, a week after her visit to Chicago. She'd gone into the office every day last week, clearing up the work she'd begun. She'd finally reached a decision as she'd lain night after night in the guest room, unable to sleep. She needed some time off, which she really hadn't had since . . . well, since January.

So she'd explained to Tom Sikes that she trusted him to take over for her for a while. He was very capable, she'd told him, and knew that to be the truth. He could handle things and, though she'd be available for calls and would stop in occasionally, she needed a week. Perhaps two.

Strolling into the bedroom she'd shared for years, Janice stood in the center, looking around. She would paint first, three of the walls, and she'd paper the fourth. Next would come new carpeting and then she'd go shopping for bedroom furniture. Something in a lighter wood. She'd never been crazy about the mahogany set Kurt had chosen.

All weekend she'd worked hard, bundling up his clothes—every last shirt, tie and jacket—and emptying his closet and dresser as well. Tom had told her of a needy family on the outskirts of town and she'd called them. The man had said he and his son would drive over tomorrow with their truck. When she'd said he could also have the bedroom furniture, he'd been elated.

Janice walked over to the window and looked out. It was raining again, a light April shower, and it was gloomy, perfectly suiting her mood. Perhaps she'd feel better once she redid the house. First she would do this room—this room she could no longer sleep in since learning of Kurt's infidelity.

All of it had to go, she thought, turning and shoving her hands into her jeans pockets. The furniture, the knickknacks they'd collected through the years, the color scheme—everything. Maybe then she could stand to sleep in here again. Maybe then, when she closed her eyes, she wouldn't see that small boy's face, so hauntingly familiar.

She'd tried, but she couldn't seem to put him or his mother out of her mind. Working at Eber Insurance was no longer pleasant, either. As she sat at Kurt's desk, in Kurt's chair, she heard his name mentioned repeatedly. By week's end she'd wanted to scream at the sales producers and at his good friend, Tom, that the Kurt they'd known had been a phony and a liar.

But she hadn't. Instead, she'd decided to sink her teeth into a project that would occupy her mind and exhaust her energy. Maybe then she could stop thinking so much and be able to sleep again. And she loved decorating.

Turning to gaze at the window, she narrowed her eyes thoughtfully. On her trips to Madison for her insurance classes during the winter, she'd noticed that a new fabric store had opened near the university. Perhaps she'd drive up, pick out some material for sheers and draperies and order a bedspread made from the same fabric. Something in mauves and blues, maybe. Yes, with a touch of ivory.

So lost in thought was she that when the doorbell rang, she jumped. Who would come visiting on such a dreary day and without calling first? Frowning, she hurried to answer the door.

"You're a difficult woman to catch at home," Anna said, folding her umbrella. "Have you got time for a cup of coffee?"

"Sure." Janice beckoned her inside and took her raincoat, leading the way into the kitchen. "Aren't you working today?"

"George had an emergency at the hospital so I have the morning off." Anna sat down at Janice's wrought-iron table. "How are you? I haven't seen you in ages."

Janice busied herself pouring them each a cup of coffee from the pot she'd brewed earlier. "Fine, but busy. I've decided to do a little redecorating."

Anna studied her friend as she brought over the coffee, then sat down opposite her. Janice was looking thinner again, with dark smudges under her eyes. Much as she'd looked right after Kurt's death. Anna had thought that with her studies and work at the office, Janice would have been feeling better about herself now. Unless something new had happened. Perhaps she could draw her out, get her to talk. "You're so good at that sort of thing. But this house is already lovely. What rooms did you have in mind to redo?" Anna sipped her coffee.

"My bedroom, for one. Then perhaps the living room."

Anna glanced at the four boxes taped shut and stacked by the back door. Kurt's things, undoubtedly. It was about time Janice gave them away, so she wouldn't constantly be thinking of her dead husband. "I think that's a good idea," she commented, nodding toward the boxes. "Those reminders only hamper your recovery."

Janice swallowed hard and blinked back a rush of tears, annoyed at these recurring emotional moments.

Misinterpreting, Anna touched her friend's arm. "I know you still miss Kurt."

Perhaps confiding in Anna would help her see things more clearly, Janice thought as she shook her head.

"No, Anna. I don't miss him and I've come very close to hating him."

Anna Kelsey didn't shock easily, but hearing the sudden new bitterness in Janice's voice, her eyes grew wide. "What do you mean?"

And so she explained. There, in the kitchen where she'd cooked and served many a meal to the man who'd hurt her like no other, she poured out her heart to Anna, telling her about finding the checkbook and receipts in Kurt's desk, of how she'd hunted for Diane Flynn, learned the truth about her and then met young Sammy.

"A son? I can't believe it."

"You would if you saw him. The boy looks just like Kurt."

"Oh, Janice." Anna squeezed her hand. "I don't know what to say."

"And I don't know what to think. I've asked myself over and over, why did he need her? Why wasn't I enough for Kurt?"

Her face was so pale, her eyes so bleak. Anna searched for an explanation. "There are some men, as we all know, who are never satisfied with only one woman."

But Janice shook her head. "If that were the case, he'd have had a whole string of women through the years. Which I almost wish he had, because then I could categorize him as one of those womanizing men. But it seems he had only Diane. This twenty-two-year-old, uneducated, quiet woman who obviously thought he was wonderful. Maybe it was because she was younger." She found a tissue in her jeans pocket and wiped at her eyes.

Anna got up to pour them more coffee. "I don't think so, Janice."

Janice sent her a puzzled frown. "Then why?"

"I'm not an expert on men, but my guess would be because of who Diane Flynn is, not merely her youthfulness. As you said, she's a waitress with a limited income and future. To her, Kurt must have seemed like Prince Charming rescuing her on a white horse. With her, he could be a hero. He didn't have to prove anything to her nor slay any dragons for her. He just was there, and probably that was enough for her."

"And you're saying that he had to prove himself to me?"

"Not in fact, but in his mind. He was always competing with the Ingalls family, the Ingalls wealth. With that woman, *he* was king of the hill, the one to be looked up to. Did you ever look at him adoringly like that grateful young thing probably did?"

Janice thought about that a moment. Anna had a way of getting to the heart of things, which was likely why Janice had always gravitated to her. "No, I don't suppose I ever made him feel special. Do you do that for Johnny?"

Anna dismissed the question with a wave of her hand. "We're talking two different men here. Johnny never felt he had to prove something to me or my family. We were on a par. But Kurt never felt totally welcome with the Ingallses, though none of that was your doing."

She knew Anna was right. "I don't suppose then that there's anything I could have done to prevent him from finding her."

"Oh, my dear, there's very little any woman can do if a man is determined to find another woman. Have you told Stefie and K.J. about the boy?"

"Not yet, but I intend to." She reached for her coffee, then shoved it away, realizing she didn't want more. She rubbed her forehead, wondering if this headache was from humidity or tension.

"You say the mother's gone back to waitressing and that the place they live in is pretty substandard?"

"Yes." Abruptly, Janice stood, carrying her coffee to the sink and dumping it out. "But that's not my problem, is it?"

Anna regarded her thoughtfully. "No, I don't suppose it is."

"You have no idea what discovering this has done to me," Janice went on. Noticing that her hands were trembling, she clutched them together. "This is far worse than when Kurt died. Every time I think of him, I want to smash something. And everything here reminds me of him. I haven't slept in...in the room we shared since I found out. That's why I have to do this place over. Or move."

Anna went to her, slipping an arm about her slender shoulders, feeling the shudders that went through her. "I can only imagine. Go ahead and cry."

But Janice shook her head. "I don't want to cry anymore. I'm so *tired* of crying." She sucked in a great gulp of air. "All right, I can accept the reason Kurt went to her. Intellectually. But emotionally, I can't. If what you say is true—that he needed someone who could make him feel special in a way I never could, especially since I didn't know that's what he needed— then why was he such a damn coward? Why didn't he just tell me he'd found someone else and ask for a divorce?"

Why, indeed? Anna looked into her friend's troubled eyes and wished she had a better answer. "It's only a guess, but I'd say because he didn't want to lose you and his children. He wanted to have his cake and eat it, too."

"Well, *damn* him for that." Janice walked to the window and stood looking out at the rain, heavier now, drenching the yard.

Empathizing, Anna followed her. "Janice, there are no easy explanations in matters like this."

"Don't I know it."

"You have a right to be angry and bitter."

Suddenly, Janice's shoulders sagged. "But I don't want to be angry and bitter, Anna. I want to go on with my life. I want to feel good again, to laugh and enjoy things. I hate this—all of it."

Anna moved to hug her. "I know, honey. I wish I could help." She glanced at her watch and saw she had to run.

Blinking back her tears, Janice turned. "You have, just by listening. By caring. Thank you." She walked her friend to the front door and waited for her to put on her coat.

"Call me if you need anything." Anna stepped out on the porch and raised her umbrella.

"I will." Janice stood at the screen door a long while after Anna's car had driven off, staring into the gray sky, watching the puddles form on the porch. She should get going, she thought. Do something. Go to the paint store, at least.

The ringing of the phone finally drew her away and she walked back to the kitchen to answer. "K.J.," she said as soon as she heard her son's voice. "How nice to hear from you." Here was someone who usually could cheer her.

They talked a minute or two, updating each other on small things, while Janice's mind raced ahead. Should she tell him about what she'd learned over the phone, or wait until he came home for summer vacation? A difficult decision. She hated to put it off, yet...

"I've got some great news, Mom." K.J. sounded elated. "At least, I hope you'll think is great. I sold a political satire cartoon to that Chicago paper I'd told you about."

"Wonderful! Which one? Have I seen it?" He'd been mailing her some of his drawings since their discussion about his career.

All but tripping over his words in his excitement, he told her which drawing, about the letter he'd received and the editor who'd written it. "But the best news of all is that I went for this interview with their editorial staff last Friday and they just called back. They want me to work for them."

"You mean to buy occasional drawings?"

"No. For that cartoon-character strip I told you about. I didn't have any samples with me when I was home, but I'll mail you a couple. It's on the order of *Doonesbury*. The editor who called to offer me the job seemed very impressed."

"That's terrific, K.J.! I hope it works into something big."

"Me, too, Mom." He hesitated a moment, then plunged in. "There is one thing. I might have to work out of the Chicago office. I mean, you can always mail your drawings in, but they prefer you to live there, especially when your stuff revolves around local politics. Hard to get the feel of the city unless you're right there, you know?"

"Sure, sure. You mean after graduation?"

"I mean for the summer, to start. Then, if it works out and the response is good and they give me a permanent spot, they'd like me to move there." K.J.'s voice became softer. "I know it's a hell of a thing to tell you when Stefie's getting married and all, now that you're alone."

Janice swallowed around a lump, realizing her baby was growing up. *Had* grown up, she corrected. "No, it's not. I want what's best for you. When would you have to be there?"

"Uh, the week after school's out."

That soon. Which meant she had to discuss the situation about his father now. "K.J., I need to tell you something as well and it's not nearly as pleasant as your news. I hate doing this over the phone, but I don't know when we'll be able to talk in person. I can drive up if you'd rather."

"Mom, what is it? Tell me." He sounded suddenly worried.

So she did, all of it, as gently as she could, as honestly as possible. She stuck to the facts, trying desperately to keep her emotions out of the telling. Through it all, Kurt's son listened silently. Janice felt her heart pound in her chest as she finished and waited for his response.

Finally, he spoke. "How do you feel about this, Mom?"

She let out a whoosh of air. "Not good, but I'll survive." We're survivors, David had said. Good grief, she should probably also tell K.J. about David. Oh, the poor kid.

"I...I guess I'll have to get used to the thought," K.J. said. "This baby—you say he's two—what's going to happen to him?"

She tried to harden her heart, but found she couldn't. "I don't honestly know."

He was silent a long moment. "It's not his fault, is it, Mom?"

She closed her eyes and leaned against the kitchen wall. "No, it isn't."

"Is there any way we can help him? I mean, he's re-lated, in a way, right?"

Oh, Lord! She supposed they were half brothers, something that hadn't occurred to her before. "Let me think about that. I—I've been having a little trouble dealing with . . . with all this."

"Mom," K.J. said, his voice strong, "I don't know why Dad did this and I'm terribly disappointed in him. But I do know he loved you and Stefie and me. No one can convince me otherwise."

Janice pressed her fingers to her lips to keep from crying. "I hope so, K.J."

"I wish this hadn't happened, though, for a lot of reasons. It wasn't your fault, Mom. I know that's what you're thinking." When she didn't reply, he went on. "I hate the fact that it's destroying the good memories we've always had. I talked with David last night and he said . . ."

She became alert. "David? You mean David Markus?"

"Yeah. I met him at our house in January. A neat guy, you know. I called to tell him I might be moving to Chicago and—"

"What did he say?"

"That he'd be glad to show me around. He even of-fered to let me stay at his place for the summer or until I found an apartment of my own. Wasn't that nice of him?"

Janice walked over to sit down at the table. So much happening so quickly. "Yes, it was. K.J., what do you think of David? As a man, I mean?"

There was a definitely pregnant pause before her son answered. "I like him. Why?"

Janice cleared her throat. "I've been seeing him." She let it go at that.

Again, he waited before responding. "You could do worse, Mom."

She smiled then, the first real smile of the day. Then she sobered. "You don't sound surprised."

"Why would I be? You're a pretty together lady. I knew some guy would move in on you in no time. And David's okay in my book." He paused a moment. "Mom, don't dwell on what Dad did. It's over and done with. I think it's rotten, but life goes on. And you're too young to sit around crying."

Janice felt the tears roll down her cheeks, only this time, they weren't hurtful. "Thank you, K.J. I needed that."

They hung up moments later, and Janice felt better than she had in many days. Quickly, before she could change her mind, she dialed David's office number. His secretary put her through directly. The moment she heard his voice, she felt a healing warmth. "Hey, fella, wanna play hooky tomorrow and help me do some painting around here?" she asked.

SHE HAD A PAINT SMEAR on the end of her nose, a dab on her forehead and quite a bit more speckled on her

T-shirt and jeans. David thought he'd never seen a more beautiful woman. Holding his brush aside, he grinned and grabbed her into a bear hug, swinging her around the bedroom floor.

Janice was not a squealer, but she squealed when she realized the brush still in her hand was splattering generous globs of paint on more than just the tarpaulin she'd spread around the edges of the room. "You're making a mess. Put me down."

He nuzzled her neck. "You're replacing the carpeting, so what difference does it make?" Deliberately, he swung her one more time before setting her back on her feet.

"Now I'm stepping in it. Honestly, David." She raised a sticky tennis shoe gingerly to show him.

He'd gladly abandoned his workday, driven up early and changed into old jeans and a shirt to help her. He hadn't played hooky when he'd been married to Eleanor, though she'd asked often. He'd been too intent on becoming successful, David thought, which had caused him to neglect his wife. Perhaps here was his second chance.

Janice was being entirely too serious, and David wanted to hear her laugh again. So he bent to yank off her shoe and toss it aside. Next, he took the brush from her and stuck it in the bucket, then fell to the rug, pulling her down with him. Nose to nose with her, he smiled into her surprised eyes. "It's break time," he said, rubbing against her sensuously.

"You want a coffee break?" Janice teased, well aware that wasn't at all what he had in mind. She'd phoned him on an impulse yesterday and then wondered this morning when he'd arrived if she'd done the right thing. Now, as she stared down into his laughing blue eyes, she knew she had.

"Not coffee."

"Oh, perhaps tea?"

His hands slid beneath her shirt. "Not even close." Rolling over, he pinned her beneath him and touched his mouth to hers. The kiss started innocently enough, then quickly heated as it usually did when it was Janice in his arms. It had been more than a week and he was hungry for her. Shifting, he unfastened her bra.

"No." Janice spoke against his lips, then pulled back.

David lifted his head, a question in his eyes. "No?"

"Not in here, David. Please, not in here." She was being silly, she knew, but she couldn't explain how she felt.

He understood. She'd shared this room with Kurt. Rising, he drew her up and pulled her out into the empty hallway. "Did you ever make love here?"

Despite her unease, Janice smiled. "Are you kidding? With all these bedrooms, why would we—"

"Because." He yanked her to him, so close that he recognized the scent of wildflowers clinging to her hair, mingled with the smell of paint. "Because it's fun, it's different and you've never done it before." Dropping to the floor, he coaxed her down, shoving off her shirt as he did. "Are you game?"

She was.

BY LATE AFTERNOON, the bedroom was painted and the cleanup chores finished. After eating two bowls of her wonderful chili, David sat at Janice's kitchen table browsing through a wallpaper book.

"There're too many here," David said, his forehead wrinkling in confusion. "How did you decide?"

Janice pulled her chair closer to his. "Slowly and carefully, like this." She held up the two swatches of material she'd picked out yesterday afternoon. "These are the colors I'd decided to use. The wallpaper needed to be simple, so it wouldn't overwhelm the effect of the drapery and bedspread fabric. I wanted something soft and restful, so I chose this!" She turned to the wallpaper she'd ordered, one that blended perfectly with fabric *and* paint.

He remembered she'd studied design years ago in college. "Did you ever take more decorating classes after you moved to Tyler?"

"No. I always meant to, but never got around to it. I just go by instinct, I guess." She turned several pages of the book, then stopped to study a particular sample. "When you decorate a room, you need to decide on a certain look, or a theme. For instance, a man might want a very masculine study with a big oak desk and a leather couch. Which is fine if he's the only one using the room." Like Kurt had been, she thought. Perhaps the study was the next room she'd redo.

"But a woman would want to change that to a more feminine room, you mean?"

"Not necessarily feminine, but a softer look. Perhaps a patterned rug. Maybe an antique desk and tie-back draperies instead of shutters on the windows."

"I see." David had seen Kurt's den and knew what she meant. He was glad she was redoing her home, removing all traces of her dead husband. Kurt didn't deserve to be idealized. He leaned back thoughtfully as she continued to thumb through the books. "What did you think of my decor?"

"Did you do it yourself?"

"With the guidance of a department-store decorator about ten years ago."

Since the choices hadn't been entirely his, she would be truthful. "I'd make a few changes. In your bedroom, for instance. You've got solid balcony doors, so the only way you can enjoy the view is if you open them. Which, in inclement weather, you can't. Privacy isn't a problem, since there's only woods behind you. I'd get glass doors, perhaps with vertical blinds so you could control the amount of light coming in, yet still see out. Just a suggestion, of course. You might hate the idea."

David smiled. "I don't. Sounds good. Maybe when you're finished here, you can help me make some changes."

"Maybe."

"Or maybe what you should do is go back to school and get your degree, then go into some sort of design work. You've got a knack for it and you seem to enjoy this sort of thing."

Janice sighed and closed the book. "We can't always do what we want to do. I've got obligations to the people at Eber Insurance. K.J.'s definitely not interested in taking over. By the way, thanks for offering to help him this summer."

"I was tickled he called me. Nice kid. And he'd got a great opportunity there."

"I should show you some of his drawings. He's really good."

He heard the pride in her voice and was pleased. At least her relationship with her children seemed good. He disliked bringing up problematic subjects, but he'd been wondering about something. "Have you told your children about your trip to Chicago?"

Janice ran a hand through her hair, pleased to see it was steady. Maybe she could even discuss the situation without breaking down this time. "I told K.J. and he took it well. Matter of fact, he said something that I hadn't thought of. That baby is his half brother."

"Does that bother you?"

"I can't seem to stop thinking of that child. They live in such squalor, David. A terrible neighborhood, graffiti on the walls, chains on the doors. What will that boy turn out like, being raised there?"

David shrugged, watching her carefully. "His chances aren't good."

"I know it's not my problem, but growing up like that, Sammy could easily get into trouble, mixed up with kids who break the law, do drugs, any number of things. K.J. said, you know that it's not the boy's fault. And he's right." She shook her head. "For a week, I've tried to hate them, tried to ignore them, to forget them. And I just can't. But I don't know what to do."

David leaned closer and reached for her hand. "I have a suggestion. How about if we see to it Diane Flynn gets a better job so she can move out of there?"

"But how? She quit school at sixteen."

"I have a lot of friends in the government, remember? There are grants for women at the poverty level who want to improve themselves. These grants pay rent, groceries, utilities, school tuition and even baby-sitters. They're low-interest loans that the recipient has five years to pay back, starting *after* she gets a good job. Did Diane strike you as the kind of woman who was ambitious enough to work hard to get out of that lousy place?"

Janice studied the hand gently stroking hers. "Difficult to tell on such a short visit. But she obviously loves that boy and is very protective of him. I think, for his sake, she'd do all right." She raised her eyes to his. "Do you honestly think you could get her a grant?"

"I can call tomorrow and check, get the paperwork started. I'd guess she qualifies. Then the rest is up to her."

"I'd appreciate that. Also, would you mind contacting her? I . . . I really want to stay out of this. It's a lot to ask, but . . ."

He squeezed her fingers. "It's *not* a lot to ask, and besides, it was my idea. I'll take care of it. Will that make you happy?"

"I don't know about happy, but it relieves my mind."

He stood, drawing her up with him as he checked his watch. "I hate to leave, but I've got a couple of appointments tomorrow that I couldn't put off."

"I understand." She walked to the door with him, glancing out the screen at the early-evening drizzle. "I wish this rain would stop for a while." She shifted, moving into his arms. "Thanks for coming, for helping."

"I was glad to. I want you to be happy, in every way. Do you believe that, Janice?"

She rested her hands on his strong shoulders. He'd come so readily when she'd called and been so agreeable all day. So much so that his affability annoyed her at times. Why was that? she wondered. Perhaps she simply wasn't used to such compliance. David did want her to be happy, she knew. "Yes, I believe that. And I am happy when I'm with you."

His arms tightened around her. "You could be with me a whole lot more."

She nodded. "I know, but I need more time. My life is still so topsy-turvy."

"Are you going in to the office tomorrow or shall I call you at home?"

"I'll be here, but Friday I have to go in. It seems I forgot that Tom and I are meeting with the C.P.A."

"You don't sound too enthused."

"I'm not. I'd rather stay here and work on the house." She gave him a small smile, not wanting to let him go on a glum note. "Got to earn the bacon, right?"

She wouldn't have to, if she'd only marry him, David thought. But he knew better than to press. "I'll call you tomorrow." His hands at her back drew her closer as he bent his head to kiss her.

Late afternoon and growing dark, the weather gloomy with rain. Suddenly, she hated the thought that he was leaving and she'd be alone. Pressing herself to him, Janice returned his kiss, her hands moving into his hair, her tongue dueling with his. Torn between her need for independence and her need for this man, she struggled with conflicting emotions as her heartbeat picked up in rhythm.

She could feel him hardening against her as his hands slid lower on her back, urging her closer. Always it was like this with David—the quick beat, the overpowering need. With no one but him had she ever felt such a shocking response. With no other man had she dropped to the floor and made wildly exciting love as she'd done earlier. With no one but David did she gladly relinquish control and let him take her where he would.

Slanting his mouth over hers, David took her deeper, wondering if he should change his plans, carry her upstairs and leave early in the morning. She was so warm, so pliant, and he was ready again. He...

"Ahem. Don't let me interrupt."

Startled, they drew apart, almost guiltily. Janice turned to look toward the voice that had come through the screen. Her mouth dropped open in shock when she saw Stefanie standing on the porch.

"Hi, Mom. I wanted to surprise you." She swung her eyes to David. "It seems I have."

CHAPTER ELEVEN

"I JUST CAN'T MAKE chili the way you can, Mom," Stefanie said as she bent to put her dirty dishes into the dishwasher. "Mine never tastes as good as yours, even though I follow your recipe."

Janice poured them each a glass of iced tea and smiled. "Must be a gift, this culinary talent." She carried their drinks into the living room, setting them down on the coffee table, then curled up in the far corner of the couch.

Following, Stefanie sat down in the opposite corner and drew up her slim legs as she turned to face her mother. "And speaking of gifts, you seem to have another. A gift for attracting handsome men." She watched the color move up into her mother's face and grinned. "That was some kiss I witnessed, Mom."

"Yes, well..." Feeling a little nonplussed, Janice smoothed back her hair. She'd been waiting for Stefie to mention the kiss she'd interrupted, hoping she wouldn't, but knowing she would. This was one predicament Janice had never thought she'd find herself in. She was delighted to have discovered her daughter on her doorstep, but she fervently wished Stefie's timing had been a bit different.

Stefanie was enjoying Janice's discomfort only because she'd thought for a long while that her mother took life too seriously and ought to loosen up. It would seem she had, in spades. She'd certainly never seen her dad kiss her mother like that. "I take it you and David have been seeing quite a bit of each other."

"Yes, we have." A mother-daughter role reversal, Janice thought, deciding to smile at the situation. David had stayed a couple of minutes longer, then had kissed her goodbye again, right in front of Stefie, though not quite so passionately. It would be foolish to deny their relationship. "I asked him for financial advice a while back. Remember I told you the last time you visited that he'd gone through the office files?"

"Mmm-hmm. And he went with you to the winter carnival. But I guess it just didn't occur to me to ask if you were still seeing him."

Janice had suspected that her daughter might be critical of her seeing another man. Stefie had been closer to her father than K.J. "You don't approve?"

Stefanie shrugged. "I don't know him really. Why, are you really serious?" She was frowning now.

Janice propped an elbow on the couch back as she leaned toward her daughter, wishing she didn't have to go through this again. Some things you couldn't prepare someone to hear. "Yes, we're serious. David's a good man, very caring and awfully kind. He's fun and he makes me laugh." She noticed that Stefie was twisting a lock of her hair thoughtfully, a habit she'd had for years when she was mulling something over. Patiently, she waited.

"It just seems a little soon, you know. Dad's only been gone a few months."

"Four and a half, I know." Janice reached to take a sip of her iced tea. Now or never, she thought. "Stefie, I need to tell you something, and it's not pleasant."

For some reason, perhaps because she hated to alter her daughter's love for her father, this telling was far more difficult than when she'd told K.J. or even Anna. By the time she finished, Stefanie's shocked expression had turned to tears. Janice moved closer and slipped an arm about her.

"Oh, Mom, how could he do something like that?" Sniffling, Stefie let the tears flow unheeded down her cheeks.

"I wish I knew." Janice handed her a tissue from a box on the end table. "Anna seems to feel it's because Dad felt he needed to prove he was as good as the Ingalls family, and with . . . with this woman, he didn't have to try to impress anyone."

Stefanie shook her head. "I don't buy that. Grandpa never made Dad feel he should do more. He used to praise him to the skies. And so did Uncle Judson."

"Then maybe it was me. I didn't make him feel special."

"Oh, that's crazy. What about him? I never remember him lavishing gifts on you or bringing you flowers." She pointed to the single yellow rose in a bud vase on the mantel. "Is that from David?"

Janice nodded, raising her eyes to the delicate flower. Winter and spring, he managed to find a yellow rose for her.

"That's the kind of thing that matters to a woman, a flower for no reason. Dad never bothered. Ross is very romantic. I can see why you're attracted to David."

Perhaps Stefie needed more of an explanation than K.J. had, being a woman. "I dated him some in college, but he didn't want to get involved back then. He had obligations to his family. When he started coming around last winter and I got to know him better, I began to care for him. And that was before I found out about...about Dad's other life. I wanted you to know I wasn't turning to David as a means to get even with your father."

"I didn't think that. You know, Mom, maybe the strain of trying to keep us from finding out about that woman and his baby had something to do with Dad's heart attack. They say stress is a big factor, especially for men."

"It's possible." If so, then it would seem he'd brought about his own death, in a way. A sobering thought. And his behavior certainly added to the stress in her own life, Janice thought.

Stefanie wiped her face, then turned to her mother. "Are you going to marry David, Mom?"

"I don't know."

"Has he asked you?"

"Yes, but, as you said, it's too soon. I just found out about this mess in Chicago a week ago. I've got to sort through things in my mind."

"Well, maybe you should do it. Maybe we should have a double wedding."

Janice smiled. "I don't think so. You just go ahead with your plans and .."

"We've moved the date up." Stefanie's eyes, the same gray as her mother's, were wide and watchful.

"Oh?" Janice studied her daughter's face. "For what reason?"

"A pretty good one." Stefanie sniffed again. "I'm pregnant."

"Well, now." Janice sat back, digesting that bit of news. It would seem that, lately, every few days brought another piece of upsetting news. Or was this upsetting? "I take it this was unplanned." She knew only too well how carefully Stefie and Ross had mapped out practically their whole lives.

"Very unplanned. I'm just sick about it."

Sick about it. What a terrible way to feel about the birth of a child. Janice frowned in annoyance. "If that's so, then why did you let this happen? I mean, we've discussed all kinds of birth control methods since you were fifteen."

"I *know* about birth control, Mother." Impatience put an edge to her teary voice. "But no method works all the time."

Oh, yes. One works very well, the one where the husband insists you have your tubes tied. Damn, if only she could get over that particular bitterness. But back to Stefie's situation. "Listen, honey, this shouldn't be such a big problem. You love Ross and he loves you, right?"

"Of course. But we weren't planning on getting married for at least two more years."

"I suppose it would be awkward if I remind you that we can't plan every phase of our lives and have everything go according to plan. Most especially when it come to babies. How does Ross feel about this?"

"He's not as upset as I am. But he's not the one who has to put his career on hold and stay home with the baby."

Shifting, Janice stretched out her legs in front of her. "A career can wait. Why don't you try to stop looking at this like a Greek tragedy, set the wedding date and be happy? Think of all the women who'd love to have a child and can't."

Stefanie sighed somewhat dramatically. "I'm being selfish, I know. It's just that this has caught me by surprise."

"Honey, we wouldn't have overpopulation in the world if only planned children were born. You can plan the next one. I, for one, am delighted for you. Two people as much in love as you and Ross should have children. A baby born into the kind of home you'll make together will be very fortunate."

Finally, Stefanie smiled. "I knew I'd feel better after talking with you. I always do." But thoughts of her own baby brought her mind back to the half brother she'd just learned of. "What will happen to that little boy? I mean, he's related to me and K.J. technically. Is he going to be all right?"

Janice was well aware that Stefie had always had a soft spot in her heart for children, as she herself did. "David has contacts and he's going to see if he can get a grant for the mother. So she can finish her education and get a better job."

"That's great. I know this is hard on you, Mom, but it's not that baby's fault that...that his father died without leaving him anything." Stefie stopped to sip her tea.

Now that she thought about it, Janice was surprised that Kurt hadn't taken out an insurance policy with Sammy as the beneficiary. He'd certainly spent a considerable amount of money supporting the child and mother. Perhaps he'd planned to, but he'd died too soon. Anger at Kurt rose inside her again and she made herself switch her thoughts. "So, when is the wedding going to be?"

"We were thinking of June, if that's all right with you. K.J. will be out of school by then and home. And can we invite David?"

"He'd like that."

"Has he been married before? Does he have children?"

"He was married years ago. His wife, pregnant at the time, died in an auto crash."

"Oh, how awful."

"Yes." They talked a while longer, about K.J.'s new job offer and Janice's redecorating plans. "I'm sleeping in K.J.'s room until I'm finished with my bedroom."

Stefanie stared at her mother a long moment. "I know why you're redoing that room. I wouldn't be able to sleep in there after what you found out, either." Seeing Janice turn her head and blink rapidly, she moved to hug her. "Dad hurt you badly, I know, and I'm sorry. I don't know what else to say."

"I'll be all right, in time."

"I know you will." She pulled back to smile at her mother. "You're very strong. I've always known that."

A survivor, as David said. Perhaps she was. "I hope so."

"I know so. And now, I think I'm going to call Ross, then go to bed." Stefie stood, picking up her glass. "Are we going to go shopping for wallpaper tomorrow? I'm pretty good at hanging paper."

"Are you sure you want to? If you're only going to be here a few days..."

"I'm sure. Good night, Mom." She leaned down to hug her mother briefly, then made for the stairs.

Janice walked to the kitchen to lock up, but the phone ringing interrupted her. Probably Ross, she thought as she picked it up.

"I just called to wish you good-night," David's deep voice said.

With a smile forming, she leaned against the wall, cradling the phone. "Mmm, how very nice of you." She wished he were here with her, holding her, about to go upstairs with her.

"Everything all right with your daughter?"

"I'd say so. She's going to have a baby."

"What? I thought she had her entire life planned ahead."

"She thought so, too. They've moved the wedding up to June."

"So, I'm in love with a grandmother-to-be?"

She paused, needing to hear him say the words. "Are you?"

"Yes. Am I invited to the wedding?"

"Certainly."

"And when they're back from their honeymoon, maybe we should take a trip. I've always wanted to visit New England, drive along the east coast, visit some bed-and-breakfast places. We could stop and see them on the way. What do you think?"

"Sounds better and better." She hesitated, then decided to tell him. "I miss you." And he'd just left a mere three hours ago.

"Good. Keep on missing me. I love you. Good night, Sunshine."

"Good night, David." Feeling warm from his words, she turned to hang up the phone and saw Stefie standing in the archway, wearing pink pajamas.

"You love him," she said quietly.

Caught red-handed, her feelings written all over her face. "Yes."

Stefanie smiled. "I'm glad, Mom."

Arm in arm, they climbed the stairs.

"IF YOU'RE GOING to wear your hair short, you've got to come in for trims more frequently," Tisha chastised Janice as she fastened the plastic cape over her shoulders.

"I know," Janice agreed, "but I've been so busy. Do you remember how you did it last time? A feather cut, I think you called it."

"Sure, sure." Tisha pumped up the chair and swung it around as she picked up her scissors. She paused, catching her customer's eye in the mirror. "Honey, I've got to say you're looking a whole lot better than the last time you were in my shop, even though you do need a trim. When was that, last February?"

"Yes, February. And here it is the middle of May." Lately, the days had flown by for Janice.

"So, what's keeping you so busy these days?"

"I work in the insurance office a couple of days a week and I've been redecorating my house."

"So I heard from Liza. I guess she stopped in to check it out."

"Yes, last week."

"She says you've got a real good eye for colors, and she ought to know. She also said you had some gorgeous guy in there painting your den." Tisha tilted

Janice's head forward so she could work on the back. "You been holding out on me, honey?"

Despite her best effort, Janice felt the heat rise in her face. "No, I just haven't seen you lately. His name is David Markus and—"

"And he's a financial adviser." She let loose with a deep-throated laugh. "From what Liza tells me, he can come advise me anytime."

Janice didn't quite know what to say to that. "He's a very nice man, actually."

"Uh-huh." Tisha brushed back a strand of red hair that had escaped from her rather elaborate upsweep. "Is he the reason you got me to stay late to get you in shape? Got a hot date tonight?"

"I don't know if I'd call it a hot date, but we're going out to dinner, driving to Madison." David had phoned last night, inviting her. A special evening at a new restaurant he'd found. Very schmaltzy, he'd said. Get something new, something yellow. She had, a soft filmy dress, different from anything she'd owned in far too long.

"Sounds romantic. Good for you, honey." Tisha clipped away for several minutes before another thought occurred to her. "Since you're so good with decorating and all, how would you advise me if I wanted to give my shop a face-lift, so to speak?"

In the mirror, Janice checked out the familiar room, with its black-and-white-checkered vinyl floor, red chairs, and walls filled with random clusters of memorabilia that Tisha had collected through the years, plus her vivid green parrot in his cage in the far corner. "Are you serious? You want to redo this shop, when it's almost an institution in Tyler?"

"Shucks, honey, you can get tired of anything. How would you do it over?"

"Well, if you're going for a more modern look, I'd probably suggest something more dramatic." Janice had a feeling Tisha with her flamboyant red hair and her penchant for unique clothes, would be attracted to something striking. "For instance, plum-colored sinks and chairs, stark white walls with some vivid framed prints and a shiny black floor."

"Sounds expensive." Tisha swiveled the chair about and went to work on the top of Janice's head. "Where would I find things like that?"

"I could probably get you some catalogs to look through."

"Would you help me decide, too? I'm not real good at picking out classy prints and so on."

"Sure, if you're serious."

"You bet I am. And I'm also wondering why you're fooling around with that stodgy old insurance business when folks say you're so good at decorating."

"Probably because that stodgy old insurance business pays the bills and I don't know if I could make a living at design. I only do that for fun and for my friends."

"That's how I started, cutting my friends' hair, and look at me now. The thing is, most people are happiest doing something they like. And if you can get paid for doing something you enjoy, hot damn, you got it made.''

"You're probably right."

"Honey, I'm *always* right." Tisha laughed to prove she was poking fun at herself, then set down the scissors. "How's that look?"

Janice ran a hand through her damp hair. "Good. Really good."

Tisha turned on a hand dryer and picked up her brush. In minutes, she had Janice's short hair dry and styled. She whipped off the cape and walked over to the register. Lighting a cigarette, she inhaled deeply.

Janice paid her bill thoughtfully. "You sure you want me to find some catalogs and bring them over?"

"Yes, ma'am. Next week be all right?"

"Fine. I'll call you. And thanks for staying open for me. I hope I didn't keep you from something important tonight."

"No problem. And you have a good time with that hunk, you hear?"

Janice smiled. "I'll try."

From the corner came a squawking sound. "*Arrivederci,* babe!"

"'Bye, Nouci." Janice waved to the parrot and his owner, then left the shop. Outside in the warm spring air, she breathed in deeply as she glanced at her watch. David would be coming for her in an hour. The thought had her hurrying to her car for the short drive home.

She'd seen a lot of him since the day they'd painted her bedroom, the day Stefie had dropped in so unexpectedly. Her daughter's visit had been short, but good, and they'd talked more as friends rather than as mother and daughter. Janice was pleased that by the time Stefie left, she was actually looking forward to her baby's arrival.

And her own relationship with David had deepened. Yet for some reason, she seemed unable to make that final commitment, to answer the question she saw in his eyes more and more frequently. She wasn't quite certain what, but something was holding her back.

The thing was, he never denied her anything, never even argued with her. It didn't seem normal. Surely he must disagree with some of her decisions. Yet he avoided discussion more often than not. Odd.

Climbing behind the wheel, Janice closed the car door and decided to set aside all troubling thoughts for tonight. Tonight, she would just enjoy.

THE MUSIC WAS MELLOW, the song familiar. Her hand on his shoulder, Janice let David dance her around the floor. She was comfortable within the circle of his strong arms, and she let the sweet sounds surround her as her blood warmed. How long had it been since she'd danced like this, felt like this? Had she ever?

David's lips were at her ear. "Have I told you how beautiful you are?" he asked, his voice husky.

"Mmm, yes, I believe so."

"It bears repeating." He tipped back his head as the music stopped. "I think that's the end of the record."

She smiled up at him. "I still hear the music."

"Me, too." He bent to kiss her.

He'd picked her up promptly at seven, his eyes telling her how much he appreciated the yellow dress she'd bought just for him, as well as her new haircut. He'd kept her close to his side as he drove to Madison and they'd had a lovely, leisurely dinner at a restaurant overlooking the lake. But there'd been no band, so back in her living room, they'd put on a Beatles record and danced.

His mouth on hers was heating her blood, as always. How long, Janice wondered, would this attraction be this strong? Would she ever tire of being in his arms, of seeing his eyes turn dark with desire for her? As his hands moved to frame her face, she doubted if she ever would.

"I love you, Janice," he said as he stared into her eyes.

He was waiting, and she knew what for. She'd never said the words to him, though she'd known for some time how deeply she cared. It was time. "I love you, too, David." She saw the pleasure and the relief in his eyes.

He kissed her then, thoroughly and deeply. Pulling back, he took her hands in his. "Marry me, please."

She was hesitant and didn't know how to explain her feelings. "Let's wait, David. It's only been a few months and..."

"Are you afraid how our marrying would look to your family and friends?"

"No, it's not that." Stepping back, she went to gaze out the window. Past midnight and a sliver of moon hung in the clear dark sky. She could smell pipe tobacco as David came up behind her.

"Is it because you don't want to leave Tyler? I could move here, if that's what you want. Or we could live in my house. It's plenty big enough and you could redecorate it any way you want. Or we could keep both."

So agreeable. Always, so very agreeable. She turned to face him. "Surely you have a preference?"

"No. Whatever you want, that's what we'll do."

Odd how she'd never thought him quite that unopinionated. Quite a change from Kurt, who had always decided quickly, then *told* her what they'd do.

"Is it your work at the office? Because I have no problem with that if you want to do it. Or if you'd rather sell the business and go back to get your degree, that's fine with me."

Janice frowned, wondering what was wrong and why she couldn't put her finger on it. "I don't know, David."

David drew her down to sit beside him on the couch, wondering what to say to convince her that they could have a good life together. "Are you afraid I'll be unfaithful like Kurt was?"

She looked up at him then, her gray eyes huge in her small face.

He took her hands again. "Let me assure you, that wouldn't be the case. I took my vows to Eleanor very seriously and I never once strayed, or even thought of it. I wouldn't with you, either. You must believe that."

She couldn't doubt his sincerity. "I do believe you."

He was running out of arguments. "I don't know what else to say. We love each other and I think we'd be happy. All I want is to make you happy."

"I'm not sure that's possible, David. A person can't *make* another person happy. Each person has to do that for himself."

"No. I didn't make Eleanor happy. I wasn't there for her when she needed me. I didn't pay attention to her needs because I was so busy getting ahead. I won't make that mistake again." He ran a hand over his face tiredly. "I remember the morning I left her, the last time I saw her alive. I'd promised I'd be home to take her to her doctor's appointment, but something came up and I had to go out of town unexpectedly. The last thing I said to her was, 'I'll make it up to you, I swear I will.'"

Janice saw the haunted look in his eyes as he turned to her, saw the plea in that look.

"I never got a chance to make it up to her. She went to the doctor alone, and died. I wanted things my way and look what happened." He shook his head. "I vowed that if I fell in love again, I'd never let that happen. I want what you want."

"But that's not right, David. It's just as bad as one person dominating another, like Kurt did with me. One person giving in to another also builds up resentments. Believe me, I know."

"You're wrong. I wouldn't resent you. I love you."

She pulled away, finally focusing on what had been holding her back from committing to David, despite her love for him. "I want a fifty-fifty marriage, David. *That's* what I've never had. Not *your* way or *my* way, but a compromise. Our way, so to speak. You win in some things and I win in other ways. Do you see the difference?"

He nodded. "If that's how you want it, that's how we'll do it."

"You're doing it again, giving in." Agitated, she rose and walked to the fireplace. After a moment, she turned and saw he'd leaned forward, his elbows on his knees, his face a mask of confusion. "David, suppose I want you to quit working, move into this house and take care of it while I work? Suppose I want to move to China, or learn to hang-glide, or become a stripper? Are you still going to be agreeable to my every whim?"

He looked up, frowning. "Now you're being silly."

"No sillier than you when you tell me that you'll put up with anything if I'll marry you. In no time, I wouldn't like myself very much, and neither would you."

He stood, his stance angry. "All right, damn it, then I'll call all the shots and *you* follow suit."

"No, thanks. I've already had one marriage like that." She stepped closer. "Why can't we be equal partners?"

"I was only trying to make you happy and you attack me. I don't seem to be able to please you tonight. Perhaps I'd better leave."

Maybe there were more differences between them than she'd let herself see, blinded as she was by that all-consuming attraction. "I guess we both have a little thinking to do."

At the door, he turned to her. Funny how you could love someone, and it still wasn't enough, he thought. "I'll call you."

"All right."

"I love you, Sunshine," he whispered softly.

Janice felt her eyes fill. Why did this hurt so much? Dear God, hadn't she had enough hurting? "I love you, too." Without a touch or another word, she saw him turn and walk away.

She closed the door, unable to watch him drive off, wondering if she could find her way upstairs through her tears.

CHAPTER TWELVE

JANICE LEANED BACK in her chair and smiled at the gray-haired man seated across the desk from her. "I really appreciate your taking the time to explain all this to me, Charles. Balance sheets, profit and loss statements, audits—they were all a mystery to me. But you make it sound almost easy."

Charles Atwood nodded acknowledgment of her compliment as he removed his rimless glasses. As Kurt's C.P.A. he'd done the books for Eber Insurance for years. A somewhat dour man, she'd yet to see him look terribly pleased about anything. However, he was very good at making the numbers come out right.

"I thought it best to wait until the fiscal year ended before I went over everything. You should know exactly where you stand financially now."

"Thanks to you, I do. One more thing." Opening her top drawer, she removed a brochure and handed it across to him. "I'd like your opinion on this as an investment."

Charles put his glasses back on and studied the booklet. "Nice-looking building. I'm familiar with the neighborhood and it's solid. Rentals in that area hold their value and long-term leases are sought after. I'd say it's a sound investment.'' Again, he removed his glasses and carefully put them away. ''Is someone you know interested in purchasing it?''

''Yes. I am.''

Charles raised his bushy white brows. ''I thought we just went over your investment portfolio and you were satisfied.''

Janice toyed with her fountain pen. ''I'm satisfied with the return I've been getting on my money. Satisfied but not delighted. According to the Realtor who lists this property, it has nowhere to go but up.''

Clearing his throat, Charles sat back and crossed his legs. ''No offense, my dear, but realtors aren't always prone to give the best advice, especially to...well, to an inexperienced woman such as yourself.'' He pursed his lips. ''Before making a move, I would suggest you consult someone whose business acumen you trust and respect.''

''I just did. You.''

Steepling his fingers over his paunch, Charles eyed her, obviously unflattered by her statement. ''But why would you consider taking money from the safety of your conservative investments and putting it into something more risky, such as building ownership? Being a landlord is time-consuming and can be costly if one is unaware of the pitfalls. And should the recession continue, vacant property can drain your assets.''

The man was a good accountant, but he was also stodgy, humorless and much too cautious for her taste.

"No pain, no gain, Charles," she said, trying for a lighter touch.

"Why are you interested in buying a building, may I ask?" His look was appraising.

She leaned forward. "I went through these papers and learned that Eber Insurance's lease with the owners of the building we're in is up in two months. We're obligated to give them thirty days notice. The new place has a vacant suite of offices on the first floor, street level. I've inspected the space and it's better than we have here. If we go ahead, we could close in thirty days and still have thirty more to renovate where necessary."

"But Eber Insurance has been in this location for... well, for nearly twenty years."

Janice was growing impatient. "We're talking a move of about ten blocks here, Charles. And our business doesn't rely on walk-in trade. Any more objections?"

Charles was still unconvinced. "I certainly couldn't recommend such a purchase without careful consideration, feasibility studies and perhaps consulting an investment counselor."

An investment counselor. Like David Markus.

He'd left her home two weeks ago, and though they'd talked twice on the phone since, their conversations had been strained and uneasy. No, she would not consult with David on her business or anything else, the way things were between them.

Dropping the pen, she met Charles's eyes. "Look, Charles, I'm not Kurt. I perhaps do things a different way, but that doesn't necessarily make my methods wrong. I also rely on my instincts more. Call it feminine intuition, if you will. I see no reason to keep throwing money away on rent when we could buy a building. The down payment is affordable and there are seven tenants on long-term leases already in the building. The interest on the mortgage would also be a tax write-off. Don't you think it's a good idea to let those tenants pay off the mortgage for me?"

Charles shifted in his chair, his expression indicating grudging agreement. "Actually, I'd suggested a similar move to Kurt several times. But he preferred to invest the cash flow in other ways. For instance, he spent a great deal on traveling to acquire more business."

Traveling. To Chicago mostly. "Yes, well, I've looked into that and decided there isn't that much to be gained by expansion. Tom Sikes does the traveling now, and we've cut down considerably on the trips. The money we save should help with the building costs. So, what do you think?"

He was not a man generous with his smiles, but he gave her a small one anyway. "I think you're a better businesswoman than your limited experience would indicate." His voice held a measure of respect that had been previously missing.

Had the quiet little man been playing devil's advocate the whole time? Janice wondered. "Thank you.

Then would you please call the Realtor—his name is on the brochure—and prepare a breakdown of costs for me?"

Charles stood. "I'll have something for you in under a week. Will you be needing anything else, Mrs. Eber?"

"Not really, but I wanted to mention that I'm turning over the day-to-day operation of Eber Insurance to Tom as of next week. I intend to meet with him one day a week only, for an update. You may call him if you need anything."

"Of course. Are you contemplating selling?"

"I'll retain ownership, for now. But I've gotten involved in another project that's occupying more and more of my time. Tom's very capable, so I expect things to run smoothly."

She rose and stretched out her hand. "That's it. Thank you, Charles."

Like pulling teeth, Janice thought as she sat down after Charles had left. Trying to get respect from the "good old boys" club was like pulling teeth. Difficult but not impossible.

She was making gains, albeit slowly. The staff meeting last Monday had been long and almost boisterous. She'd asked each and every employee for input as to how they could keep Eber Insurance strong and forward-moving. After an initial hesitancy, suggestions had poured in, some very good, a few too petty to consider. She'd promised to carefully examine each.

Opening the folder in front of her, Janice couldn't help but be pleased. Numbers, at least, never lied. Five months after Kurt's death and they were doing well. Business-wise, that was. Personally, she wasn't nearly as confident.

Swiveling the chair around, she looked out the window. It was the first week of June, a beautiful summer day, but unseasonably hot. It had rained last night, complete with thunder and lightning, but there were few signs of the storm lingering. The office was hot and stuffy, the humidity overtaxing the ancient air conditioner. Twice she'd called the landlord and twice he'd promised he'd send a repairman. No one had arrived yet. But soon, hopefully, they'd be out of here and in their own place.

Walking to the window, she felt a pang of longing as she inhaled the scent of newly mown grass. The geraniums in David's flower bed were probably in bloom by now. Perhaps his rosebushes were solidly anchored to the trellis he'd undoubtedly finished by now. She wondered how the little squirrel was doing.

Damn. She was back to being lonely. This business of being in love wasn't the panacea to problems, that was for certain. Perhaps she'd have been better off if David hadn't come to Kurt's funeral, if she'd not seen him again.

Involuntarily, Janice shook her head. No, she wouldn't want to have missed getting to know him again—the shared laughter, the moments in his arms—for anything. But would she ever be with him again?

Neither of them seemed able to get past this hurdle. Well, she would live alone, missing him, rather than be an unequal partner in another marriage.

It was too nice a day to stay in. The work on her desk would wait for her. Anna had just phoned to say she was leaving the office early and wondered if Janice could do the same. Janice hadn't talked with her, *really* talked, in weeks. Maybe she'd even confide in her friend about David. And maybe she'd have a good laugh or an overdue cry in Anna's kitchen, where the two of them had shared many a cup of coffee along with lots of chuckles and a few tears.

Picking up her purse, Janice left her office.

ANNA KELSEY WAS BORN a good listener and had perfected the talent through the years, raising four children and living with a husband who enjoyed talking things over with her. She was a good friend, too, always willing to drop what she was doing to have a chat. The Kelsey backyard was a peaceful spot, Janice thought as she sat down at the painted wood table on the porch while Anna poured iced tea for both of them.

"Too hot for coffee today," Anna commented as she dropped into a chair. "Awfully early for this heat wave, don't you think?"

"I certainly do." Janice slipped off her shoes and wished she hadn't worn panty hose today.

"You just missed Brick. He was here with Michael Youngthunder."

"I've met Michael. He seems like a nice young man, don't you think?"

"That he is, but right now, he's quite worried. It seems his grandfather, who's in his nineties, wandered away during last night's rainstorm. Michael's looked all over for him and finally asked Brick to help."

"That's a shame. At his age, that old man could easily get disoriented and not be able to find his way back home."

"They wanted to know if I'd seen any signs of him, but unfortunately, I haven't. Michael seems to think his grandfather's looking for the old Indian burial grounds. He's been upset, according to Michael, about the renovations taking place at Timberlake, with that new wing being added to the lodge. The old man feels the excavating might have disturbed the burial grounds."

Janice shook her head sympathetically. "I hope they find him before too long. In this heat, I don't know how well he'll fare unless he's found some shelter."

"The humidity's beastly." Anna patted her damp brow, then looked over at her friend. "But you look pretty cool. That's a lovely dress." It was amazing how vastly improved Janice's wardrobe had become over the past months.

"Thanks." Janice sipped her tea, watching a robin on the limb of a nearby maple tree.

"How are things at the agency?"

"Fine."

"And the kids?"

"K.J.'s out of school and in Chicago for his summer job." And seeing David regularly, she knew.

"I sure hope that works out for him. He's so talented."

"I hope so, too. And you got the invitation to Stefie's wedding shower?"

"Yes. I meant to call, but I haven't had a chance."

Janice dismissed the apology. "Stefie's flying in next week for the shower and so we can go shopping for her dress."

"Why the sudden change of plans?"

"She's pregnant."

"Oh, my. And upset, I'll wager." Anna had known both of Janice's children from babyhood and was aware that Stefanie had mapped out her whole life years ago.

"She was, at first. However, she's adjusted to the thought by now, and Ross seems happy."

Anna removed her glasses and busied herself cleaning the lenses. "How's David these days?"

"Fine."

Even without her spectacles, Anna could see that something was bothering her friend, and she had a feeling the problem centered as much around David as it did around the other things Janice had been coping with lately. Anna was not one to pry, but she knew most women felt better after sharing their feelings. "Have you seen him lately?"

"Not for a couple of weeks." Janice hesitated, then plunged in. "We quarreled."

Bingo. "Do you want to talk about it?"

"He asked me to marry him, Anna."

Obviously, there was more. "Do you love him?"

"Yes, very much." Now the anguished eyes swung toward Anna. "I never thought I would feel this way again. It's stronger, deeper, than when I first began to care for Kurt." She looked down then, balling a tissue in her hands. "But sometimes, loving isn't enough."

"It can be. What did the two of you quarrel over?"

"It wasn't a shouting-match quarrel. We'd gone out to dinner and come back to my house. David's been wonderful throughout this whole mess with Diane and the baby, very compassionate. He volunteered to get her into a grant program, which was something I hadn't even thought of, and he's taking care of all the details for me. He's such a caring man."

"That should help her."

"Yes, and I talked things over with K.J. and Stefie. We've set up a trust fund for the boy. For his education."

"That was a very kind thing to do, Janice."

Janice dismissed the praise. "As angry as I've been, I've come to realize you only hurt yourself if you hang on to bitter feelings. And we all three agree that none of this is that little boy's fault."

Anna knew it was important to let Janice tell the story in her own way. "But getting back to David..."

Janice cleared her throat. "Yes. As I said, he asked me to marry him. He's asked before and something always held me back from answering. I finally discovered what it was. David's vision of marriage is different than mine."

"How do you differ?"

Janice tossed the shredded tissue into the ashtray on the table. "You know, Anna, I adjusted my life to Kurt's needs and wants all the while we were together. I didn't question, didn't demand, rarely even stated a preference. I just went along. And I became so dependent on that man that when he died, I was left floundering. I hadn't ever bought a car by myself, or balanced a checkbook or picked out one stick of furniture without consulting him." She shook her head, still amazed at her own naiveté. "I never want to be like that again."

"There's no reason why you should be. Is that what David wants you to do, to bend to his will on everything?"

"Quite the opposite. He's willing—no, insistent—on doing whatever I want. His main goal is to make me happy, he says. Because of his first marriage." While Anna sipped her tea, Janice told her about David's relationship with Eleanor, including the last day he'd seen her alive. "So you can see *why* he feels the way he does. But that kind of lopsided marriage isn't for me."

Anna understood. Janice was afraid of entering another marriage where decisions weren't shared equally. However, as she replaced her glasses and studied her friend for a moment, she felt as if these two people both wanted the same thing but just weren't communicating. "Janice, what is it *you* want?"

"You mean out of a marriage?"

"Out of a marriage, out of life. Do you want to continue at the agency, keep it going, make it a huge part of your life? Do you want to stay in Tyler in the house you shared with Kurt, especially with Stefanie settling down in the east and K.J. in Chicago?"

Janice drained her glass and sighed. "You ask tough questions, Anna. All right, let me see. The agency. I feel proud that I was able to rise to the occasion and take over. But do I want it to be a huge part of my life? I can't say I do. Insurance was Kurt's choice, not mine. I wanted to prove I could do it, but I've done that now."

"So you're selling it?"

"Not yet. I've made arrangements for the firm to buy a building, because it makes good business sense. When I do sell, that should make it more appealing. But I'm turning over the actual running of the agency to Tom Sikes."

"Good for you."

"As for my house, frankly, it's filled with too many memories. Especially now that I've learned about Kurt's other life. Even the good memories leave me with a bad taste. I've redecorated most of the rooms, yet I'm no longer comfortable there. I'm not quite sure where I want to live."

"So a change of scene is probably in order," Anna suggested mildly. "And what will you do with all your newfound leisure?"

"I've enrolled in summer classes at the university, taking another shot at design. I really do enjoy decorating. If it works out, perhaps one day I'll open a design studio of my own."

"That sounds like a wonderful plan," Anna said, very pleased with how far Janice had come in decision making. "Now for the big question—how does David fit in with all this?"

Janice gazed off into the maple tree. The robin had hopped up to a higher branch and was carefully feeding several tiny birds in a nest wedged into a leafy crevice. The babies chirped noisily and the bird patiently continued stuffing their open mouths, while nearby on the same branch, the robin's mate waited, a worm dangling from its beak. They were a family, something she'd once been a part of. Would she ever be again? Janice ran a hand through her hair and turned to Anna. "The truth?"

"Yes, the truth. Tell me how you really feel."

"All right. I would love to marry David and live in his lovely home, to share my life with him. K.J. likes him and Stefie seems to approve. But Anna, I need him to realize that *both* of us have to have input into what happens in our lives. I want him to see us as individuals with needs of our own, active partners who should each be involved in every decision that affects us both. Is that so wrong?"

Anna reached over and took her friend's hand. "Not wrong at all. But your telling me isn't the solution. You need to tell David how you feel."

"I tried, but he wasn't listening."

"If you love him, you'll try again and *make* him hear you."

After a thoughtful moment, Janice managed a hesitant smile. "Perhaps I've been so busy being righteously indignant that I didn't really spell out everything as clearly as I should have."

"Then go to him. Tell him all you've told me. I'd be willing to wager that I'll be invited to two weddings very soon."

Suddenly, Janice lost her confidence. "You don't think I'm being ridiculous, do you?"

Anna reached over and hugged her. "Now you're worried you'll chase him away. Listen, I think that David's been attracted to you since you were a girl back in college. I don't think wild horses would actually chase him away. But he's a man, and men are stubborn and find it difficult to admit their ideas might need changing." She rose, smiling. "He'll come around, wait and see."

Feeling enormously better, Janice stood and picked up her handbag. "Thank you. I don't know what I'd do without your insight. If I do move away, I hope we can still stay close."

"Of course we will. Chicago's less than two hours from Tyler." Arm in arm, she walked with Janice to her car. "So what are you going to do now?"

"Go home and get a good night's sleep. Then tomorrow, call David and ask if I can come see him.

Hopefully, by then I'll find the right words." She opened the door to her Capri.

"Start by telling him you love him. The rest will follow." Again, she hugged her friend. "And afterwards, call me. Let me know what date you've set for your wedding."

Settling behind the wheel, Janice sent Anna a skeptical look. "I wish I had your confidence."

"You will have. Love and a good marriage can give you lots of confidence." She watched Janice back out of her drive and wave as she headed home.

Glancing at her watch, she hurried inside. It was time to start dinner. She could hardly wait for Johnny to come home, to share with him the story of Janice and David. A romantic at heart, Anna loved happy endings.

THE MOMENT Janice turned onto her street, she saw the gray Lincoln parked in front of her house. Heart in her throat, she passed it, noticing that no one was inside, and swung her Capri into the drive.

David was sitting on the front-porch steps, his back against the post, his arm resting on one bent knee. Turning off the engine, she sat for a moment looking at him, then got out and slowly walked over. Near the bottom step, she stopped.

He didn't move, just looked at her, his eyes as blue as the afternoon sky. He'd evidently left his jacket and tie in his car, for he had on dress slacks and a white shirt open at the throat. His face was tanner than she remembered and he looked altogether wonderful to her hungry eyes.

"Hello, stranger," she managed.

"Hello, yourself. I stopped in at the agency, but they said you'd gone for the day and they weren't sure where you were."

"It was too nice a day to be inside. I went over to Anna's for a while. We sat on her back porch and talked." She moved up to sit alongside him, leaning against the opposite post and angling her body so she could look at him. But not touch him. She knew if she touched him, the speech she'd rehearsed all the way home would be forgotten.

"I've missed you," he said quietly.

"I've missed you, too."

His expression was serious, unreadable. "I talked to Tom. He says the company's in great shape, that you're considering buying a building and moving the agency into it."

She nodded. "It seems to make good business sense to own instead of renting. My C.P.A. thinks I should discuss the decision with my financial adviser. So what do you think?"

David shook his head, his eyes suddenly sad. "I don't think you need my advice, business or otherwise."

"Did Tom tell you the rest, that I'm turning the day-to-day operation over to him to run while I go back to school? What do you think of that?"

He seemed surprised, but his eyes didn't brighten. "You seem to be doing just fine. It also looks like you have no room in your busy life for me."

"That's not so."

David struggled with a myriad of emotions.

He was hurting and finding he wasn't very good at hiding the fact from her, which upset him further. He'd had a business appointment this morning not far from Tyler and had decided last night to drop in on Janice afterward. He'd carefully rehearsed what he had to say, which basically amounted to an apology. He'd been wrong to be so compliant. How could she love a wimp? Compromise was the answer to any good relationship.

But he'd come to realize, after talking with Tom and now seeing her, that he was too late. She was happy and successful with her life here. She didn't need him. Not only did she not want to leave Tyler, she likely wasn't even interested in a compromise. He'd lost her again, and both times it had been his own doing.

She could see he was wrestling with his feelings. It would seem she'd have to make the first move. "David, talk to me. I need to know what you're thinking, what you're feeling."

He straightened on the stoop, leaning forward with his elbows on his knees, his hands clenched together. "That's been one of my problems. I've never been good at sharing my deeper thoughts. Oh, I can talk for hours, but not about my gut feelings. When my dad died, my mother had to work so hard she had little time left over for heart-to-heart talks. My sister was years

younger. So I learned to keep my own counsel, to solve
my own problems and to make my own decisions.
Eleanor and I were together such a short time and I was
gone so much. I've never even had a close male friend.
Maybe that's why talking serious things over is difficult for me."

She could relate. "It's difficult for me, too. Kurt
never gave a damn about my opinion, much less asked
for it. But women are fortunate. They can open up to
each other more easily and share confidences. It's sort
of a bonding thing." She took a chance then and
moved closer, placing her hand lightly on his arm. "I
want a relationship where I can share my feelings with
the man I love, even if we don't always agree."

He turned to her then and she could see the pain in
his eyes. "I want that, too." He took her hand,
squeezed it. "I came to tell you that I've been wrong.
About a lot of things. I not only didn't share with you,
but I didn't take your feelings into consideration. I just
was so hell-bent on trying to make up for not being
there for Eleanor that I nearly smothered you with my
good intentions. And I lost sight of an important fact.
I've always wanted what you want, an equal partner. I
just didn't think I'd ever find one who'd want that,
too. I didn't think I'd ever find you."

"Oh, David . . ."

He clutched both her hands now, wanting badly to
hold her, but knowing he had to get it all out first. "I
said it all wrong the last time we were together. Let's

talk, let's plan our future together. The main thing is for us to be together. I love you so much, Janice."

"I love you, too. But there's more here. I—I can't give you a child, David, and that's been bothering me. You'd be a wonderful father and you can still find a younger woman who—"

He'd begun shaking his head halfway through her recital. "I *did* want children once, I admit. But I'm perfectly happy being a stepfather to your two. They seem to like me...."

"They do. And soon there'll be Stefie's baby." But she had even more to say. "I'm as guilty as you for not sharing my feelings, yet expecting you to know how I felt. I've been struggling with decisions, wanting to be independent, and I've proved I can make a few. But I've often wished I could talk over a decision with you. I *need* that kind of input so I can make up my mind."

He smiled. "Anytime, sweetheart. I'll be glad to hear you out and share my opinions from now on, I promise." David touched her face, her beautiful face, his hand lingering on her soft skin. "Just don't let's go through another week like these last two. Lord, I've missed you."

She smiled. "Ditto."

David stood, drawing her up with him. "Is this really happening? Are you really going to be my wife?"

"If you still want me."

"*If?* Dear God, it's all I've been thinking about." Pulling her close, he kissed her then, unable to hold off. The kiss was tender, then grew more heated, as the memory of their torturous days apart increased their need.

While she was still able, Janice drew back. "It's a little public here. Could we go inside and finish this?"

"Mmm, yes. I want to make love with you very slowly and for a very long time."

Janice felt the warmth inside spread. "Let's go."

Arms entwined, they walked up the steps together. David took her key and unlocked the door, then paused. "I don't believe we've done justice to the sofa in the living room."

She smiled. "And there's the couch in the den...."

David bent to nibble at the corner of her mouth. "I don't care if it's the floor, but let's hurry. It's been way too long already."

Laughing with sheer joy, Janice followed her love inside and closed the door behind them.

And now,
an exciting preview of

ARROWPOINT

by Suzanne Ellison

the seventh installment of the
Tyler series

Artist Renata Meyer tangles with Winnebago Indian Michael Youngthunder over the rights to the land on which her family ranch is built. She tries to tell him that it's all in the past, but Michael insists that until he fulfills his grandfather's deathbed promise to the Thunderbird clan, the two of them can never have a future. Meanwhile, Alyssa has a memory flash of the night her mother disappeared, and Edward suspects that his father may have murdered Margaret.

CHAPTER ONE

IT HAD RAINED all night, but by the time Renata Meyer saw the sign that said Tyler, Three Miles the sky was only dripping, a misty remnant of the deluge she'd left an hour ago in Milwaukee. It wasn't quite summer yet, but for the past month it had already been so hot that this cooling thunderstorm was more a relief than a burden, especially considering where Renata was going to spend the weekend. Her Milwaukee apartment had a feisty air conditioner that kept her chilled most of the time, but the old family homestead north of Tyler had poor insulation, few windows and only one ancient oak tree for shade. The improvements made since her great-grandparents' time had been minimal. Air-conditioning was not one of them.

As a free-lance artist, Renata didn't have a lot of income, but she did have a lot of freedom as to where and how she spent her time. She lived on the periodic sales of her paintings and her more frequent free-lance commercial assignments, which embarrassed her artistic pride but kept a roof over her head. At this point she found that being in the city—where she could brush shoulders with gallery owners, better-established artists and sympathetic art-buying friends—was a tremendous help to her fledgling career. But living in the thunderous rattle of Milwaukee wore her down from time to time, and it was always a relief to know that there was somewhere to go to renew herself. When life got to be a bit much, she turned north and headed back to Tyler like a homing pigeon, even when she hadn't received a summons from an old friend.

Alyssa Ingalls Baron wasn't a friend in the intimate sense of the word; she was more a fixture of Renata's tiny hometown. She was of Renata's mother's generation, though the two had not been particularly close. Everybody knew Alyssa, at least by name, and everybody liked her, even if they were a bit jealous of her family's wealth. Renata's family had been in the area just as long, but since for the past four generations they'd unpretentiously run a farm that barely broke even, nobody had ever paid much attention to the Meyers. The Ingalls clan, on the other hand, had the Midas touch. They owned land and a thriving business, and kept a guiding hand in local politics. Fortunately, Alyssa wasn't snooty about her wealth and power—she was a sweet and gentle person—but when she suggested, as she had to Renata, that a Tylerite "volunteer" to do something for the good of the town, it somehow felt like an order.

Renata had loved the warmth of her hometown as a child and hated it as a teenager. She hadn't been Tyler's wild child as a girl—Alyssa's younger daughter, Liza, had sewn up that title—but she had been a bit eccentric in the town's eyes.

Renata had always been more interested in painting than pom-poms. When the rest of her high school classmates were swimming in the summer or skating on winter ice, Renata was alone at her easel. Kicking local tradition in the teeth, she had skipped the junior prom, the senior homecoming game and one of the Ingallses Christmas parties—by accident—when she'd started painting after dinner and forgotten about the world till after midnight. Tyler people still teased Renata about her early paintings and her dramatic choice of clothes. She couldn't wear her paintings, so she tried to make a statement with fabric art whenever she could. And when she couldn't do that, she usually found herself wearing a paint-spattered T-shirt and watercolored jeans.

There had been times when she'd found herself in such bad straits that she'd had to return to live in Tyler for several months—once it was a whole year—but Renata had never been poor enough to consider selling the old place. Regardless of the demands of her ambition and her art, she took deep comfort and joy from the knowledge that twelve acres of lush farmland had remained in her family's hands for nearly 150 years. Granted, the house was old and drafty—a two-story box with a pair of upstairs bedrooms, one bathroom with a hand-held shower, an old-fashioned parlor and a kitchen that hadn't been updated since World War II. Every time she came home, Renata vowed to start remodeling the old place, but she was never there long enough to justify the expense. Someday she knew she'd want to come home for good, but at the moment it would be too inconvenient to live in Tyler full-time.

And too lonely.

She pulled up at the mailbox and rolled down the window of her old red truck before she remembered that one of the Hansen kids picked up her mail once a week when he checked over her house, watered her roses and mowed the lawn. She couldn't really afford to pay him, but his mother, Britt, was so strapped since her husband's death that Renata hadn't been able to turn Matt down when he made the offer. Even knowing that the mailbox ought to be empty, Renata felt a twinge of sadness to find it that way. When her parents were still living, a mound of good tidings and junk mail had arrived every day.

Before she had time to get maudlin, Renata was startled by an eerie, distant sound. At first she thought it was merely the whisper of the storm, but it almost sounded like humming. No, it wasn't humming. Not exactly. But she couldn't exactly call it singing, either. It sounded human. Well, not human so much as not-animal. Sort of other-worldly.

Heyeh, heyeh, heyeh, hiyayayayayaya, heyeh, heyeh. It was a chant of some sort, a weird, eerie chant that made Renata's flesh crawl. It was soft, which either meant it was loud at the source and very far away, or else . . . or else it was coming from just up the road.

And the only house up this deserted gravel road was Renata's.

Maybe it's just the rain, she told herself stoutly. *Sometimes the trees creak in a high wind and sound like someone moaning.*

It was a reassuring notion, but Renata didn't really think the noise had anything to do with the weather. Someone—friend or foe—must be up at her place, expressing himself or herself in some kind of bizarre mantra. But the sound of one voice didn't mean that there was only one person. It could be one of those devil-worshiping cults! Renata hadn't been home in a long time, and everybody who lived in Tyler knew it. What better place for weird cult gatherings than an isolated spot like this?

But what kind of a cult gathers at nine a.m. in the rain? a more rational voice asked. Maybe it was just Matt Hansen, humming whatever was hip among the high school crowd these days.

In the end her curiosity overcame her apprehension. After all, Renata prided herself on her acceptance of new things. She'd always been a bit of a radical, moving through life at her own pace to a drumbeat all her own. She wasn't a rebel, in that she didn't fight society anymore; she just ignored it when it got in her way. Renata sought her own brand of happiness, and she pursued it with joyful glee every day of her life. She wanted no less for the people around her, but she never tried to force her ways on them.

As she drove on toward the house, she realized vaguely that it was starting to rain more heavily. But she didn't care. She was too consumed with curiosity to roll up her window. Curiosity tinged with a tiny bit of fear.

Concern and awe washed away the fear the instant she pulled into the gravel driveway and got a good look at her front lawn. Renata had to blink a couple of times. She couldn't believe what she saw.

Under the shaggy oak tree sat an old man—a very, *very* old man—hunched cross-legged on a tattered blanket that was drenched and saturated with watery mud. He was wearing buckskin leggings, moccasins and some kind of beaded deerskin shirt. He wore several strands of bones and shells—bears' teeth, maybe?—around his wrinkled, leathery neck. Feathers dangled from the two long braids that hung halfway down his chest.

Renata knew that Tyler had once been part of the hunting grounds of the local Indians—she couldn't recall which tribe—and she knew that her grandfather had loved to tell stories about running into them now and again as a child. He even had a collection of old Indian artifacts he'd found on the property; it was still somewhere down in the basement along with the beading loom kit Renata had fussed with as a child. But in Renata's lifetime, Tyler had been virtually devoid of Indians. She knew some native people in Milwaukee, of course—had taken art classes with more than one—but they were, for all practical purposes, assimilated. She couldn't imagine any of them sitting on a blanket in buckskin in the rain, chanting to…well, to whatever deity this leathery-skinned Methuselah was probably directing some sort of tribal prayer.

Renata did not particularly care that the old man was trespassing. She wasn't even dying to know what he thought he was doing or why he'd chosen her place. At the moment her thoughts were more practical and pressing. This old fellow looked as frail as parchment and he was obviously soaked to the bone. There was no telling how long he'd been here, but it took no genius to realize that he was in danger of getting pneumonia. She had to get him dried off and warmed up at once. And that meant she had to get him inside.

His eyes were open and he was more or less facing her way, but he showed no sign of seeing Renata. She wondered if he might be blind. She wondered if he might be crazy. She wondered how on earth he'd gotten here without a car. Surely nobody would have left this old man out here all alone!

She took a few steps forward, then crouched before him. The lawn was saturated now and the rain was lashing the ground again. She knew that if she didn't move him soon, she'd end up soaked to the bone.

"Excuse me, sir," Renata said quietly, afraid to startle the spooky old fellow. "I'm Renata Meyer. I live here. I've got warm blankets inside and I can have some hot coffee going in no time. Wouldn't you like to come in and dry off?"

The chanting continued. His eyes showed no sign that he knew another person had joined him. Could he be deaf and blind? she wondered. Or was he in some sort of trance?

Uneasily, she moved closer and risked laying one hand on his arm. It was a thin arm, devoid of muscle, but it didn't even twitch.

"Please, sir. Maybe you don't care about the rain, but I do. I'm getting cold. Can't we go inside and talk?"

The chanting changed pitch then—higher, more ee-rie. It occurred to Renata that maybe the old man didn't speak English. She had heard that there were old Indians who still spoke their native tongue. And this one looked old enough to have ridden against Custer . . . or maybe Columbus.

Renata bit her lower lip and tried to decide what to do. She felt absolutely helpless. She still remembered her own dear grandfather, who'd died at the age of ninety-six but hadn't recognized any of them at the end. If somebody had found him wandering around, befuddled and confused, she would have wanted them to take care of him.

She knelt in the mud right before the old fellow, put both hands on his shoulders and tried one more time. "Please, sir. I know this is important to you. But get-ting you warm and dry is important to me. Can't we go inside now? Later, when the rain stops, you can come back and finish. Or you can even chant in my living room."

This time his eyes flickered over her in what almost looked like sympathy. He brushed one hand in her di-rection, as if to say, "You go inside. Don't worry about me." But he did not stop chanting. And he did not rise.

It was pouring by now. Renata couldn't see herself forcibly dragging the old man into the house even if she'd had the physical strength to do it. There was a dignity about him that made her feel awkward about calling some authority to take him away. But she'd rather have him mad at her than have him die of exposure right here on her lawn.

"Is there anybody I can call?" she asked. "Do you have family or friends near here?"

It occurred to Renata that Timberlake Lodge was a stone's throw away from the back of her property, and it was feasible that he'd hiked here from there. When the lodge had belonged to the Ingallses, Liza and Amanda had sometimes walked over to her place to visit, and since Edward Wocheck had turned it into a resort, she'd encountered a few tourists nosing around on their morning meanderings. But Edward's resort catered to a ritzy crowd. Renata couldn't see this wilted old guy as a typical guest or morning jogger. He seemed more like a candidate for Worthington House, the convalescent center in town.

Relieved that she'd finally thought of a few leads to check out, Renata said, "I'm going to try to find out where you belong, sir. If you change your mind while I'm gone, just come on in and I'll fix you some breakfast. I'm going to put on some coffee."

He kept on chanting as she turned and headed for the house, oblivious to the thunderous new cloudburst that nipped at her heels.

"COME IN, BRICK," squawked the radio in the police car. "I've got a message from the captain."

Under other circumstances, Michael Youngthunder would have grinned. He remembered when he'd first met Lieutenant Brick Bauer, a kind, decent man struggling to pretend he wasn't madly in love with his female precinct captain. Beautiful Karen Keppler—they called her "Captain Killer" now—had ruled the station house with an iron hand, but she'd been kind to Michael and his elderly grandfather. Now she was married to Brick, publicly admitted she adored him and actually allowed her dispatcher to convey messages to her husband when he was on duty without using the complex county police code that was more trouble than it was worth in such a small town. Everybody knew everybody else's business anyway.

Michael had no interest in Tyler's business, and he would never have come to Tyler at all if his grandfather had not begged him. Last winter Grand Feather, as he'd affectionately called the old one since childhood, had heard about the proposed expansion of Timberlake Lodge near Tyler around the same time he'd heard that some Native Americans in other parts of the country were reclaiming sacred bones from white museums and preventing development on traditional burial grounds. Tyler, the old one insisted, had been built near the site where his ancestors were buried...on land "stolen" by white people 150 years ago.

Michael, the manager of a busy Katayama Computers retail outlet, had better things to do with his time than root through the countryside searching for nonexistent Indian bones. But the suit and tie he wore to work each day could not totally obliterate the part of him that was still Winnebago, and the nice paycheck he earned could never compete with his love for the old man who had raised him. So six months ago he'd come to Tyler, talked with Captain Keppler and Lieutenant Bauer, who'd been kind enough to spend a day driving Grand Feather to all possible sites for the burial ground, which allegedly could be identified by a horseshoe of oak trees. They hadn't found anything and that had been the end of it.

Until last night. Until news of the scheduled ground breaking of the new wing of Timberlake Lodge Resort had been broadcast on the only Madison station that his grandfather's puny television picked up in Wisconsin Dells. An hour later Michael had received a call from his uncle, who now owned a tiny remaining piece of allotment land near the old shack where Grand Feather still lived and where Michael himself had grown up. It broke Michael's heart to see the old man live in such squalor, but Grand Feather would not be moved. He said he'd lived as a true Winnebago on that patch of land back when the old ones still taught ancient rituals that they'd learned from their foreparents before the arrival of the whites. He was born a Winnebago, he had lived a Winnebago, and he would be buried as a Winnebago when the time came. More than once he'd claimed that he was ready to die and could not rest until he knew he would not be buried among white strangers.

Although Michael lived in Sugar Creek, a good hour and a half from Wisconsin Dells, the family always called him when there was a problem with Grand Feather, partly because they knew that nobody loved the old one more and partly because Michael was the best equipped of all of them to deal with white people in the outside world. He was the only one with a college degree and a VCR, the only one who stood out like a sore thumb whenever he went home to visit. His cousins called him a half-breed, even though he wasn't, and treated him like a white, even though his heart was still Winnebago. At least he thought it was; he knew he wanted it to be. Most of the time he was too busy to think about it, a condition that was easier to handle than was grappling with his tangled cultural roots.

This morning he was too tired to think, but he had never felt his Indian status more keenly. For twelve solid hours he had been trapped in this police car, searching for Grand Feather in the storm-soaked farmland surrounding Tyler. It was an all-night walk here from the Dells, and a long hike even if the old one had caught a bus or hitchhiked to Tyler proper. And it had been raining all night long. Michael's fear was a living thing, a serpentine rope of nausea that threatened to choke him. He knew he'd disappointed his grandfather terribly by choosing to follow the white man's road, but he worshiped the old one and would have done anything, anything at all, to protect him.

"Go ahead, Hedda," Brick Bauer said into the radio.

"Captain K says she got a call from CeCe Scanlon at Worthington House that might relate to your search for the old Indian. Apparently Renata Meyer is in town for the weekend and called over there to ask if they were missing anyone. They're not, but later CeCe heard your grandma talking to your aunt about how you'd been up all night looking for somebody, and it occurred to her that there might be a connection." Brick's eyes met Michael's as the dispatcher continued, "It occurred to the captain that one of the places you took the Youngthunders before was out to the Meyers' old place. Renata's line is busy, but Captain K thought you might want to swing by there."

Michael took a deep breath, relief and fear twisting his innards into tiny knots. "It's my grandfather, Lieutenant," he told Brick Bauer. "I know it."

To the radio, Brick said quickly, "We're on our way."

RENATA HAD ALREADY MADE a dozen futile calls by the time she heard a car pull into the gravel driveway behind her own. A quick glance outside told her the police had arrived, but she wasn't sure if that was good or bad. She'd deliberately avoided calling the Tyler substation because she didn't want to get the old man in trouble. Somebody else must have, or else their arrival here was just coincidental. Either way, she was at her wit's end, and she was grateful that there was some authority she could turn to.

As Renata hurried outside, wet and shivering, she felt a flash of relief as she recognized the policeman getting out of the black-and-white cruiser. Brick Bauer wasn't a close friend, but she was on good terms with him—or had been the last time they talked, a few years ago—and she knew she could count on him to be gentle with the old man.

"Hi, Brick!" she called out, pulling on a jacket to fight off the worst of the rain. "I heard you got married!"

Brick smiled back, both dimples deepening, looking a little bit embarrassed and terribly pleased. "It's true, Renata. Married my boss. Finally found a woman who could keep me in line."

It was during this brief exchange that Renata realized somebody else was bolting out of the car, somebody in a rumpled suit and loosened tie who was sprinting toward her so fast it was frightening. She only got a glimpse of him—young, dark, good-looking—before his gaze fell on the old Indian. He slammed to a stop, clutching the side-view mirror of her truck for support. The sight of his painful swallow filled Renata with a great ache for him. Love for the old man was written all over his face.

It was a magnificent face, the kind any artist would love to use as a centerpiece of a painting. But Renata knew at once that it wasn't the artist in her that responded so keenly to this man's barely veiled virility and passion. He was tall and lean, with dark brown eyes and thick lashes and a strong jaw. His bronze skin and handsome, angular features hinted strongly at some sort of Indian ancestry.

But Renata only had time to register his compelling good looks and his panic before Brick said softly, "Renata, this is Michael Youngthunder. We've spent the whole night looking for his grandfather."

Brick was wasting his breath. Michael Youngthunder didn't even see Renata; he certainly didn't hear Brick or respond to his courteous introduction. Every nuance of his attention was directed toward the old man.

Under other circumstances, Renata would have resented being so totally ignored. But she had loved her own grandfather, and she understood the anguish in Michael's bloodshot eyes. Even without Brick's explanation, she could have guessed by his haggard demeanor that he'd been searching for the old man all night.

Instinctively, Renata stepped toward him and laid one hand on his arm. "He's all right," she said quickly, even though she knew Michael could see it for himself. "I found him about half an hour ago and begged him to come in. He won't budge, but his voice isn't getting any weaker."

Michael's well muscled arm was tensely knotted beneath Renata's fingers, but a mighty sigh of relief escaped his invitingly full lips. For the first time he glanced at Renata, but even now she didn't think he really saw her. Habit more than conscious thought seemed to prompt him to murmur, "I'm sorry for the intrusion. It may take me a few minutes to persuade him to come away."

"Don't worry about that," she assured him. "Just let me know what I can do to help. I draped a rain slicker around his shoulders—" she gestured toward the yellow vinyl garment sprawled across the grass "—but he just let it fall to the ground."

Again Michael's beautiful mahogany eyes met hers. "Thank you," he repeated in a choked voice.

When she felt the ripple of tension in his biceps, Renata realized belatedly that she was still holding on to him. Abruptly she let go. But Michael wasn't paying any attention to Renata. His gaze was once again on the old man, who was still chanting. Not once had his eyes even flickered toward his grandson.

"I tried everything I could to make him come in and dry off," Renata explained apologetically. "He acts as though he doesn't see me. Doesn't hear. I think he's in some kind of a trance."

"Trance?" Michael repeated, as though the single word alarmed him.

"Well, I don't know what else to call it. It's as though he's gone somewhere that I can't reach."

Michael closed his eyes, shook his head, then whispered, "I'm not sure I can reach him, either."

At that point Brick joined them, laid a hand on Michael's shoulder and said, "This is like talking down a jumper, Michael. I'll speak to him if you want me to. I would if you weren't here."

Quietly Michael said, "Thanks, Lieutenant, but this is something I have to do myself. If he doesn't finish, he'll find a way to come back here later. The best thing for me to do is to hurry him along a little."

"Finish?" said Renata. "He sounds like he's just repeating the same thing over and over again."

This time Michael's gaze focused on her face for a long, dark moment before he turned away. For some reason she could not fathom, Renata knew she'd disappointed him.

Hugging herself for warmth, she stood beside Brick and stared at Michael as he crossed the lawn to join his grandfather. They couldn't have looked more different: young, old; business suit, Indian clothes; utterly contemporary, locked in another space and time. Still, there was a family resemblance, or at least a tribal one, in the coppery skin and straight, masculine nose. The old man's hair was very long and braided, already thin and gray. Michael's black hair was longer than average—thick and straight as it flowed over his broad shoulders—but it was such a magnificent mane that a proud display of it didn't strike Renata as peculiar. In her arty crowd, lots of people cherished eccentricities in their appearance. None of her Milwaukee friends would have looked twice at Michael's hair even if he'd worn it in feathered braids.

"I met Michael when Edward Wocheck came back to town and started talking about expanding Timberlake Lodge," Brick explained sotto voce. "Old man Youngthunder's got some idea that there's a sacred burial ground around here. We drove through your property before but the 'spirits' didn't speak to him."

Renata was astounded. People were right when they said truth was sometimes stranger than fiction! The only burial ground nearby was the family plot out toward the barn, and nobody had been buried there in seventy or eighty years.

"So why do you think he came back here this morning?" she asked Brick.

"Edward's having a ground-breaking ceremony for the new wing of Timberlake Lodge tomorrow. Last night Mr. Youngthunder heard it on the news."

Michael was squatting in front of his grandfather now, meeting his eyes, but Renata found it odd that he still had not spoken. The old man was chanting again, and for some reason Michael's head was nodding ever so slightly as though in time to the distinctive rhythm.

"Why doesn't he say something to his grandfather?" Renata asked. "Aren't they on good terms?"

"Very good terms. Winnebago terms. Don't let the suit throw you. Michael still knows how to be an Indian when he has to, and I think he's going to have to act Winnebago to get through to the old guy."

Brick was right. A moment later the handsome man in the rumpled suit—a suit that looked as though it had fit him magnificently before his night in the police car—folded his long legs and sat down on the mud-soaked blanket in front of his grandfather. Then he held up both hands the way the old man was and started to chant right along with him.

Renata stared disbelievingly at Brick, then back at Michael again. She knew Michael loved the old man, so she wasn't surprised that he was willing to do anything to get him to come inside. She might have been willing to sit in the mud herself, especially in her jeans. But Michael was wearing a suit! And he wasn't just sitting there pleading with the old man. He was joining in the ritual, raising his hands, chanting the same syllables.

It took Renata a moment to realize the symbolism of that simple act. He wasn't feigning understanding. *He knew the chant.* He knew the sounds, the words, the gestures! He knew why his grandfather had come to this place, knew what he was doing, knew why he wouldn't just get up and leave. And he clearly shared some part of his grandfather's way of thinking, something that Renata guessed he couldn't put into English words.

She battled the weird feeling that she was sinking into quicksand. Right before her eyes, this terribly attractive businessman had turned into an Indian! All he was missing was the buckskin and braids.

Suddenly there was a crackle from the cruiser. Brick quickly strode back, picked up the mike, barked a quick response and waved a hand. "Got an emergency," he called to Renata. "Tell Michael I'll be back for him as soon as I can."

In an instant the black-and-white car had pulled away, leaving Renata feeling like an interloper on her own property. It had been strange enough starting the day with one rain-soaked Indian doing eerie chants on her front lawn.

Now there were two of them.